I0580498

FANDOM

FAMOUS BOOK 3

EDEN FINLEY

FANDOM

Copyright © 2020 by Eden Finley
Cover Illustration Copyright ©
Eden Finley

Professional beta read by Les Court Services.
https://www.lescourtauthorservices.com

Proofread by One Love Editing
http://oneloveediting.com/

All rights reserved.
This book or any portion thereof may not be reproduced or used in any manner
whatsoever without the express written permission of the publisher.
For information regarding permission, write to:
Eden Finley - permissions - edenfinley@gmail.com

Names, characters, businesses, places, events, and incidents are either the products
of the author's imagination or used in a fictitious manner. Any resemblance to
actual persons, living or dead, or actual events is purely coincidental.

DISCLAIMERS & TRIGGERS

Mason and Denver ended up being heavier than anticipated. They very much still align with Eden Finley's brand of snark and light heartedness but do deal with/address/or mention the following heavy topics:

Addiction

Death

Suicidal thoughts

If any of these are likely to trigger a negative response, it might be best to skip this one.

CHAPTER 1
DENVER

THERE ARE EYES ON ME. I can sense it.

I mean, it's understandable. This is my house, my party, and I have one of the most recognizable faces in LA, if not the world. Conceited as it sounds, I always have eyes on me, so it's nothing new.

But this is different.

I'm standing on the balcony of my Malibu mansion, overlooking my brightly lit pool, sipping scotch, chatting with people I'm supposed to know but honestly don't, and I hate myself.

Not in the *oh, I'm so depressed, I hate my life* kind of way.

But here's my deal. I know I'm privileged. I know I'm fortunate. Yet, everything is being held together with sticky tape. Not even the good duct tape serial killers use. No, mine is covered in fingerprints and fur, rapidly losing its adhesive.

Dating celebrities for publicity feels pointless, but it buys me time. Actresses are batshit crazy. *Who knew?*

These stupid "networking" parties I throw are empty gestures for a tabloid story so I can stay relevant in this industry. My albums sell, but I'm no Harley Valentine with his Grammys and number ones.

I've signed on to be a judge for a reality talent show, but after months of off-camera auditions and legal crap production has been dealing with, it might not even get off the ground. Filming has been postponed twice now.

Hence throwing myself another party for attention. Because I know what's coming. If this show goes under, it's going to take me with it. I only agreed to do it because it was my manager's latest effort to keep my career alive.

Next thing will probably be selling vitamins on infomercials.

My career is on life support, and my fate lies in the hands of network execs. I'm learning they're very similar to executives at a record label. Any title with the word *executive* in it can't be trusted.

I need another drink, but my feet are glued to the ground. I can't find an opening to slip it into the conversation that I'm leaving. I don't even know what these people are talking about.

"So then the woman said, 'Where I come from, I'm treated like a princess.' And the guy replied, 'Well, in West Hollywood, I'm a queen, so I outrank you.'"

Oh, yay, unfunny jokes with homophobic undertones. I force a laugh. *Ha, ha, ha, fuck my life.*

"Excuse me, guys." I finally break away from them and head inside.

That's when I notice someone standing in the corner of my formal living room. The guy looks out of place in amongst all my expensive, asymmetrical furniture. According to my interior designer, it's modern. All I've ever thought is it's uncomfortable. It's why I only ever use this room for parties. I have an actual, usable living room that has my big-ass comfy couch. I'm tempted to go there now and shut out the rest of the party.

But there's something about Mr. Hazel Eyes, who's in tight jeans, a white T-shirt, and an undone vest. He's got a blond man bun, and I have no idea who he is. Then again, I don't know a hell of a lot of these people, but I at least know I *should* recognize the others. This guy doesn't look like the usual crowd who show up to these things. My defenses go up because if he's a reporter or is about to pull out a camera from behind his back, I'll be pissed.

I want the media to know *about* the parties, but they're not invited to the intimate details.

I down the rest of my drink and then head in his direction. "Hey, man." I hold my hand out for him to shake.

"Hey." He smiles easily.

"Uh, I don't mean to be rude, but have we met?"

His smile widens. "No, we haven't, but, uh, I feel like I know you … Denny."

There are only a handful of people in this world who would use that name. My eyes narrow. "Who in Eleven do you know?"

The presence of someone appears at my back. No, not someone: multiple someones.

I turn and come face-to-face with Harley Valentine himself and Ryder Kennedy. Behind them is Harley's wall of a bodyguard.

"What's happening? Did someone die?" I ask.

They grin.

I hope no one's dead if they look so happy about it.

"We have a proposition for you," Harley says. "But we might want to take this somewhere else." He glances around the busy space where more than one person's attention is on us.

Three of the five ex-boy band members together? It's practically a reunion.

I usher them into my casual living room and gesture for them to take a seat on the oversized couches. Harley's bodyguard closes the sliding doors behind us and stands guard.

"What's up?" I take a seat on an armrest on the end. "It has to be serious if you're both here." I glance at the guy they used as bait. "And … whoever you are."

He and Ryder share a look.

"Ah." I nod. "Got it."

Ryder's a weird closet case. He kept it a secret from us and the rest of the guys a long while, but it was never from self-hatred or shame. More self-preservation. He's always been comfortable with who he is but has trouble labeling it.

And don't I know what that's like.

"I'm starting my own record label," Harley says.

My head swivels in his direction so fast the room spins. "Really?"

On one hand, good for him. On the other … jealousy tries to make an appearance.

I love Harley like a brother. But brothers can get competitive. I always knew he'd succeed when Eleven broke up, but I also thought the rest of us would be there with him. Except for Ryder, who wanted out completely.

Harley nods toward Ryder's partner. "Lyric is the first act I've signed. He's amazing."

I'm … confused. "Okay." I drag out the word. "What does that have to do with me?"

"Well, the second act I'm hoping to have on my label is Eleven."

That clarifies absolutely nothing. "That will never happen."

"Come on," Harley says. "If I can get *Ryder* to agree, I have to at least hope the rest of you will jump at the chance."

"Why? Because we're so much crappier than you? Because we need you to succeed? Fuck you."

"Denny." Harley sighs. "You know that's not what I mean."

I stare down at my empty hand, wishing another drink would magically appear. "Then what do you mean?"

Harley and Ryder look at each other and say at the same time, "We miss it."

"We miss being part of a group," Harley adds.

"I just miss recording," Ryder says.

I frown. "Are you guys high? You want to go back to living on top of each other, fighting, bickering …" Accidentally falling for your bandmate and making a fool of yourself in front of him …

"Yep. We miss it all," Ryder says.

"But your daughter."

Ryder shrugs. "Her mom's back in the picture, and Harley's agreed to touring over summers where they can come with us."

I turn to Harley. "You're a Grammy Award–winning solo artist."

"Shit, am I?"

"I have my talent show and another album to cut." If my label gives me a new contract, that is. "So, thanks, but no thanks." I can't go back.

Even if touring with the guys was the best time of my life. It was carefree, and while there was pressure, it wasn't as heavy when there were four others to help handle it. Plus, our albums sold so easily. We could've had a record of us reading the dictionary, and teenagers everywhere would've gotten smarter from it.

Going back to that could be the resurrection of my career that I desperately need, but it will come at a cost.

I'd have to swallow my pride, and that's something I've never been good at doing.

Look at the smoke-and-mirrors show I'm putting on out there for everyone to see.

My career is going down in flames, and I'm sitting and watching, telling myself everything is fine.

"Come on," Harley says. "You were supposed to be the easy sell."

"Why do you *want* to go back? It doesn't make any sense to me. We've all moved on." I stand. "Besides, you think Blake is going to give up the silver screen? Hell no. You think Mason is going to come out of hiding?"

Ugh, just saying his name sends a twinge through my chest.

Mason and I were best friends once upon a time. We were closer than Harley and Ryder, even.

I must've said the wrong thing because Harley's face lights up.

"You know where Mason is?"

"No." *Yes.* Well, I have a fairly good idea.

His family owns land in the middle of nowhere Montana. After Eleven hit it big, he built a "cabin" out there. And by cabin, I mean a mansion. I'm not certain if he's there, but I'm assuming he is. He took me there whenever Eleven was on break because I had no one to go home to.

With a drug addict for a mom, I was raised by my grandmother when the state took me away from Mom's toxic behavior. I'm pretty sure I'm the result of her making a deal with either her pimp or her dealer, so yeah, the first few years of my life were delightful. Luckily, I was too young to really remember much before my grandmother reluctantly took me in.

She raised me and cared for me right up until she passed away when I was sixteen.

By that point, I was in a famous boy band and could prove to the courts I was able to provide for myself.

Pro tip: don't let sixteen-year-olds dictate their own lives.

When I was eighteen, I needed a financial advisor to keep my spending under control.

I had the habit of shopping for expensive and meaningless things to fill my house. Because when you grow up with nothing, the constant reminder you can afford a twenty-thousand-dollar duck statue fills that void. His name is Bill, and he's essential to my mental well-being.

Harley says the one thing that could tempt me into caving to this stupid idea. "We were like family. Even families have reunions."

All I ever wanted was a proper family. When I did visit with Mason, his life was so … normal. He might have lost his dad at a young age, but his mom, sister, and he are the definition of close family.

I've told myself for years that the bond I had with Mason was pure envy over what he had. That I was somehow confusing admiration for attraction. But I can't help acknowledging the hole his absence has left in my life and in my chest.

I long for someone who was my best friend even though I haven't had the balls to contact him since Eleven broke up.

I can't face him after what I did.

I turn to Harley. "I can't. I'm sorry, but I'm out. I guarantee the others will say the same." *Especially Mason.*

CHAPTER 2
MASON

THE DEEP VOICE on the other end of the line is soothing yet authoritative, and I find it hard to say no to the man who had been like a father to me for seven years. Cameron Verikas, Eleven's manager, was the replacement dad for me after having lost mine at ten years old. It was nice having that fatherly figure in my life again after going through my teen years without one, but right now I'm remembering why overbearing parental figures can be annoying.

"Just take a meeting with Harley. It's one meeting. What have you got to lose?"

My dignity, for one. "I don't think you can hear me, old man. Have you got your hearing aids in?" I bite my lip to stop from laughing because I know what's coming.

"I'm fifty-two. I don't need no damn hearing aids."

I'd believe his anger more if he wasn't laughing with me. "I think you do because you clearly can't hear when I say I'm not going back."

I breathe in the Montana mountain air and stare out at the vast land before me. There's a comfort in knowing that while it's isolating and lonely out here, it's consistent. Unlike Hollywood and everyone in it.

I remember back to when Eleven broke up, when I couldn't wait for creative freedom and to take responsibility over my own career. I was a naïve motherfucker.

Apparently, when trying a new sound, surrounding yourself with *yes people* is a bad idea. Everyone on my team showered me with praise to the point I thought I was doing amazing things, and while I love the album I ended up cutting, seeing it from an industry perspective, it wasn't a sellable record. It was all over the place with no real theme or genre.

It's great to have a creative outlet, but I wish I'd hired a manager who could rein me in when I went too far out of the mainstream box. I wish I still had Cameron, but he made it clear when the boy band broke up that he wouldn't pick sides.

The only person I have to blame for choosing the wrong team of people is myself, but I'm still salty about it anyway.

When everything fell to pieces, it was the first time I realized I was truly alone in the industry, which is why I came running back to Montana with my tail between my legs and why I have absolutely no interest in what Harley has to say to me now that it's convenient for him.

"Are you going to make me shlep all the way out there again?" Cameron asks.

"Hey, you're always welcome to visit."

Cameron's the only one from my old life I've kept in contact with over these last eighteen months since being home, and that's only because I respect him too much not to return his calls.

He's come out here twice already trying to convince me to come back—he even offered to be my manager again—but I can't bring myself to make him break his promise that he wouldn't choose between us. Why I still have that loyalty, I'm not sure, because the rest of Eleven can go fuck themselves for all I care.

Wow, maybe I'm even more bitter than I realized.

"I'm sure you've heard Harley is trying to get Eleven together again. I think it could be the right move for all of you."

I've had a million missed calls from Harley, and all the voice-mails about getting back together were deleted immediately. "I can't go back."

"There's something you're not telling me," Cameron says.

"I have no idea what you're talking about. I'm done with Hollywood and music. That's all."

"No, you're not."

"Oh really. I'm not, am I?"

"Nope. Because I know you loved those guys like brothers, so to go from being that close to nothing, something happened, and I want to know what it is. Because if that's your only roadblock, I'm going to find a way to fix it."

Of course he is.

"I … can't. I'm really sorry, but I can't go into it." Because it would involve outing someone I used to care about. Still care about. Maybe. I don't know. I'm still too angry to work out my emotions when it comes to Denver Smith.

And out here, in the middle of nowhere, I don't have to deal with it at all. That's how I like it, and that's the way it'll stay.

But talking to Cameron about it does make me flash back to that night, the last night Eleven was on tour, just hours before the announcement that we were breaking up.

The screams were deafening, and the crowd was going insane for us like they always did, but it was as if they all knew that it was our last show ever. Or maybe I knew that it was the last show we'd ever play together, so I was focusing on it more.

The last few years had felt a little lackluster when it came to performing. We were all burned out. We were ready for a break, and we wanted to do our own things.

It was our last encore. The last song.

All five of us on stage breathed heavily as the song finished and we stared out at our adoring fans.

Denver purposefully stepped in front of me when it was time to take our bow, and I laughed as I shoved him out the way. His shaggy light brown hair was dripping with sweat, his aqua eyes were shining, and he'd never looked happier than when he was onstage performing. The guy had gone through some serious shit in his life, but you wouldn't have known it looking at him in that moment. With the lights shining down on him, he had an ethereal glow about him.

He threw his arm around my shoulders while the crowd took photos of us all lined up next to each other. Those were the types of shots that got posted all over social media, but this particular one would go down in history as the last time Eleven ever played onstage together. Not that the crowd knew that yet.

Eleven breaking up was massive news, and hearts were about to break all over the world. Telling rambunctious fans their favorite band was dead was a good way to get someone trampled if they did it at the wrong time. The label had prepared statements to release into the world after the stadium had cleared out.

The fandom was manic, but there was no doubt we did something special.

I thought the only sucky thing would be saying goodbye to them all, particularly Denver. He was like my kid brother, and we hadn't spent more than a few days away from each other since we were first signed to the label. Even on breaks, if we weren't with my family, he'd drag me on some tropical island vacation somewhere. We were tight, and I didn't want to lose that, but we both needed to spread our wings.

I knew it would be hard, but I had no doubt we would support each other through this next venture. He would still be in my life.

Boy, was I fucking wrong.

I had no idea my life was about to implode. I was too excited about moving on and becoming a grown-up for once. Signing a major record deal when I was nineteen years old was a lot to process, and I hadn't slowed down in seven years.

With everyone wanting me, a very full bank account, and endless accessibility to everything one could ever dream of, being in a boy band froze time for me.

I still felt like I was that nineteen-year-old, but I was ready for more responsibility and more artistic freedom.

Denver leaned in and said in my ear, "We did it."

I didn't hesitate to turn and pull him into a hug. That too was photographed and posted all over the internet, but it was okay with us. The media was too obsessed with #Ryley4Ever to even contemplate something going on between Denver and me. Then again, there were too many incriminating photos of Denver and me partying with girls over the years.

Blake was on the end of the line, quietly looking like he was going to have a panic attack. Out of the five of us, his voice wasn't the strongest. He was usually reduced to harmonizing and backup vocals.

It was nostalgic leaving the stage as a group for the last time. The same sadness that hit me must've been getting to Denver too because his eyes became glassy as we went backstage.

We were ushered to our dressing room where Diva Harley got first dibs on the shower. He'd been a real pain in the ass toward the end there—more so than usual. He had been through a nasty breakup and had plans to marry a woman for publicity. It was messy.

We only had to get through a few more VIP appearances, and then we were out of there in time for our label to announce Eleven was over.

"What'll it be for our send-off?" I asked. "Party? Club?"

"I'm out," Ryder said. "Gotta get home to Kaylee."

If Ryder had been anti-partying before, that was nothing compared to when he became a dad.

"Won't she be asleep? She's a baby," I argued.

"She's three, dude."

"Since when?" How had the last three years gone that quickly?

"Since you didn't come to her birthday party two months ago?"

Oops. Kids and I were not a great mix.

When you get engaged at nineteen with plans to immediately have a big family and love and happiness, it kind of puts a sour taste in your mouth when you find out your future wife was in it for the fame.

The Eleven fandom killed her budding career when they found out she cheated on me. Especially when they found out it was with a One Directioner.

Oh, the blasphemy!

That's what the tabloids said, anyway. It was all alleged. I might not have known for sure if she fucked a 1D guy, but I did know I walked in on her in *my* house with some random producer who'd promised to cut her album seeing as my label refused to sign her because she couldn't sing. Even me asking for a favor didn't get her a deal with them.

After that, I said fuck relationships. Fuck marriage. And fuck having kids. That ties your life to someone else forever, and after that kind of heartbreak, I wasn't looking for more.

Temporary and casual. That had been my motto since *she who shall not be named* moved out.

"All right, Ryder's a no," I said. "What about Harley?"

"Harley's probably going to go home and record his first solo. We all know he's been planning this for months," Blake said.

"Okay, so it's us three."

Blake shook his head. "Nah, I'd rather not be out when all the shit goes down. Plus, what am I supposed to do now? I need to make a plan."

"A plan? You keep recording. It's what we do. It's what we love."

Blake ran a hand through his blond hair. "You guys maybe. I get the feeling this is the end of music for me."

"Damn, brother. That's heavy," I said.

He moved toward the bathroom. "I'm gonna kick Harley out of there. I need … I need to not be in here."

I turned to Denver. "You and me, then. What do you say to bottle service at … wait, what city are we in?"

"If it's all the same to you, I'd rather go back to the hotel and chill."

I slumped. "You all are no fun in your old age."

Denver grinned. "I'm only twenty-two."

"And you've been in this industry for seven years already. In Hollywood years, you're at least forty."

"Oh, so your age?" he quipped.

I jabbed him in the ribs. "You're a funny fucker, aren't ya?"

"You're welcome to join me," Denver said. "But I'm out. I don't feel like being *on*. Don't you want to be the real Mason?"

"That's the whole point of ending this, remember? But it's our *last* night."

Denver reached for a bottle of whiskey. "I think we've all been checked out a while, though."

"Fine. We'll chill in your hotel room."

It was always better with just me and Denver anyway. I loved the other guys, but Denver and I had something real. It wasn't a *manufactured by proximity* friendship.

I thought we'd all at least be together when the announcement of our end would come out, but after smiling for fans and being vague about our next nonexistent album, it was me and Denver, more whiskey, and Netflix on his hotel suite couch.

The notifications started pouring in a short time later.

"Here we go." I looked at my phone.

"I turned mine off." Denver was on the couch next to me, glass in hand, his shirt unbuttoned with a mess of loose curls falling into his eyes.

Then I noticed how utterly exhausted he looked.

Denver had a baby face, so it was like he couldn't seem to ever age, but in that moment, he looked almost thirty. It was the first time I'd really seen him haggard, and after countless nine-month-long sold-out tours, I'd seen him at his worst.

"Hey, are you okay?"

He sipped his drink and looked contemplative. Over the years, I'd seen Denver in many different stages of drunk. From happy to sloppy and everything in between. He'd done it all.

This moment was his philosophical *what is life?* phase.

"I'll be fine," he said dismissively. "It's just surreal at the moment."

"But exciting. We get to do our own thing. Aren't you ready for it?"

"I am, but ..." He bit his lip. "I'm ... scared."

I loved that he wasn't afraid to admit the emotional stuff to me. If I could help him, I would, and when he confided in me often, it made me feel needed. "What are you scared of?"

He shook his head. "Never mind. I'm being stupid."

"Tell me. It's *me.*"

"What if none of us sell? What if this isn't only the end of Eleven but the end of our careers?"

"Denny ..." I used his real name so he'd know how serious I was. "You have so much talent. Don't let any labels or industry assholes tell you any differently. We're all going to succeed. I trust in that."

"What if you and I get too busy for each other?"

"Will never happen."

"I'm used to seeing you every day. You're my rock. You're ... everything to me. What if—"

I gripped his arm. "Stop with the what-ifs and look at the facts. We have millions of fans. Even if we don't sell half of what we do now, we're still going to be hitting charts and making names for ourselves. And you are gonna shine. I promise. I also promise I'll be at the sidelines cheering you on every step of the way."

"How can you be so positive about this?"

"I can't help it. I'm naturally Zen." I smirked.

"You so are not."

"Namaste and all that other bullshit." I threw my arm around him and brought him closer. "You and I are solid. Always will be."

He turned his head to look up at me. "Promise?"

"Only if you promise back."

"No matter what happens?"

"You could kill a man, and I'd still love you. You're like my ki—"

Before I could get the words *kid brother* out of my mouth, Denver pressed his lips to mine.

Shock doesn't begin to describe what I was going through. It took more than a second to get my bearings and a half second more to push him off me. "Wait, wait, wait, what the fuck is happening?"

Denver pulled out of my arms and stood. "You said you loved me."

"Like a *brother*."

He blinked at me.

"You … you know I'm not into guys, right? I'm not some closet case like Ryder and Harley. It's cool if you are, but I didn't think—"

He threw up his hands. "I'm not."

"Then what—"

He ran his fingers through his shaggy hair. "I'm freaking out about Eleven breaking up, about the future, about being *alone* … I thought … I don't know what I thought, but whatever it was, it was wrong. I'm sorry."

I slowly stood. "Hey, it's okay."

"No, it's not. It's really not."

I tried to touch him, to pull him into my arms so he knew I was there for him no matter what, but he flinched away.

"Don't." He sounded pained, and I didn't know it was possible for one word to be filled with so much regret.

"Denver." I wanted to reassure him that it was fine. It was a mistake, but it didn't change anything.

He averted his gaze. "I … I should go."

"But—"

All I could see was Denver's retreating form as it disappeared through the door. He vanished so quick I didn't even have time to point out we were in *his* hotel room.

I didn't know it then, but that would be the last I'd see or hear from Denver Smith.

CHAPTER 3
DENVER

I'M KNOWN as the nice one. The one with the sweet face and kind heart.

Anyone who believes our perceived personas needs a pat on the head and a condescending "Oh, honey." But it's a role I've played for years. I need to keep up appearances.

That might go to hell if I'm forced to sit through another terrible audition. I'm this close to stabbing something with my pen. Preferably my ears. I suddenly understand why Simon Cowell is the way that he is.

Finally, after all the red tape and months of delay, *Fandom* is happening. And this first week has been a complete shitshow.

To save my voice, I should make up a sign that says, "Good try, but no. Sorry."

And these were the ones who made it through prescreening auditions? Jesus H. Christ.

My fellow judges look as over it as I am. We've been on set for close to fourteen hours, and all the faces of the contestants are blurring together.

I take a sip of water which has the makeup artist running over to apply more ChapStick, and while she's at it, she powders my face for the countless time today. My lips are shiny, and my skin is not.

This is saving my career.

Supposedly.

Am I regretting turning down Harley's offer to get back together? Maybe. If it weren't for the fact I haven't spoken to Mason since Eleven broke up, I would probably take the leap.

But, I just … can't. I don't want to face him.

We promised we wouldn't drift apart, but after I kissed him and ran away, it's exactly what we did.

When his debut album tanked, I should have reached out, but I was too busy making sure my own career didn't suffer the same fate.

Also being a good friend after my humiliation didn't come easy. There's a reason pride is one of the seven deadly sins, and that's because it can fuck up entire friendships.

In the seven years Eleven was recording and touring, Mason and I grew close. When you spend every single day with someone for that long, it's impossible not to bond. Then for someone as naïve as me with abandonment issues, that bond can get … confusing.

To this day, I still don't know if what I felt for him was real or exaggerated in my mind. I've never had the urge to kiss another guy. Before or after Mason. But without a doubt, whenever I think about that night, longing pangs my gut. For our friendship, for more? I don't even know anymore.

Like always when I start dwelling over my old friend, I force myself to ignore it and focus on my work. It's the only thing I have left.

Alondra Casey, pop sensation from the nineties, is in the judging seat next to me, and she leans over. "I know I'm supposed to be the motherly one, but it's really hard not telling these kids they'll be eaten alive in this industry."

I snort. "Right?"

"Do you think if I fake a diva tantrum, they'll let us go home?"

She's barely spoken two words to me all week, but I decide right here and now—I like her.

"Please do," I beg.

She laughs.

Luckily, they call it before she needs to bring out the big guns. Thank God. Two whole days off.

"Might need to save that one for next week," I say to her as we exit to our trailers. I need to get out of the clothes the wardrobe department picked out for me. We turn them in every day so they can wash them and rewear. We need to be in the same clothes for all the auditions on tape. That way they can mix the auditions up in edit and it will look like it was filmed in that order.

I climb the steps to my trailer and throw open the door. My shirt's over my head, and my belt's unbuckled a second later. Then a throat clears, and I practically jump out of my skin.

"Motherfucker," I hiss.

"Now, now, Denny. What kind of good role model are you for the kids on this talent show?"

I know a lot of people love Harley Valentine's voice, but right now I can't think of anything more grating to my ears. And that's coming from a long-ass week on a judging panel of what I'm beginning to think is a prank show. At the end of six weeks, some B-grade celebrity is going to jump out and go, "Ha-ha, gotcha!"

"I already said no," I say and continue undressing.

Brix, Harley's bulky bodyguard-slash-boyfriend, covers Harley's eyes.

He swats him away. "It's nothing I haven't seen before. Trust me. Seven years on tour with the guy, it's impossible to be attracted to ... that." Harley waves his hand in my direction.

"Wow, way to butter me up. Where do I sign on your new label?" I quip.

"Denny," Harley whines.

"What?"

"I'm not here for that. I'm here to offer to take you to dinner."

My gaze narrows. "And to try to get me to sign on a dotted line?"

"Me? Never."

"Mmhmm, sure."

"We're going to dinner with an old friend, and I want you to come."

"Which old friend? And who's *we*?"

"Do you not trust me anymore?" Harley blinks innocently at me.

"I'm not even going to dignify that with an answer."

Harley sighs. "Only you and me. Oh, and my wall of muscle." He points with his thumb to his boyfriend.

"And who's the friend?" A lump gets stuck in the back of my throat. For some reason, I'm expecting him to say Mason even though logically, it couldn't be.

"It's Blake, okay? I wanted Ryder to come too, but he has the kidlet with him tonight."

I haven't seen Blake in a long time, and it would be nice to catch up. But … "What's your play?"

"Play?" Harley's voice breaks.

"Yeah. There has to be an angle here."

Harley turns to his boyfriend. "I told you it would be easier to lure him with candy instead of merely asking him."

"That might work with you," I say. "Honesty works better with me. Just level with me."

"Okay, so I had a crazy idea that if we showed a united front, Blake would say yes, and then you will change your mind, and then there's only one more person to get on board. One for all and all for one and all that."

Ugh. He is not going to let this go. The thing is, I do want to see Blake. And I'm not naïve. If this reality show thing doesn't work out, or our ratings tank, *Fandom* might be the death of my career. Toying with Eleven getting back together is a smart thing to do even if it never eventuates.

Having said that, the thought of having to see Mason again scares the shit out of me, and if Harley gets his way, it will happen eventually.

But what are the chances Blake will say yes? He's a movie star now. Even if Blake is up for getting back together, that doesn't mean I have to say yes.

Harley bounces. Literally bounces. "Please, please, please, please, please?"

"Fine. But I'm not saying yes to getting back together. This is dinner only."

"Dinner only." Why does the glimmer in Harley's eye terrify me?

As I buckle my seat belt on the private jet, I glare at Harley. "You neglected to tell me Blake was on set of a movie in the Nevada desert."

"Did I? Oops."

I shake my head. "I'm starving now, and it's at least an hour flight. You better have snacks."

"Who do you think I am? Of course I have snacks." He opens a compartment, and a bunch of sugary confections falls out.

"I see your sugar addiction is under control."

"Eh. Brix reins me in. I swear he and my trainer are in cahoots."

"Cahoots?" I laugh.

"They're both against me."

Brix wraps his large arm around Harley. "Not even. I always tell you to eat whatever you want."

"Then you make me work it off!"

"Because you ask me to. And you never seem to complain when we *work it off*." Brix waggles his dark eyebrows.

Seeing their easy back-and-forth makes a longing feeling stab at me, but that doesn't make sense. I'm used to being alone. I've practically been on my own since I was sixteen. The closest thing I had to someone stable in my life were the guys from Eleven.

The last few years by myself must be catching up to me. "On second thought, where's the alcohol cabinet?" I ask.

Brix leans over and opens a panel that's a hidden minifridge. "What would you like?"

"Jack."

"With?"

"The bottle."

Brix hands it over.

"Tonight's gonna get messy," Harley says.

I lift the bottle. "Cheers to that." I take a large gulp and then hand it to Harley, who takes out a glass and pours himself some with Diet Coke.

He offers some to Brix, but Brix shakes his head. "I have a feeling I'll be needing to look after you two tonight."

Even though it's Harley's boyfriend, the mere thought of having someone look after me makes my chest ache. "Yeah, I'm gonna need more alcohol."

"Want a glass this time?" Harley asks.

"Fine. Make me use my manners and shit."

By the time we land at a private airfield outside Vegas, I'm a little tipsy and buzzing happily. We go straight from the plane and are ushered through the private terminal and into an awaiting stretch Hummer.

I stare at Harley, like, *really*?

"I figured we'd do this trip in style," Harley says.

"Mmhmm, style. This would have nothing to do with drawing attention to the three members of Eleven hanging out so the tabloids catch wind of a reunion and having the fans beg for it until we all relent?"

"I am a pillar of innocence," Harley says.

I have to admit, his passion for us getting back together is alluring. He doesn't need the publicity like the rest of us, so I don't get the impression he's using us for a PR grab. He genuinely wants it to happen.

"Where to now? Driving to the middle of nowhere?" I ask.

"Yep. Then we're gonna kidnap him from the set and go to a late dinner at the Catalina Casino."

"Wait, does he know we're coming?"

Harley grins. That motherfucker.

"You're having fun with this, aren't you?" I turn to Brix. "Isn't this the type of thing you're supposed to rein in?"

"Hell no," Brix says immediately. "I'm assuming you know how he is when he gets something in his head."

"Definitely."

"Oh, look! Minibar." Harley pulls out a bottle of champagne and hands it to me. "Keep drinking. If you have liquid in your mouth, you can't talk about me like I'm not here."

"I'm not really a wine kind of person." I pop the cork anyway and take a sip straight from the bottle. "On second thought. This isn't too bad."

"All the whiskey probably helps," Brix mutters.

Harley and I drink, we ask the driver for some music, and when an Eleven song comes on, we can't help laughing and reminiscing.

"Remember when Blake's clumsy ass fell off the stage because he was too busy trying to read a fan's sign and kind of just kept walking to get closer?" I howl.

"Hey, how many times have you fallen over in public?" Harley argues.

"I never fell off the *stage*. And mine was never from being clumsy. It was pure drunkenness."

We bring up story after story from our touring days, but I'm conscious of bringing up Mason. I've always been scared to talk about him to anyone because I'm paranoid about people seeing right through me.

The drive out to the desert feels way shorter than it should.

When we pull up to a gated area, Harley stands and pops his head through the sunroof. "Harley Valentine to see Blake Monroe."

Unsurprisingly, we're let right on set. Oh, to have the powerful name of Harley Valentine. Not that my own name doesn't come with perks. Denver Smith will get me into clubs and some paparazzi interested, but it doesn't have the same pull as Harley's. The name I grew up with—Denny Mariano—will get me nowhere. No one even knows it. Unlike Harley, where a quick Google search will tell you he changed his name, the label wanted to bury my past. Well, more specifically, my birth parents' past. When the guys from Eleven call me Denny, people think it's a nickname. It's not.

The driver pulls the monstrosity of this tank up to a row of trailers much like they have on the set of *Fandom*.

A production assistant approaches with his finger to his headset. "Come this way. We'll take you to where you can watch. We're almost wrapped for the day."

I'm delightfully wobbly as we follow the dude to a fake eight-story building with scaffolding all around it. The whole set is lit up with industrial lights, and it's hard to make out what it's going to look like postproduction. Are we supposed to be in a city? Is that a high-rise? Or is it supposed to look like a construction site?

"They only have one take of the action sequence, so we need quiet on the set," the PA tells us. He ushers us closer to some more crew who are watching. There are screens showing multiple camera angles, and Blake stands on top of the building wearing all black, a bulletproof vest, and holding what looks like an assault rifle. Coby Godspeed, eat your heart out.

I've lost count of how many movies they've shoved together in this franchise in two and a half years. He's so busy filming them back-to-back, he might be making Coby Godspeed films forever.

We all watch on in fascination as there's some cheesy dialogue about the building about to blow, and then in the next second, Blake turns and runs for the ledge, but before he can leap over it, the director calls, "Cut."

"Well, that was anticlimactic," I say.

They reset for the next shot, only this time, it's without the dialogue. Blake is in a harness, and he runs at the wall, but this time, he keeps going.

I gasp as his figure flies over the top of the building, free-falling a few stories in seconds.

Blake grabs onto a ledge and dangles there for a moment, but then an explosion shakes the ground and the building above, and he drops again to the next ledge.

I go to open my mouth to ask when Blake got such good upper-body strength when I remember I'm supposed to keep quiet. I don't really feel like donating money toward reshoots.

The top of the building is on fire, and another explosion rocks through the crumbling building, this time on the other side.

There's a quiet snicker beside me, and I turn to find Brix trying not to laugh. I don't know what he finds funny.

Then with agility I didn't know Blake had, he turns and lets go completely, diving onto the awaiting inflatable pillow underneath.

"Cut," the director says again.

"Whoa," Harley says.

"No shit," I agree.

Brix scoffs. "So unrealistic."

Ah, guess I now know what he found so funny.

A voice comes from behind us. "What the fuck are you two doing out here?"

We turn to come face-to-face with Blake. He's still in his Coby getup, but— "Uh ..." I glance toward where the guy I thought was Blake climbs off the safety thing and then back at Real Blake. "Harley, are we drunker than we thought? There are two Blakes."

"Stunt double," Blake says. "You really think they let me do any of the fun stuff around here?"

His blond hair is all wet and slicked back in that Coby Godspeed way, and his smile still brings the same comfortable warmth it always has. When it comes to our manufactured personalities, I'm the nice one, Harley's the star, and Blake's the quietly charismatic one. Which is why I was surprised when he'd landed a role as this big, super badass on film because it can't be further from who he is in real life. I guess he's a good actor because he can pull it off.

"Blake!" Harley exclaims. "We missed you."

Blake looks at me as Harley wraps him in a hug. "I'm going to answer your question with I think Harley is drunker than you thought. What are you doing here?"

Harley pulls back and pouts. "You've been avoiding my calls."

"I've been working."

"He's trying to get Eleven back together," I say. "I'm still a firm no. But he tricked me onto the plane here by saying we were going to dinner with you. And that you knew."

Harley puts his finger up. "Nuh-uh, I never said he knew about it."

Blake's gaze flits between us both. "Is this for real? You guys really want to get us back together? What, for a reunion tour?"

Brix clears his throat. "Have you got a trailer we can discuss this in? There are a few stares coming this way."

Blake frowns. "Who are you?"

"My bodyguard," Harley says and grabs Blake's hand. "Are you done for the night? We have reservations."

"Yeah … I just need to … wait, reservations for where?"

"More drinks!" I say excitedly.

It's a lot easier to get Blake to agree to come to dinner than it was me. In less than ten minutes, he's showered, changed, and we're back in the Hummer on our way back to Vegas.

"So …" Harley says.

Blake slinks down in his seat and throws his head back. "It's starting already."

I reach for a fresh bottle of whatever's left in this car and hand it to him. "Here. Drinking helps drown him out."

"Oh, so that's what you were doing for seven years on tour? Trying to drown out Harley?" Blake grins.

"Ha, ha, ha, so funny." Though if that was my excuse for drinking in excess back then, I don't know what my reasoning has been for the last two and a half years.

Oh, wait, yeah I do. His name is Mason Nash.

"Just you two wait," Harley says. "I'm going to get you to agree to something by the end of the night."

"We already agree you're an overbearing workaholic, doesn't that count?" I blink innocently at him, and Blake snorts.

"I'm not agreeing to anything unless all five of us are on board," Blake says and then turns to me. "Mason's still a hard no on this, right?"

I'm supposed to laugh, but it doesn't come. Instead, I frown because I have no idea what Mason thinks. The more I try to think about where his head would be at, I'm reminded of the last time we saw each other, and that just depresses me.

"Done with this?" I take the bottle back off him and take large gulps.

"It's like old times," Blake says.

Yeah, it is. Harley's focused on work, Blake's as laid-back as he always was, and I'm drinking to forget.

It's exactly like old times except for two big differences. Ryder's missing, and so is the only voice of reason I've ever had: Mason.

A hand tries to rouse me from sleep, but I let out a muffled "Fuck off" and cuddle into … leather? Where am I? What is that loud humming? And why does it taste like I ate a bag of cotton balls last night?

I crack open an eye, and then Harley's face comes into view. He looks perfectly perfect in every way, like he's not as hungover as I am.

A laugh bounces off the walls of wherever we are, and when I sit up, I realize we're back on the private plane and in the air. "Wha—"

"Who let Denny drink so much?" Blake.

I turn my head to where he is in a seat across the small aisle from me. "Why are you … Shouldn't you still be in Vegas?"

"Road trip! Oh wait … Air trip?" Blake shakes it off. "We all decided last night to ambush Mason. Don't you remember? We agreed if Mason says yes, we'll all do the Eleven reunion."

Those cotton balls suddenly feel like lead. "M-Mason?" I half expect him to be on the plane too, but when my gaze darts around the small space, it's only the three of us and Brix.

Harley sits in the seat in front, the one facing me. "About that. Want to tell us what last night was about?"

Of all the times to get blackout drunk, last night was not the night to do it. Over the last ten years, I've built a tolerance to alcohol, and it takes a lot to make me forget. Trust me, I've tried. I usually don't touch the stuff unless it's at one of my parties—the ones I throw to try to stay relevant because they remind me that I'm not. Which makes me drink just to get through them.

"I remember jack all after everything we drank. What the hell was that? And why don't you two look half as bad as me?"

"We stopped drinking after we decided to come to Montana."

My eyes widen. "Montana? You know where Mason is?"

"You told us where he is."

Oh fuck. "No. I mean … I don't know if he's definitely there or not."

"We've heard from numerous sources where he is, but his address is difficult to locate. Even for Brix, who has hackers on speed dial."

"He does?"

"Oh, you wouldn't believe half the stuff Brix has access to. I will say, C4 is super fun to play with. But anyway, you told us how to find Mason. You've been to his house before."

Oh shit, oh shit, oh shit. "We can't go to Montana," I blurt.

"And why is that?"

I shift in my seat. "This thing got parachutes on board? I'll let myself out here."

"Hey," Harley says softly. "What happened between you and Mason?"

I swallow thickly. "Nothing!"

I'm sweating, and all I can smell is alcohol.

"Why don't you want to see him?" Blake asks. "You two were solid back in the day."

"Exactly. *Back in the day.* Want to know the last time we saw each other? The last night on tour."

Both Harley's and Blake's eyebrows shoot up high.

"How is that possible?" Harley asks.

"We promised we wouldn't drift apart and we'd keep in touch and then …" Then I kissed him. I can't tell them that. I also can't tell them the entire reason for radio silence now is me. I avoided Mason's phone calls like the plague until one day he finally gave up.

Guilt, regret, and confusion have followed me around ever since.

"Then what?" Blake asks.

"Then we just … didn't keep our promise."

Harley and Blake share a look like they don't believe me.

"Denny ..." Harley says. "Coming to get Mason was your idea."

I groan. "I'm never drinking again."

"So are you going to tell us what the real deal with you and Mason is?" Harley asks.

Fuck no. "I already told you."

"We're about to land, so is that your final answer?"

I swallow hard and nod.

"We still need you to show us where he lives. Can you at least do that?"

What am I going to do? If I say no and refuse to get off the plane, it will only bring more questions. Like why I'm so strongly against seeing him. If I say yes, I actually have to see him again. Plus, he'll be pissed I sold him out.

Oh, who am I kidding. Mason's going to be mad at me no matter what.

I fucked up, and then I ghosted him for two and a half years. Do I really think he's going to greet me with open arms?

Ugh. I take it back. I'll never drink again starting tomorrow.

CHAPTER 4
MASON

WHEN MY SECURITY system tells me the front gate to the property is opening, I'm stunned still for a moment. My sister and her husband are on vacation with their kids. Mom is right in front of me.

"Expecting company?" Mom asks.

"Maybe Ria is back early? No one else knows the gate code."

"Apart from those rock stars you let stay here over Christmas."

Dread sinks and lands in my gut. "Those fuckers sold me out."

Theoretically, it could be Cash or maybe Thorne. When the band stayed here over winter, Thorne, Cash's manager, and I kinda bonded. He or Cash might be back to catch up. Though, why wouldn't they call first? It could be Cameron, but each time he has visited me out here, he's used the buzzer. He doesn't have the gate code.

Deep down, I know who it is. I've been waiting for it.

I knew trusting Cash to keep my location a secret was a mistake, but he already seemed to know I was in Montana, and if he'd told the guys from Eleven, they'd know exactly where to find me thanks to Denver. Cameron has known since I moved home, so I doubt he'd sell me out now. Unless he was getting too impatient about me coming back.

The sound of a car pulling up outside gets me out of my chair and moving toward the front closet where I keep my father's old hunting rifle. It's not loaded, but whoever's outside doesn't know that.

I throw open the front door and stomp outside into the frigid spring air, raising the rifle to point at the car.

As suspected, Harley tumbles out with his hands up. Someone tries to pull him back, but he swats them away.

"Whoa," he says. "I'm Harley Valentine. I'm looking for Mason Nash."

Ugh. Another person who doesn't realize I'm me. In a way, it's been great because I've been able to go to the store without being recognized. In other ways, it makes me self-conscious about how much I've "let myself go."

"Why do you think I haven't lowered my gun?" I snark.

His face morphs from confusion to surprise. "Mase? Is that … you? What—" His mouth slams shut, and I know what he was going to ask.

What happened?

Oh, you know, moved home to be close to my mom, have lived off home-cooked meals and brownies and all the delicious food that took away my hurt. I might have put on forty or so pounds since moving home. I've also grown out a beard, stopped trimming my thick black hair, and traded in my designer clothes for flannel.

And I like it. Because like this, I'm not Mason Nash.

I lower the rifle. "What are you doing here, Harley?"

"We came to get you back."

"What makes you think I'd want to come back? I don't even know why you'd want to. You had your own career—your own success." Then his words register, and it hits me all at once. "What do you mean by *we*?"

Another guy gets out of the car, someone I don't recognize. He's built like a tank. He takes a protective stance next to Harley, and I'd have to guess he's a bodyguard. I would say bringing a bodyguard is overkill, but I guess I did just point a weapon at him, so yeah, valid.

As the next body climbs out of the car, I hold my breath because out of everyone in this world, there's only one person I'm desperate to see yet want him to go to hell at the very same time. My heart plummets when I see a head of blond hair.

Not my Denny, then.

It's Blake.

"Plenty of boy bands have moved from five members to four. You don't need me." And I sure as fuck need none of them.

"Nope," Harley says. "It's all or nothing. That's what we've all agreed to."

"Then it's nothing. Sorry you wasted a trip, but you can turn around and go right back to the airport."

I spin on my heel and go to march inside, when I hear a voice. A distinct, croaky, upset voice. My back stiffens. I know exactly who it is without needing to turn around.

"Mase? Please hear Harley out."

I look back over my shoulder. Denver stands there looking nothing like the guy who abandoned me in a hotel room and hasn't spoken to me since. His hair is no longer shaggy like it once was. It's cut short and styled on top. His baby face is still young-looking, though the bags under his eyes and his tired expression age him some.

"So you're the one who sold me out," I say. It wasn't Cash at all.

"I ..." Denver's mouth closes.

"I don't want to hear what Harley has to say. The only person I need an explanation from is you." I spin back around, and this time I get to the door before that damn voice stops me again.

"I'm sorry," Denver calls out.

What for? For running away after he kissed me, for fucking up our friendship, or for ignoring my calls for months, and then not being there for me when I actually needed someone.

I remember sitting in my mansion in Palos Verdes, overlooking the water, and thinking, *This is how my career in Hollywood ends.* And who was there for me? Absolutely no one.

With Harley, Ryder, and Blake, it stung. From the person who had been my best friend for seven years, it was soul-crushing.

And because why? Why did he ghost me? Because he was going through an identity crisis? Did he really think I would hate him for kissing me? I want him to be happy and comfortable in his own skin. I would've been there for him to work through it all, but no. He didn't want me there. Apparently, rejecting his kiss and wanting to talk about it was too much for him.

I haven't decided if I actually want to hear him out or not when I sense him behind me.

"I know this has been a long time coming," he says, his voice low. "And if Harley hadn't dragged me here, I'd probably still be ignoring it."

I scoff. "Good to know you're only doing this because Harley forced you to."

"No, that's not what I meant. Please, can I … can we come in?"

I make the mistake of turning and looking into his unnaturally aqua eyes. I don't want to give in—I'm mad at each and every one of them—but for the first time in over two years, Denver is in front of me, and I have always been ridiculously bad at saying no to him.

He's the youngest of us all, and I'm the oldest. I've always felt protectiveness toward him.

"We're going to go get hangover food," Harley calls out where he still waits by the car. I get the sense he wanted to move closer, but his bodyguard's beefy hand is wrapped around his arm, stopping him. "You two talk your shit out, and when we get back, we're all having a serious conversation."

Maybe it's time we bury the hatchet, but I don't know if I'm ready.

Harley takes it out of our hands by getting in the car and backing out the drive, leaving a terrified Denver on my doorstep.

"Come inside." If I don't take this opportunity, I might not get another one.

CHAPTER 5
DENVER

MASON LOOKS ... insanely different. Gone is the smooth square jaw and cleft chin. Gone is the short hair. Gone is the lanky, skinny guy I once knew, replaced by this huge mountainous man with a dark beard and hair that sits below his chin. His arms are thick, his chest is bigger, and his face and stomach are rounder. If it weren't for his expressive brown eyes, I would've thought some random man was pretending to be my best friend.

Ex-best friend.

I follow him inside the insane mansion he calls home. It's an amazing wood-and-stone structure, and when there's snow everywhere, it looks like a picturesque ski resort.

Inside is exactly the same as the last time I was here. Soft, plush couch in front of a stone fireplace. Hall to the right leading to guest rooms. Stairs to the left leading to more bedrooms.

Sitting at the informal dining table is Mason's mom, and even that feels the same.

Mason's outward appearance may be drastically different, but I get the distinct impression nothing else has changed.

Mason's mom stands. "It's been so long." She approaches me

and hugs me in a way only a mother can. Or, grandmother in my case. Fuck, I miss my nanna.

"Way too long, Mrs. Nash," I say.

"Mom, can you give us a few minutes?" Mason asks.

"Sure thing. I was about to head home anyway. It was great seeing you again, Denver. You boys talk, and I'll bring up some food for dinner later."

"He won't be here for dinner," Mason says.

I knew he wasn't going to make this easy on me, but by the sound of it, he's not even going to hear me out.

I've apologized a million times in my head, but now the moment's here, I have no clue what to say.

His mom's gaze flits between us before she plasters on a smile. "I'll make extra just in case. If you aren't here when I get back, Mason won't let it go to waste." She pats her son's stomach on her way past, and he winces.

I'm starting to see how he piled on the weight so fast. He might have a bit of extra padding, but if I'm honest with myself, I find him even more attractive now than ever before. And that's saying something because I've always thought he was gorgeous.

Don't start that shit again, Denny.

Not even in his presence for more than a few minutes, and my thoughts are already drifting back to all those times on tour where I caught myself staring at my best friend a little too intently and pushing every confusing thought back down into a box labeled *I don't want to deal with that.*

"Coffee?" Mason asks.

"Thanks."

We move toward the kitchen, and he gestures for me to sit at the table. There's this weird tension between us that never used to be there, and I have no idea where to start or what to say.

Maybe we should start with small talk.

Yeah. I can do that. "What did your mom mean when she said she was going home? She lives here."

"When I came home for good, she moved back into her house. She's still close by."

I frown. "You live up here all by yourself?"

Mason presses the button on the coffee grinder and holds his hand up to his ear as the whirring noise fills the space to say he can't hear me. Or he doesn't want to hear me.

I guess I don't have a right to know about his life anymore. The thought of some beautiful woman with long, flowing brown hair coming down the stairs at any moment makes my gut twist.

Mason always had a thing for brunettes. After his blonde fiancée—*she who shall not be named*—cheated on him and they broke up, he swore off blondes. Actually, he swore off relationships. He was twenty when it happened. Well, according to the public he was nineteen, but that's neither here nor there. When Mason signed to Joystar, just like they changed Harley's and my names, they changed Mason's birth year. Apparently, a nineteen-year-old serenading young teen girls was too creepy. If you ask me, making sure we were all underage was creepier to me, but we did a lot of things that didn't make sense thanks to the label.

Harley and Ryder hid their sexualities. We all played our own assigned part.

Why are we thinking about going back to that? For money? Harley says his new label will be different, but will it?

Mason makes our coffees while all the millions of memories fill my head. When he slides over a cup, I take a sip and moan.

I'm hungover as fuck, my head hurts, and part of me can't believe after two and a half years we're finally face-to-face.

"Rough night?" Mason asks.

"Apparently. I can't really remember, though."

He nods knowingly. "Wouldn't be the first time you've spilled a secret while drinking. I should've changed my gate code, huh?"

The gate code is his birth year—his *real* one, not the manufactured one.

I go to argue, but I can't. Apparently, I did sell him out even if I don't remember it. "I'm so sorry."

"Are you, though?"

"Definitely. If I'd kept my mouth shut, I wouldn't be here doing something I should've done a long time ago but haven't had the guts."

"I don't understand, Denny."

My name is weighted with disappointment and hurt. Like I wasn't feeling horrible enough already.

"You and me both," I mutter.

"Can you at least tell me why you disappeared from my life immediately after promising you wouldn't?"

Is he kidding me? "You mean apart from making a fool of myself by kissing you?"

"It has to be more than a stupid kiss."

That's what he doesn't understand. He didn't that night either. It wasn't just some stupid kiss to me.

It was all the confusion that had been building over months—no, *years*. It came down to two quick seconds of his lips on mine followed by the crushing reality of rejection.

"I ..." I have no idea what to say to that.

"Was it because you didn't think I'd be supportive of your sexuality? Or that I'd try to convince you to keep it a secret or ... that I'd disapprove? You know I have absolutely no issues with people living their truth."

"I'm not ... it's not ..." I grunt. "I still haven't worked any of that out, okay?" *Because you're still the only guy I've ever been attracted to.*

"Then what did I do that was so wrong you felt you had to cut me out of your life? It's not like you were in love with me or anything."

My gaze flies to his, and his mouth drops open.

"Oh, shit, was it?"

"No," I say quickly. Maybe too quickly. I try to cover. "Check your ego."

"I don't get it. I did nothing wrong. And then … then when I needed you …"

"Y-you needed me?" Why does that idea call to me? Mason needing me. Wanting me.

Ugh. Ugh. Ugh. Stop it.

"I needed someone to tell me everything was going to be okay when I had no faith that it was," Mason says. "I needed someone to encourage me to keep trying, and when everything that mattered to me blew up in my face, I needed a friend. You broke my heart."

You broke mine first.

I *can't* say that. I don't have the courage.

"All I can say is I'm sorry." And I know it's not enough.

We sit in silence while we drink our coffees. I try to think of something to say. Anything. But nothing comes close to being good enough.

The security gate tells me the others are back, and we're no closer to coming to any sort of civility.

Mason glances toward the door. "Tell Harley I'm still not interested. I can't … we can't …" He shakes his head. "I don't think there's any coming back from this. For you and me or for Eleven."

If possible, this might be worse than when he didn't kiss me back. My heart twinges. It *hurts*. I want to take it all back. Everything. From kissing him to ghosting him, I wish none of it had ever happened.

Maybe then we'd be in each other's lives. Maybe then I'd still have my best friend.

I need to find a way to apologize and have him truly hear how sincere I am.

I messed up, and I've spent way too long avoiding this moment. "At least take some time to think about the Eleven reunion. The only reason I've said no so far is because of you. Because I didn't want to have to face my mistakes. Your solo career might not have gotten off the ground, but this tour could save it. If you're happy to live here by yourself, then fine. Do that. But you can't let this opportunity pass by because of our bad blood."

Mason purses his lips. "Calm down, we're not Taylor Swift levels of hate. I'm just not willing to put myself in a position to be disappointed again. I don't want to go back to an industry that sees me as expendable. No one will care if I'm there or not."

"Not true. There are millions of fans out there hoping for it. Screw the execs and the industry people. Do it for the fans who made us all who we are."

For the briefest moment, I see a crack in his tough exterior, but it doesn't last long. "Not interested."

The Mason I knew was always warm and inviting, and he would've gone to extreme lengths to make any of us from Eleven happy.

New Mason's bitterness is like a slap in the face.

I guess I was wrong. Mason's physical appearance isn't the only thing that's changed about him.

I wish I knew how to fix it.

Fix *us*.

I don't think I can.

And for the second time in two and a half years, I walk out of Mason's life.

CHAPTER 6
MASON

MOM PICKS up pancake mix and chocolate chips from the shelf in the supermarket, and I promptly put them back.

"You need to stop with overfeeding me," I grumble.

All those times where I wasn't recognized on the street and felt really good are tainted now by the look Harley, Blake, and Denver gave me a few days ago. It was similar to how I felt when Cash's band didn't recognize me over Christmas either. Though, with them it was tolerable because while we ran in similar circles once, and I would consider Cash a friend—loosely—when the people you spend seven years on tour with don't recognize you? Maybe it's time to hit the gym and stop eating all of Mom's food.

"Nonsense," Mom says. "You're stocky and healthy. I swear when you were away, they didn't feed you ever, and your label was okay with that. It's like they wanted you all to look like little boys instead of men."

This is not the first time I've had this conversation with my mother, nor will it be the last. She was supportive of me moving to LA to pursue my musical career. She was not okay with me dropping out of college at the end of freshman year because I got a record deal to be in a boy band. She didn't expect it to happen that fast, and she was worried it would all blow up in my face, and then I wouldn't have a career or a diploma.

She was half-right. It happened *eventually*.

"I'm not saying I need to get as skinny as I was when I was touring. I'm talking a few pounds here." Twenty-ish. Twenty-five, maybe.

"You don't need to lose anything, but if you're doing this for yourself and are serious about it, I'll stop bringing all my leftovers to your house."

"Thank you."

She puts the pancake mix and chocolate chips back in the cart. "This was actually for your niece and nephew, not you. Geez, one visit from your old friends and suddenly you think the world revolves around you again."

I laugh and then realize something. "Wait. If you're not going to cook for me anymore, does that mean I'll finally need to learn how to do it myself?"

You'd think living alone for this long, I would've learned something, but Mom's house is literally a two-minute drive away. It's on the same property with acres of land between us, but it's easier to go there for food than drive all the way to Big Sky where we are now for our usual grocery run. I always bring Mom to the store so we can stock up and not have to come back for a few weeks.

When I first moved home, I used to wait in the car while Mom did her shopping so I wouldn't be recognized, but then I found out putting on forty pounds and growing my hair and beard made me invisible.

We finish our shopping, Mom puts in some healthier foods and promises to show me how to cook them, and then we make our way through the checkouts.

As we're putting the bags in the back of my truck, the telltale sound of a camera shutter flicking a million miles a minute startles me. The sound is like nails on a chalkboard to me even after eighteen months of complete silence.

Sure enough, when I turn, some asshole has a camera pointed in my direction. But ... how do they know it's me? I'm in invisible mode, damn it.

"Mason, have you been hiding up here this whole time?"

Fuck.

I turn back around so he can't get a good shot of my face. "Mom, get in the car now."

My fifty-something-year-old mom, all five foot four of her, ignores me. She storms over to the paparazzo, who found me God knows how, and starts yelling at him. "Can't you leave him alone? He gave so much—all of him—and you're still tormenting my boy."

"Mom! Let's go." I have to drag her back to the car.

We get in the truck, and I speed away as fast as I can get out of the spot so they can't follow us home. Not that they can get on my property without trespassing. Paparazzi are invasive, and they know how to skirt the law, but they never completely break it.

"How many times do I have to tell you not to give them anything?" I bark.

"Why are they even here?" Mom asks.

I know she means well, and her heart is in the right place, but I'm dreading the headlines tomorrow.

Ex-Boy Bander's Mom to the Rescue.

"I'll give you two guesses, but you really only need one. What has changed in the last few days? I guarantee word got out about Harley Valentine and Blake Monroe being here—no doubt when they came into town to get food."

"I'm so sorry, honey."

"Yeah. Me too. I'm going to have to lie low for a while."

"Or ..." Mom looks at me like I should come to her conclusion on my own.

"Or what?

"Or you could maybe go back to LA and face them. Why were your old friends here? You never said."

I shake my head. "They want to get Eleven back together. I'm not interested."

"Why not? You were never happier than when you were performing with them."

Ugh, I can't go through this again. "I'm just not, okay? They're not even my friends. They're ex-work colleagues. At least, that's how they've treated me since we split, so fuck each and every one of them."

"You don't really mean that, do you? Denver loves you. He was practically part of the family once upon a time."

I scoff. "Denver's the worst of them all."

"Oh. Oh, dear. What happened between you two?"

I still don't know why he avoided me. Not entirely.

"Did you fight over a girl?"

"Hardly." I wish it were that simple.

"I still think you should consider it. You're miserable at home, and don't lie and say you're not. You miss that life. You miss performing."

I grit my teeth. "It's not going to happen."

"We'll see."

"No, we won't see. It's not happening, end of story."

Apparently, it is happening.

Go to LA, she said. *Try to get back your old life.*

Motherfucker. What am I doing here?

As I stare at Denver's Malibu home, I curse my mother and the millions of paparazzi swarming Big Sky.

Denver's house is still the same as it was. It's not your typical

Hollywood celebrity home where the house is hidden by trees or a long driveway with a locked gate out front. There is a gate, but the front door is visible from here. The gate is closed and locked, but it's late, so he might be inside, or he might not. I'm just trying to build the courage to hit the intercom button.

With one extremely unflattering photo published of me, the media turned up in droves to try to get a photo of, and I quote, "The Train Wreck That Used to Be Mason Nash."

Yeah, the headlines were *worse* than I was expecting.

Speculation about my weight gain has started. Apparently, according to one source, I have a rare blood disease and the medication for it makes me appear bloated.

That's good to know.

Someone in town who knows where our property is must have a big mouth, because reporters and paps were camping outside my damn house along the fence line.

Mom's solution? Get the hell out of Dodge.

Coming here, though, I might have made a mistake. This thing with Denver … I don't think I'm ready to put all of that behind me.

I was prepared to come out here and hide in a hotel suite for as long as it took for the world to realize I'd left Montana, but money is tight. I still have some royalties coming in from the Eleven days, but I have no savings. My gut twists when I acknowledge that I'm basically broke. Well, not technically, because the millions of dollars I earned from Eleven went to building my house and bailing out my family on the failed tree farm. The land in Montana is technically all mine, but I'm not going to divide it and sell off blocks to support a hideaway location for me. I had the perfect hideaway, and then Harley fucked that up by showing his face in my town.

Now I'm here, after a sixteen-hour drive, regretting the choice to pick Denver to turn to. Not that I had many other options. Ryder has his daughter, Blake's on location I think, and Harley …

Yeah, no, I don't want to have to make a deal where I say yes to a reunion so I have somewhere to sleep for a while.

Both Harley and Denver owe me—Denver for our past and Harley for the current predicament I'm in—but I went with the lesser of two evils. Not that Harley's evil. He's just intense. Especially when it comes to work, and especially when he gets an idea in his head. He almost always gets his way.

If I were going to even consider going back to Eleven, I'd need Denver and me to be okay again. Even if it means swallowing my hurt and *trying*.

Yeah, this whole trying to convince myself I'm doing the right thing is not working.

I turn on my heel to head back for my truck when Denver's Maserati pulls into his drive. The headlights blind me, and I hold up my hand.

He doesn't drive into his garage. The car door opens, and his tall frame appears in a silhouette, hidden by the lights. "Mase?"

"I need a place to crash."

Silence. Denver stands stock-still. Maybe it was a mistake coming here.

"Or I could go somewhere else. It's fine."

Denver leaves his car door open, the engine running, and rounds the hood to approach me. He looks exhausted again. Or still. I thought it was because he was hungover when he came to Montana, but he can't be hungover now at nine o'clock at night. I hate my first instinct is to coddle him and make sure he's okay, but I refrain.

He steps in front of me. "Don't go anywhere else. You can stay here as long as you want. I, uh … This is not what I was expecting after …"

"Yes, well, after you guys visited me and made your presence known, paparazzi followed the story and found me. I don't have many other options."

He stares at me. The vibe between us never used to be like this.

I don't know if we can get back what we once had, but I hate what we have now—strained tension.

"I'll go put the car away and show you the guesthouse."

That should fill me with relief—staying with him but technically not—but I've stayed in his guesthouse before. It's a small hut out by the pool that has a bed, a TV, and a single bathroom. If I want anything to eat, I have to go to the main house. It's no different than giving me the room right next to his because we will inevitably still run into each other.

You'd think the long-ass drive down here would have prepared me for this, but it hasn't. I'm torn between wanting to hug him and yell at him.

I still think we can't come back from the last few years, and I hate that I'm here having to swallow my pride because I have nowhere else to go, but there's a part of me who has missed Denver so much, it's already made peace with him.

I already know it's going to be a constant fight with that side of me to stay mad.

Denver parks the car in his garage and goes through the house to meet me at the front gate.

He leads me inside, through his expansive foyer and living room that's filled with more god-awful trinkets and "art" than last time I was here, and as he passes that horrible duck he's owned forever, he pats his head. "Good boy."

"I can't believe you still have Bill."

"He's my good-luck charm." Denver goes out to his back balcony, and I follow.

His house is built into the side of a hill, so his entry level hides the whole underneath part of the house where he has a gym and a music room.

We go down the stairs and walk across the grass to the stand-alone square hut I guess I'm calling home for a while. At least until everything blows over.

Denver slides open the wooden door and lets me in. "Umm, so

I'll be on set again tomorrow all day. We're pulling long hours on this stupid reality show, so you'll have the place to yourself."

I read he'd signed on to be a judge on a reality talent show, and I'd wanted to call him to congratulate him but knew it would go unanswered.

So, I don't congratulate him now either. "Okay."

"'Kay." He spins on his heel but pauses. "I'm really happy you're here."

I wish I could say the same, but maybe I'll get there.

Is there a self-help book for that? *Forgiveness for Dummies*. I'd buy it.

CHAPTER 7
DENVER

HAVING Mason in my guesthouse is weird. Especially because I'm gone from sunrise to way past sunset throughout the week, so we haven't run into each other.

Every night I get home from the set, I can't help looking out at the light streaming from his window. It's tempting—so tempting—to go out there and talk to him, but my days are long, and I'm too mentally drained to muster the energy. Or the courage.

Offering him a place to stay is the least I can do, but I know it's not enough. If I could, I'd give him everything he needs, but putting myself in that position opens me up to the confusion and longing I developed the last time we got close.

I can't live through that again. I drank myself stupid and threw myself into working as much as possible so I'd be distracted. Hell, I'm still on that path, and my body can't take it for much longer. If it wasn't for the long hours I've been putting in at Fandom and coming home utterly exhausted, I'd drink just to forget Mason's in my backyard.

It's not until the weekend that I actually see Mason again.

He wanders into the house in low-hanging sweatpants and a loose tank top. His hair is down, his beard still mesmerizingly thick, but it's his arms that my gaze gets stuck on as he walks into the kitchen.

My hand freezes on the coffee machine's On button.

Mason may have put on weight and have a bit of a foodie gut, but it's as if he spent that entire time out in Montana swinging an ax. I remember when I stayed with him during a tour break, he made us go chop our own firewood. Fuck, he was so sexy. Even as a scrawny guy, the sight of him splitting wood … it made me *spring* wood.

I have to wonder if it had something to do with Mason being confident and strong-willed. He was responsible for his family and the land they owned, and he took it so seriously. When his dad had passed away, Mason took it upon himself to become the *man of the house*. Everything he did—moving to LA for college to get a smart degree and chase a pipe dream, and then landing a gig with one of the highest-selling acts of all time … He did it all for his mom and sister.

I remember the year we had our first taste of success, and we were performing on a morning talk show. The anchors were buttering us up about how we were the biggest thing since One Direction. It was probably the most relaxed I'd ever seen Mason.

He was relieved that he'd made it and didn't have to go home penniless or without a way to substantially support his family.

Mason carries the weight of the world on his shoulders, and I abandoned him because of my crushed ego. Okay, and heart. Can't forget the crushed heart too.

I can play it off as being confused all I want. I know the truth deep down.

The reason I haven't been able to face him for so long is pure and utter heartbreak. I shouldn't have put that on him, and I shouldn't have been such a shitty friend.

How do I make it up to him without sacrificing my heart again?

"Morning," he mumbles, and yep, there goes my cock thinking it's two and a half years ago.

My heart's in on it too.

Traitorous body.

I give him a manly up-nod. It's all I can do to stop my tongue from falling out my mouth.

"I haven't seen you all week." His morning rasp sounds like the old Mason. The one who'd wake me on tour with room service at my hotel door whether I was alone or not. He'd even order extra food in case whichever fangirl was with me was hungry. He was always taking care of others.

"The schedule for the show is tight," I say. "We were supposed to film over ten weeks, but production got put on hold, so they've reduced it to six with the plan to still cram everything in."

Mason frowns. I wait for the protectiveness he once would have shown me, for him to ask if I'm handling it all, but it doesn't come. "Makes sense" is all I get.

How do we get things back to normal?

"Do you have any plans while you're here, or is it to lie low and pretend Harley and the rest of the world aren't looking for you?" I ask.

"You didn't tell Harley I was here, did you?" His eyes are colder than they've ever been.

"I wouldn't do that."

"Like you wouldn't tell him where my house is?"

"That's different."

Mason cocks an eyebrow. "How?"

"I was drunk then."

"How new for you." He grunts and moves to the fridge. After perusing what's in there—not much at all seeing as I'm eating on set every day and haven't ordered food in a while—he closes the doors. "It's official. I've eaten everything remotely edible in your house. I keep telling myself to get to the store, but I keep chickening out. I'm not ready to show my face anywhere."

"I can do a food order today and have it delivered. Just tell me what you need."

"Anything that's already premade." Mason smiles weakly. "You'd think all that alone time living near my family, one of them would've taught me how to cook."

"I'll see what I can do. Did you want coffee?"

"Want? No. Need, yes please."

I make our coffees with my back turned to him, and I stare intently as it takes an eternity for the coffee to drain into the pot.

"What are your plans for your weekend?" he asks. I don't know if it's to try to fill the silence, if he's genuinely interested, or if he's as awkward as I am and trying to grasp at anything normal between us.

Usually, I'd be calling the people who always come to my parties and throwing myself into the mindless PR-grabbing stunts, but I don't have the energy for that. Plus, the last thing Mason wants is to deal with people. He doesn't want anyone knowing he's here.

"Catching up on sleep," I answer. "Maybe trying to write for my new album that may never get made. Sleep."

"Why won't your album get made?"

I don't answer him. I can't tell him this reality show was my last-ditch effort to save my dying career when his is already dead.

The coffee machine finally does its thing and finishes, so I pour us two cups.

I hand Mason's to him, black, just like he likes it.

He looks at it and then me. "Yeah, I'm not as hard-core as I once was. I need creamer now."

"Really?"

"For a while I cut out coffee completely. Turns out there's no need to stay awake when you have nothing to fill your time, so coffee wasn't really a necessity."

And yep. That's exactly why I'm not getting into my career problems with him.

"What did you do up there?" I ask as I get him the creamer.

"Not a lot. When the lumber business was going downhill ten years ago, and before I left for LA to go to college, I planted some fir and pine trees, hoping to grow a Christmas tree business. My family had been looking after them while I was on tour and kept it going. The first seedlings were fully grown when I moved home. Like they knew the whole time when I'd be back. I'd already paid off the land and didn't really need the money, so I donated them to local businesses over the holidays to give out for free. Caring for them and harvesting them gave me something to do with my hands."

"Wow. That's …" I blink at him. "Really cool."

Mason shrugs. "Everyone deserves to have Christmas. Those who want it, anyway. It's a time that should be joyful."

Seeing this big, bearded man spout shit about Christmas joy is surreal, but it's so the Mason I know.

"I spent my last two Christmases alone."

His gaze flicks to mine, and his eyes soften, but then, as if catching himself caring, he shakes it off. "What about your entourage? I'm assuming you have one now."

"I have people. But not …" *No one like you used to be.*

"Not what?"

"You remember what it's like. Constantly surrounded by people without actually knowing if they're there for you or for the fame they can get by being seen with you."

"I remember it all too well." Mason takes another sip. "There were only a handful of people I knew who weren't like that, and it was because we were all in the same spot. I never had to question the loyalty when it came to you guys in Eleven. Well, not until the end there when you all fucked off."

My chest aches. For him. For me. For *us*. "I … I was embarrassed, okay? I practically threw myself at you. I couldn't face you or what was going on with me back then."

His deep brown eyes meet mine. "What was going on with you?"

My heart stops dead. I've been avoiding it for so long. And now too much time has passed between us, too much to forgive and forget that he doesn't give me enough time to answer him. It's not a simple answer.

"Got it, you don't want to get into it. Look, I want us to be friends again if it's possible. It's hard for me to be here, and I can't do it if you don't explain to me what made you ghost me. I can't fix whatever problems we have if I don't know what they are."

Tell him.

No, I can't.

Do it.

I take a deep breath. "It wasn't a spur-of-the-moment mistake."

"What?"

"The kiss. I had super-confusing feelings for you back then, so it wasn't just embarrassment, even though that's what I tell myself to feel less guilty. It was rejection, hurt, but most of all, I couldn't understand why I wanted to kiss my best friend or why it shattered my heart when you pushed me off you and said you could never see me that way."

Mason's stoic face doesn't change. I think he's frozen.

I tell myself I've said enough, but my mouth keeps going. "I've avoided seeing you so I could avoid feeling any of that again."

He blinks at me.

Yep. Mason's been staying with me for less than a week, and I've broken him.

Way to get us back on track.

CHAPTER 8
MASON

I ... Yeah, I have no idea what to say to that. At all.

Denver looks small and young, like the kid brother I once saw him as. It makes me want to coddle him and protect him. But he hurt me. Just like I hurt him apparently.

"I had no idea," I say. "None at all. We were drinking, we were celebrating, and we were about to go our separate ways. I figured ..." What did I figure?

A million different scenarios have run through my mind over the last two and a half years. They all consisted of theories where Denver's confusion over his true sexuality made him run. I thought I handled the situation with empathy, but maybe I was wrong.

I had no idea what was going through his head when he kissed me. I'd even chalked it up to Denver drinking and he always did things out of character when he was drunk. Never, not even once, did it cross my mind that Denver had any sort of romantic feelings for me.

The other day when I'd said it wasn't like he was in love with me, something flashed in his eyes, like I'd hit the nail on the head, but then he shot that down, and I believed him.

I had no reason to think otherwise.

"I didn't know," I say again. "I'm sorry."

"It's not like there's anything else you could've done in that situation. I kissed you, you're not into guys, end of story. It's my shit to deal with."

"I still would've helped you if you were honest with me."

"Hey, I have a thing for you, and you don't feel the same way. Want to sit by a campfire and sing 'Kumbaya' while we dissect my sexuality? Sounds like that would've been fun."

I step closer to him. "Denny—"

He shakes his head. "You don't get to do that. You don't get to use that voice on me."

"What voice?" I do a voice?

"Your 'Aww, poor Denny is so lost. I must coddle him like a little lamb and bring him Christmas joy with all the other kids.' It's condescending as fuck."

"I ... I didn't realize caring about you was being condescending."

Denver closes his eyes, and I get the impression I've said the wrong thing again. Somehow.

All my bitterness toward him is suddenly replaced with wanting to make things right. He made mistakes, but apparently, I did too. I've been so obsessed with how much he hurt me I didn't consider what he could've been going through.

Because he never fucking told me.

"I want us to be friends again," I say and actually mean it. "How do we make that happen? Do ... do you still feel that way about me, or can we move past this?"

His aqua eyes hold firm even though he sucks his bottom lip into his mouth. He always does that right before he tells a lie. "I've had plenty of time to get over you. I'm not that sad."

My heart stutters because I want to believe he's telling me the truth even though the signs say otherwise. I love Denver so much, and the last thing I want to do is hurt him.

"Can we sit?" I gesture to his white dining table that looks like a glass bubble. God, he really has bad taste in furniture—that hasn't changed. "Maybe if we talk it all out, we won't have to walk on eggshells around each other while I'm here."

Denver relents and takes a seat at the head of the table. It could be a power move. This is his house, I'm the one who needs a place to stay, and he's in charge.

I'm okay with that. He can have whatever he wants. I want to fix him and make him happy any way I can. If he asked for the world, I'd find a way to give it to him.

I purposefully sit next to him in the closest spot possible, and then silence filters through the room. I guess I need to start this off. "Can I ask … have you ever been with a guy before?"

"Never."

"Not even after …" I roll my hand in a "you know" kind of way for him to get to the conclusion himself. I'm sure he doesn't want me bringing up the kiss between us a million times.

"Nope. No other guy has ever caught my interest."

"Did you try?"

"Really? You think I was going to risk going on any gay dating apps or hooking up with guys to test a theory? My career—" Denver's mouth slams shut.

"Your career, what?"

"You know what it's like for Harley and Ryder. They've kept their secret for a freaking decade. Knowing my luck, I'd meet some guy and then bam, front-page news the next day is a picture of me and him kissing."

"So, it's still entirely possible that it's not a *me* thing, and that you could possibly like men as well as women, but you haven't given it a chance."

"Possible, but not likely."

"Why not?"

His mouth drops open. Then closes. "No, you're right. It's entirely possible."

"Do you have any gay friends you can test that theory on? You know, ones you trust or maybe have an NDA? Like someone from the show?"

Denver huffs. "Uh, hooray, sexual harassment case?"

"Damn. You're right. I was looking more for the whole contracted to stay silent about your sexuality thing, but now I realize how creepy it sounded. What about Harley or Ryder?"

"Hell no. Even if they weren't both in serious relationships, that would still be a hell no."

"What about—"

Denver's eyes narrow. "Are you seriously telling me to go proposition guys to see if I like it? That's ... weird."

I run my hands through my hair. "Sorry, I'm trying to problem solve here."

"Thanks, but it's my problem to solve."

"I don't like this," I say. "The whole, you being smarter than me thing."

A genuine smile crosses Denver's face, and I think it's the first time I've seen it since we reconnected.

"I've always been smarter than you," Denver says. "You just think because you're *so* much older than me that you know better."

"What's with the *so* much older? Three years is nothing."

He fake coughs in between saying, "Four."

"Hey, according to the world, it's only three."

"Yeah, but I know the truth. I know you're ..." He sucks in a breath. "*Thirty* next year."

I glare at him. "Low. Blow."

Denver bursts out laughing into an actual, uncontrollable laugh, and I realize how much I've missed the sound.

Seeing as I'm obviously shit at gay dating advice, I switch topics in hope I can keep getting him to smile and laugh like that. "What's the reality show like?"

"It's fucked-up."

"How so?"

"Okay, so you know all the different talent shows that have been around? *The Voice, American Idol, X Factor* ..."

"Yeah."

"The producers of *Fandom* want to mesh them all together. We have teams, we have knockout singing battles, but most importantly ... we have people with hardly any talent. So extra bonus fun."

I shudder. "Sounds like torture."

"It is. I mean, don't get me wrong, I have one or two people on my team who I think have potential, but the rest are too green to try to fix all their bad habits in weeks. It would take months to retrain them."

"Whoever's on your team is lucky. If anyone can be supportive and encouraging, it's you."

"Ugh, way to make me feel guilty. I *should* be looking at this from a mentor's perspective instead of the giant waste of time I think it is. I signed on with good intentions, but ..." He presses his lips together.

"You can tell me anything, Denny. I mean that."

"My career is hanging by a thread. I might look like I have my shit together, but I really don't. My manager said if this show doesn't succeed ..."

"You'll become like me."

"Well, he didn't say that specifically, but yeah, that was the implication. And so there's a lot of pressure for it to do well, but the show has been surrounded by legal crap because the other networks pretty much know we're trying to rip off the big talent shows, and they've stopped production from going ahead at least twice now."

"Hence the scheduling problems."

"Exactly."

I know exactly what he's going through. All those doubts about his career, I've lived. But then my chest twinges, and instead of being sympathetic toward Denver, it focuses on my pain and reminds me that when I was the one dealing with the same thing, he wasn't there for me.

I'm torn because I wouldn't wish that kind of loneliness on anyone, let alone my best friend, but being that comfort he needs is a lot to ask.

"Out of us Eleven guys, it seems you and I are the ones who need the Eleven reunion the most," I say.

"And the ones who are most reluctant."

"Why are you reluctant? This could be the thing you're looking for."

Denver averts his gaze. "I was reluctant because of you. Because …"

"Because we're both dumbasses who hurt each other, and now it's hard to get over ourselves?"

"Yep."

I lean back in my seat. "Say we really try here, and we get back to how we used to be, do you think you'll say yes?"

"I'll say yes if you need me to. I owe you so much after what I did. And I know it was wrong."

"Let's not do that," I say.

"Do what?"

"Keep tally of who owes who, who hurt who more, and who was wrong. I think we can agree we both made mistakes. Yours were just more conscious. I'm sorry if I ever hurt you. You know that wouldn't have been my intention at all. Ever."

"I do know that. And that's why there's so much guilt over ignoring you, and then by the time I got past that, you'd gone home, and I … It became one of those things where I'd left it too long, so the problem between us only grew and festered. I should've made the effort sooner. I'm so, so sorry." His emphatic tone, the genuine regret in his eye, this apology finally eases some of the hurt. It's the first one I've believed.

"No more apologizing for the past, okay? Let's focus on getting us back to being friends. If you think we can work together again, I'll consider coming back to Eleven."

Denver's face lights up.

I point at him. "But don't get ahead of yourself. And definitely don't tell Harley."

He crosses his heart. "Scout's honor."

"That's not how you—" I shake my head. "You know what, never mind." I cross my heart too. "Scout's honor."

"What were your plans for the day? Can we hang out? Maybe watch a movie? Go down to the beach?" It's cute how animated Denver is now we've talked through our issues, and I really don't want to say no to him, but …

I lower my gaze to my stomach. "I'm not … I'm not really public ready."

"Why not?"

I cock my head and look at him as if to say *Really*? "Hmm, so you haven't seen the recent headlines like 'Who's the Fatass Who Ate Mason Nash?'"

"Are you serious? Who would write that?"

"Who do you think? Nearly every publication in Hollywood."

"There's nothing wrong with the way you look. It's not the Mason everyone is used to, but you still look hot."

My lips twitch. "Still?"

Denver rolls his eyes. "Well, I wasn't attracted to you for your brains now, was I?"

Joking about this awkwardness has to be a good thing, right?

"I had no other plans than hitting your gym, so we can hang after my workout."

"Or we could work out together," Denver says. "I haven't even had the chance to exercise since we started filming. It could be nice to have someone there encouraging me to push. A few weeks ago on my day off, I got on the treadmill and did maybe five minutes before I gave up and said, 'Fuck this. This is my day off, I should be sleeping.' And then I went back to bed."

Having an accountability partner would probably help lose the extra pounds faster.

"Okay, you're on."

CHAPTER 9
DENVER

OFFERING to help Mason work out was a dumbass move. Because not only are we spending time together and cracking the occasional joke between us like we used to, but now I get to watch him sweat all over the place and moan.

Jesus H. Christ, that moan.

He has these thick legs that he never used to have, and this round ass that definitely used to be flat. And as I watch him on the elliptical machine, I'm mesmerized by it bouncing in front of my face.

Okay, maybe I am attracted to the male physique after all. Maybe Mason's right and I need to look at other guys. He's certainly not going to start looking at me differently merely because he knows I have feelings for him. Had. *Had* feelings. I can't be thinking in present tense lest anything slip out.

But sitting here on my rowing machine, *not rowing*, my gaze is stuck on him. His new body turns me on even more than the skinny version of him. Am I attracted to it because it's Mason, or is it his actual body doing it for me? If he was some random guy in a random gym, would I be looking this fiercely?

His eyes catch mine in the mirror in front of him. Oops. "What's wrong? You look like you're in pain."

So much pain. Sexually frustrated and confused pain.

He stops his machine. "Did you hurt yourself?"

"No. Not hurt. I … uh … I think I'm done for the day? I'm all … sweaty." And horny. When was the last time I had sex?

"Okay. I'm almost done. I want to do one more set of weights and then a cooldown on the treadmill."

I don't like the way he's determined to lose weight. He sounds like an exec from our old label when Harley gained weight.

"No one wants to be known as the fat one." The guy said that with a pointed glare in Harley's direction.

I understand Mason's need to feel good about himself before going out in public, but at the same time, Hollywood's standard of beauty is so hard to maintain. I started drinking liquor straight because it's less calories than drinking whiskey with Coke. This coming from me, who's never had weight issues. That type of thinking is ingrained in Hollywood life. Plus, if I did drink sugary soda with my alcohol, I'd probably weigh more than Mason.

I hate what the media is doing to him. This story is going to be what he's known for now that Eleven is over unless he loses the weight and reappears like his old self.

"You don't have to push this hard. You *shouldn't* push this hard. You're doing this for an industry who, in your words, thinks you're expendable."

He climbs off the machine. "I know, but …"

"But what?"

"I used my weight as a disguise on purpose. When I realized I'd put on so much and my beard kind of hid my identity, I made sure that I didn't lose any weight. I kept going down that path because I felt like my true self for once, not some label-manufactured pop star. But now … now that the media has caught wind of my great method of staying incognito, it no longer feels like a disguise but a target."

"A target?"

"Something they can exploit and use against me." He pants from pushing himself too hard. "If Eleven gets back together while I'm still ..." He gestures to his body. "And say we're as successful as we once were, and then, I lose some weight. What is the number one question I'm going to be asked in interviews?"

"How you lost all the weight," I mutter. Of course it will be.

"There's a photo of it out there already. It might even still be too late to turn it around. But—"

"You want to try. I get it. I do. I just don't like seeing you like this."

"Red-faced, splotchy, and almost vomiting? That's a good thing, right? It's hard to be attracted to someone who's about to vomit. Don't want those old feelings being dredged up."

Too late.

"Here's the call sheet and the schedule for the film crews to be at your house next week." The production assistant shoves papers in front of me. "You'll also be emailed a copy."

"Wait, what?"

"Did your manager not tell you? The contestants left on your team by the end of this week will come to stay with you for three nights for mentoring."

My head hurts. It's been another long day, and what he's saying makes absolutely no sense.

"Why is it at my house? That wasn't in the contract." *Was it?*

The PA holds up his hand. "Please don't shoot the messenger."

This can't happen. It can't.

Mason and I are finally being friendly again. He's even welcomed me home each night this week, and we've hung out.

I've woken up twice on the couch with a blanket over me and Mason gone to his bed.

It's literally like old times.

My attraction still burns hotter than ever, and the longing stings, but I've missed my friend. I've missed him fussing over me. I just got that back.

If I go home now and tell him film crews are coming, he's going to bail. Maybe he'll go back to Montana already. I was hoping our reconciliation would give the Eleven reunion a higher chance of happening, but we have so far to go yet. This detour might derail any progress we've made to get back to normal. Well, our brand of normal.

I storm off set and go to my trailer while fishing my phone out of my pocket. My manager, Keith, is on speed dial, but it's ten o'clock at night, so of course he doesn't answer. Keith is the type of manager who only answers for his most profitable clients at random times of the day. I leave an irate phone message and then make my way to my car.

I have ten contestants left in my group. Where are ten people supposed to stay at my house? I have five bedrooms and the guest room, but they're full of queen and king beds. I'm fairly certain forcing contestants to share beds will break some sort of law.

I need to fix this.

Halfway home, Keith calls back, and the Bluetooth picks up in the car.

"What the fuck is going on?" I growl into the phone.

"It's in your contract."

"Did you tell me that?" I'm not a complete moron. I know to read over contracts before signing them, but all the legal jargon goes over my head, and I skim. Keith is great in the sense he tells me the important stuff in layman's terms so I understand. He's *usually* great.

"I told you it was an unlikely possibility that they would film at your house because it was one of the things other networks would try to contest. Rip off of *The X Factor*, I think."

"And it wasn't contested?" Of course it wasn't. None of it actually got blocked. We still have all the stupid gimmicks, and our show is put together with a million different elements to make one big Frankenstein's Monster of a production.

"They also said they only had it in there as a possibility but were probably not going to take that angle."

"Mm, convenient. Please sign this so it could possibly maybe definitely not happen. Oh, look at that, it's in the contract, and we changed our minds?"

"Tomorrow, you're culling your team by half, and the remaining contestants will stay at your house. It's four days. They'll only be sleeping there three nights."

Three nights where Mason will have nowhere to go.

"I don't have enough room for five people in my house. I have four spare bedrooms. This is a massive invasion of privacy."

"You're not really in a position to be demanding things, Denver."

"What does Alondra think about this?" I ask.

"As far as I'm aware, she's on board. You're the only one who threw a hissy fit at a production assistant."

Wait, what? "I did no such thing. Where did you hear that?"

"You know people talk in this industry. Diva-like behavior doesn't stay quiet for long."

"Yes, but I said one whole sentence to a PA asking if it was in the contract, and now suddenly I'm a diva." Fuck, I hate this part of my job.

"Put your head down, do as they ask, and just … don't play into any drama, okay?"

I end the call with him, and by the time I get home, I'm pissed off, upset, and nervous about telling Mason he has to go. I want him to stay, but I know he won't.

I amble inside, my defeated mood sending Mason's protective

instincts into gear. What does it say about me that I love it? God, I'm a masochist.

"What's wrong, what happened, why does your face look like that?" There's the Mason who always had my back. Always worried. Always *cared*.

"Why does my face look like what?" I deflect.

"Like you sucked on a lemon."

Ugh. I have to tell him. I can't keep quiet and hope he doesn't notice the cameras next week.

Can I have a shot of tequila for courage first?

Ugh, no. I shouldn't.

I hand him over the papers the PA gave me. "They're using my house for the show."

Mason's dark gaze skims over the details. "Oh."

"I'm guessing you don't want to be here for that."

"You'd guess right."

"But you don't really have anywhere else to go, do you?"

"I can afford a hotel."

"Can you?" I figured there was a reason other than wanting to reconnect with me that he decided not to stay at a hotel originally, but I didn't want to bring up the subject of money with him. I'm not stupid.

"Nothing fancy, but definitely doable. All my money is tied up in my family's land. I think I also have some stocks somewhere. I have to contact my accountant."

"You don't really want to stay at a cheap motel, do you? What if you're recognized? Imagine the headlines *then*. I hate to say it, but you kinda need to keep up appearances."

"Shit, good point."

"You could stay at Harley's?"

"No," he says quickly. "I'll … I'll think of something. It's three nights. Three nights in a five star won't break the bank." Then he keeps reading over the schedule, and I see his mind turning over. Problem-solving Mason at work. "Although, we could totally work around this. They're only filming on days one, three, and four, with day two being a solo mentor day, whatever the fuck that means. And they're giving each contestant one hour. That's only five hours. Plus, one hour for area shots."

"And if they go overtime like they've been doing every single day?"

"I have Netflix. I'm all set. And hey, starving me will help me lose weight faster."

"Healthy," I say. "Real healthy. Staying in your room sounds ridiculously boring. Not to mention, that's only the film crew who will be here for that long. The contestants are staying the whole time. Am I going to have to feed them? Water them? How often do they need to be walked?"

Mason laughs. "It's fine. I'm assuming they have NDAs in place for the show."

"Yeah, they went through that with them all on the first day. Anything that's not caught on film is strictly confidential."

Mason smiles at me. "I can handle a few hours in my room per day. I don't care if the contestants see me. Well, I do, but I'm assuming they're too green to be an industry vulture yet."

"Green might mean they won't know how to shut their mouths."

Mason purses his lips. "We'll work something out. If they're here a day and they freak out or whatever, I'll go to a hotel. And if the film crew do happen to spot me, I won't sign a release, so they legally won't be able to show any footage they take of me."

"If … if you're sure?"

"Definitely."

My heart returns to a normal rate, and I can breathe again.

Mason's not leaving.

CHAPTER 10
MASON

THE FIRST DAY of having the film crews at Denver's does go overtime like he thought it would, but it's okay because I've spent the whole time thinking I've made a mistake. I should've gone to a hotel after all. I realized I'm going to have to go into that house. Which has people in it. *People.* My peopling skills are a little rusty. Not only that, I have to trust them not to tell anyone where I am.

It's probably why I spend the afternoon in the bathroom, trying to look as presentable as possible. The beard is still there—it hides my double chin—but it's trimmed now and looks a lot less like a bird's nest.

My hair is the next thing to go. I find clippers in the bathroom cabinet, so I shave the sides of my head and use scissors to trim the hair on top so it's still long but not ponytail long. I have no idea if it's even or not, but I use product I find to spike it up. It doesn't look half-bad if I do say so myself. I'm more "Hey, isn't that guy Mason Nash?" and less "Hey, who's the Sasquatch who kinda looks like Mason?"

I'm starving by the time the film crew has gone for the day. They were here extra early, turning two of Denver's guest bedrooms into shared rooms for the contestants with separate beds. Three guys and two girls are who he has left. Denver's been texting me throughout the day to keep me updated and offered numerous times for me to make my escape.

I should've taken it, because as he texts me that pizza is in the main house and he's going to tell the contestants I'm here, dread fills my stomach.

My time hiding away in Montana might have given me stage fright. Or maybe it's my lack of confidence in who I've become.

I don't mind the way I look, and I was happy at home tending to my trees and not having to worry about much, but Mom was right. I do miss performing. I do miss LA. And the current me is not what is expected of an ex-A-lister.

I was burned when I walked away from this life, so coming back to it, I'm still heartbroken, yet there's that little part of me that craves approval. It's fucking twisted, and maybe I should see a therapist about it.

I suck in my nerves and try to swallow them as I make my way across the lawn and up the back steps onto the balcony.

Denver's voice stops me just short of the door. "So, I have a little secret to share with you guys, and it's really important when I say you can't tell anyone. No producers, no friends, nothing."

"Is this where you induct us into Scientology or something?" one of the guys asks. Smartass.

Denver laughs. "Uh, no. I have a friend staying with me at the moment. Someone who's trying to stay out of the spotlight for a while."

There's a beat of silence.

"Can I trust you all to keep his location to yourselves?"

There's a feminine squee and a couple of half-hearted promises.

"Need us to pinky swear?" a girl asks.

"Nah, this type of thing needs a blood oath," the same smartass voice from before says.

"Your word will be fine. As long as I can trust you won't break it." Denver's using his professional voice. The charming, nice, and manufactured one.

He was given the nice-guy role. The naïve persona. Probably because he was the youngest of us. In reality, he drinks like a fish and swears like a sailor.

I was given the bad-boy persona after the label used my heartache over my fiancée cheating to their advantage. I treat women like dirt, and no one can tame me. Apparently.

That's the story they give. I'd love someone to tame me. I want to wake up next to my soul mate every day and make love to them every night, but fame changed all that. After that first crushing heartbreak, I didn't know who I could trust. So I leaned into the bad-boy reputation. It's no surprise I've ended up alone.

"He should be here any minute," Denver says.

"I'm here," I croak and step around the corner and through the sliding door.

"I knew it!" I'm guessing the brunette is the one who squeed before.

I glance at Denver, wondering if he's thinking the same thing as me. The fandom of Eleven never gets old. But instead, he's staring at me, his eyes wide, his lips parted.

Oh, right, my hair. "Did I fuck up my haircut?" I run my hand through the product-heavy tufts.

"No. It, uh, looks good." He turns to his contestants. "Everyone, this is Mason. Mason, this is Cece, Declan, Henry, Isla, and Reggie." Denver points as he goes, but I'll probably remember them as Super Fan, James Blunt 2.0, Preppy Boy, Blondie, and Token Black Guy. With Super Fan being Latina, I guess they've hit their diversity quota.

I wave awkwardly. "Hey."

There's a spot saved for me at the opposite head of the table to Denver.

"Dig in," Denver says about the pizza boxes laid out in front of us.

We all grab ourselves some pizza, but there's a weird vibe around the group. I don't know if it's because I'm here or if they're nervous or what. I raise an eyebrow at Denver in silent question, but he looks as confused as I do.

I lean back in my seat. "I take it from your silence, you all have questions for me."

"There he goes with that ego of his," Denver snarks but smiles at me.

"Where have you been?" Blondie asks.

"Montana."

She rolls her eyes. "We know that, but I mean why?"

"Oh. Uh, to be close to my family. It's where I grew up. I was tired of Hollywood bullshit."

Five pairs of eyes blink at me.

"We're supposed to be trying to get these people interested in the business, Mase," Denver says.

"Right. Oops." I put on an over-the-top voice. "Get a record deal, kids. It's great." I throw them two thumbs up.

Denver's not impressed. "Okay, now you're plain scaring them."

"You guys are funny," Super Fan says. "So it's really true, then? You guys are actually friends?"

Wow, hello, loaded question. Not that they know any better. Denver pierces me with that aqua gaze I have such a soft spot for. He wants me to answer this? Fine.

"Best of." Rule number one in Hollywood. Stick to the script. Once upon a time, it wouldn't have been so difficult to say how close we are. Now ...

"He's lying." Denver smirks. "He's just here for the food."

"That too," I agree.

The James Blunt lookalike turns to me. "I've seen what's been said about you after that photo ... and, uh ... I don't really know proper etiquette when it comes to this stuff, but I wanted to say, they're assholes."

I snort. I actually like these kids. And by kids, I mean they probably range from eighteen to twenty-five, maybe. God, Denver is a mentor to people his own age. "Thanks, but it's all part of the business."

I hate that I still have that ingrained response fall from my mouth, and my instinct is to defend an industry that is full of body issues and impossible standards.

"Actually, you know what?" I say. "You're right. They are assholes. A lot of people you'll meet in this industry are. But if you call them out on it, it will only look bad on you."

"Mase," Denver warns.

"No, they need to hear this. If you're all serious about having a music career, you're going to need to hear some hard truths. Changing your image, putting on weight, having a different hairstyle is always going to make you a target for online hate. Remember when Harry Styles cut off his long hair?"

"Teenage heartache around the world," Denver says.

"If you're going to be a public figure, you need to have thick skin to survive. Is it right? No. Should someone take a stand? Probably. But there's already enough pressure on new acts to be mainstream enough without having to worry about scandal. Managers see troublemakers and run the other way. Record labels drop acts without warning." *I know. Trust me on this.*

"Now that Mr. Grumpy Pants has brought down the mood, there are good things to the industry. Right, Mason?" Denver stares at me intently as if to say I need to fix this.

"Fine. I will say there is absolutely no better feeling than being onstage"—my eyes meet Denver's—"with your best friend, and watching as thousands of fans scream for you. That kinda makes all the bullshit worth it. It's hard work, but you get to see the world, you perform for packed stadiums to people who have paid so much money to come and see you. The fandom of it all is intoxicating."

Their smiles are back, and Denver's is too.

Later, after I clear all the plates away and put them in the sink, Denver sidles up to me. "Admit it. You miss it."

I do, but I gave my everything to this industry and walked away heartbroken and lonely. I can't do that again.

Denver's breath on my neck makes me hyperaware of how close he is, and I realize we haven't even touched since I've been back.

No playful shoves, no bro-hugs, nothing. I'm sure I've brushed against him at some point—when I'm covering him with a blanket maybe—but I can't be certain.

I miss Denver's hugs. We were affectionate once upon a time, but he's been purposefully holding back. I don't want our issues to come between what we used to have.

I turn to him and grip his shoulder. Warmth fills my gut, and the feeling of coming home tries to consume me. It makes me want to pull him to me, crush his body against mine, but I refrain because we aren't there yet.

"Tell anyone I miss it, and I'll kill you." I say this as serious as I can, but when Denver's eyes widen, I have to laugh. I nudge him out of my way. "You're too easy, Denny."

He watches me walk away like some pod person has taken over my body.

There are a lot of things I miss about Hollywood, but the thing I probably miss the most is my old self. Not my appearance, but the old *me*. The guy who thought he could conquer the world and saw pessimism as a useless and unproductive emotion.

I want to find that guy again.

CHAPTER 11
DENVER

I'VE BEEN CONSCIOUSLY TRYING NOT to touch Mason because while we're on the right path, we're still nowhere near where we were. But last night there was a spark. Just a simple moment where he squeezed my shoulder, made a joke, and then walked away.

It's good, but … while Mason's trying to get our friendship back to normal, my heart's running about ten paces ahead. It's bypassing friendship and shooting right for cartoon love heart eyes.

Hell. No.

Make it stop. Please make it stop.

Today, I have private one-on-one time with each of my contestants, and when they're not with me, they're hanging out by the pool. Declan asks me if any celebrities are going to drop by, to which I reply by pointing at the guesthouse and saying, "I've already brought you a celebrity."

I've spotted Mason out there with them a couple of times, but he hasn't gone in the pool.

The show has given me an entire day to prepare a song for each of the contestants which they'll perform for the cameras over the next two days.

I'm pretty sure the people of *The X Factor* never had to put up with this stuff. I'm sure all those "judges' houses" visits were not a twenty-four-hour thing. But we have to be bigger and better than all those other shows.

It's not like I'm not used to having people in my space, but all those meaningless parties I'd throw had an ending. I usually didn't know when. I'd wake up hungover with my house trashed and people gone. That worked for me.

It also doesn't help, and I'm not being harsh when I think this, that out of my five acts, I think maybe Reggie and Cece have the potential to make it really big.

Right now, I'm with Isla, and every flat note makes me cringe. I've thought about turning it into a drinking game where I take a drink every time she screws up, but getting blackout drunk always gets me in trouble, so I refrain.

Knowing this industry, Isla will probably win because she's blonde and has the right look even though her vocals need some work.

This is the other thing. Yeah, I used to sing in a boy band. I've had vocal lessons. But I'm not a vocal coach. I have no idea how to give these contestants what they need to make them great.

I'm not good at this stuff.

Mason would be brilliant at it, and I'm two seconds away from asking him for help because my head's about to slam into the piano top in front of me.

"You're frustrated with me," Isla says.

"Not at all," I lie. "I'm frustrated because I don't know how to help you. I want to, but I don't have the skills to teach. If you were on Alondra's team, maybe you'd be getting real advice instead of trying a billion different things that don't work for your voice." Hell, even if she was on Brian Kimble's team, the top music exec, he'd be able to tell her how to be marketable with what she's got.

Maybe that's the angle I should take.

Isla steps away from the microphone and moves to stand next to me at the piano. "What do I have to do to get through to the next round?"

"You need to work hard and try to get your best performance on film."

She squeezes onto the seat next to me, her shoulder bumping mine. "Are you sure that's all I can do?" Her voice takes on a sultry tone.

I turn my head and blink at her. Did she just …

The sliding door to outside opens, and I flinch at Mason's voice.

"Hey, I thought I'd come check in to see how it's all going in here."

Thank fuck he came in when he did. Although, he looks really unhappy about it, and I can understand. Isla's sitting a bit too close and suggesting things that will no way ever be appropriate.

I'm not naïve. Hell, I've dated actresses who have been dealing with casting couch situations for years. It's disgusting and the biggest problem Hollywood has. I will never, ever contribute to that culture. No exceptions.

"We're struggling," I say to Mason. "I could really use some help. You were always so good at helping me back in the day. Why don't you stay and see what Isla has to offer?" Oh no, did that sound as sleazy as her innuendo? "Musically. Of course. Duh. I mean, what else would there be?" *Dig a deeper hole, Denny.*

I'm either doing a great job of covering what actually just happened or a terrible one. Either way, Mason eyes me suspiciously as he agrees to stay.

I turn to Isla with a forced smile. "Go on. Back to the microphone."

Mason folds his arms and stands at the other end of my piano, and hell, even I'm intimidated. Isla has no hope.

Surprising me, though, she sings it the best she's done the

whole session. Maybe she likes being under pressure. Even though it's an improvement, it's still not good enough.

"You have her singing in the wrong key," Mason says.

"We've tried different keys, different arrangements, different … everything," I say.

"Okay, so you've probably confused the poor girl. Let's strip it back and start from the beginning." He walks over to her, and the soft, encouraging Mason I've always known comes out. "Sing from your heart, not from your head. Sing it however you feel it. And most importantly, sing from here." He takes her hand and rests it on her diaphragm and then steps back.

I start in on the piano, but he stops me.

"Have her sing a cappella first so she's not trying to compete with your rendition of the song."

She looks scared now but clears her throat. When she begins to sing, her voice wobbles.

"Diaphragm," Mason says.

She belts out a note that she hasn't hit all day, and I want to scream *hallelujah*.

"Better." Mason smiles politely. "Now, do it again. With music."

I knew Mason would be better at this than me. He should be in my position. He should be on this show.

The rest of her session goes smoother than the first half ever did, but as she leaves the room, I turn to Mason to thank him when he cuts me off and says, "Dude, what the hell was that?"

I don't know if he means how he found us or her serious lack of understanding the basics of singing and how she's gotten so far in this competition.

"She was all up in your business."

I laugh, but it's awkward because yeah, I didn't like that at all. "All up in my business? Is that what the kids call it these days?"

"You know you can't go there, right?"

"Of course I do. I was about to tell her to back off when you came in."

Mason's gaze narrows in that way it does when he's trying to call bullshit.

"Honestly. She'd sat down and said something totally inappropriate. At least, I think it was inappropriate, but I can't be sure, because you know, it's in that gray area."

"What were her actual words?"

"She asked what she has to do to get through the next round." And now that I've repeated it, yeah, it sounds even worse. "Okay, I see it now. It's not gray at all."

"Why doesn't the production team have someone out here to make sure this kind of thing didn't happen?"

I lower my voice. "They offered, but I already have too many people in my personal space. I see where that might have been a poor choice."

"Do you mind if I stay for the rest of your acts?"

"Could you?" I'm way too excited about that. He can actually help these people. Maybe if they perform their asses off, some of them will still get record deals.

"Who have you got next?"

"Reggie. You'll actually like him. I think he's my number one pick to take this thing out."

Mason's brow furrows. "You've already made your decision?"

"What?"

"On who you're taking to the final round?"

I scoff. "You say that as if I have a choice. I haven't picked any of my team. The producers threw the groups together and told us who to reject and who to put forward based on their personalities. They want big personas who will do well with the reality aspect. They don't care about talent."

"That's messed up."

"I know. It's why I want to make sure that people like Reggie and Cece perform the shit out of their songs so they might catch the attention of a label that's serious about music, not just the fandom."

"I'll help. Let's do this."

"*I could kiss you*" almost falls off my tongue, but I don't let it. Because I really could kiss him again.

I won't, though. I learned my lesson the first time.

Reggie is a great person to work with. He listens and doesn't actually need that much coaching and reassurance. He's confident but not cocky. The song he's performing is Labrinth's "Jealous," and even though I've heard this song a million times, when he starts singing, my gaze gets stuck on Mason.

My fingers move over the piano effortlessly. This is one of the first songs I learned on the piano. It came out around the time the label wanted us to learn more instruments.

Reggie has so much emotion when he sings, it sends a shiver down my spine. It throws me back to every moment when Mason and I were apart where I thought about him and what he'd been doing. It was self-preservation that kept me from contacting him, but until he ran away to Montana, I was following him every step of the way.

I know people hated his solo album because, as the critics said, it was erratic and misguided, but if they had bothered to sit down and listen to each song individually, they would've seen the amazing artist Mason is.

I wanted to reach out and tell him how much I loved his album. How I had it on repeat. But I couldn't. I was jealous of every single person who got to work on that album with him, and I hated seeing him at publicity events. He looked so happy.

Then his singles failed to hit any charts, and I got busy throwing myself into making sure the same didn't happen to me.

Reggie finishes the song, and I find myself having to wipe away a tear.

"That was perfect," Mason says, his voice raspy.

"Really?" Reggie's eyes light up.

"Do exactly that during filming, and there's no way labels won't notice you," I say.

He looks like he's sweating. "Oh. Okay. Umm, pressure."

"You've got this," I say. "Want to go through it again?"

"Yeah, let's do it."

The second time around, I force myself to look at Reggie the whole time because if I even glance at Mason, all this emotional shit will bubble to the surface when I'm trying like hell to push it all down.

Reggie's eyes are on me too, and it helps to keep me focused. One of the first things I told my group is I know how easy it is to get overwhelmed onstage, and the best practice is to pick a spot to stare at and block out the rest.

He finishes it as flawlessly as the first time, and I'm confident enough to cut our session short.

As soon as he's out the door, Mason's shaking his head. "Fucking hell."

"What?"

"Do all your contestants want you?"

"What?"

"That guy is into you."

"No, he's not. He was using me as a focal point."

"It was more than that."

"If you say so." I stand from the piano and move to the minibar in the room. "Water?"

"Thanks."

I pull two out and hand him one.

He runs his tongue over his top lip. "Shame he's a contestant. You could've done that experimenting thing with him."

Except Mason still doesn't get it that the only guy I've ever had eyes for is him.

"Yeah. Shame," I say half-heartedly.

"Do you think you're going to be okay staying in the house overnight with all these hot, young people lusting after you?"

"I'm sure I'll manage. I did last night."

"My door's always open if you need a place to hide."

My mouth opens to say I'll be fine, but … sharing his room? His bed? I really shouldn't take him up on that. "All good."

"Offer's there. I don't like the way either of them looked at you."

I grunt. There he goes with the big brother act again. "I know how to turn down an aggressive fan, remember? We did it together for seven years."

"You know how to run away," Mason says. "There's a difference. Where will you run to in your own house?"

That's actually a really good point, but I don't think the answer is his bed.

I have to be strong and not take him up on his really tempting offer.

Don't do it, Denny. Do. Not. Do. It.

CHAPTER 12
MASON

SOMETHING STILL ISN'T SITTING RIGHT with me as I try to get to sleep. I punch my pillows, trying to fluff them up, but it doesn't work. I can't get comfortable, and I don't think it's purely a physical problem.

Sure, I could say that I'm being my overprotective self when it comes to the way those contestants were looking at Denver, but it's something deeper than that.

When I dropped by to see how things were going because he seemed to be taking longer with Blondie than the others, it was only to warn Denver that the mutterings out by the pool were that he was giving her extra time.

After hearing her sing, I can see why she needed it, but I wasn't expecting to walk in and find her practically in his lap.

I trust Denver not to cross professional lines because he's been in the industry long enough to know it could fuck up his entire career by sleeping with a contestant. Despite that, the scene I walked in on was just too ick.

Then the Jealous kid sang all puppy-dog-eyed, and I wanted to tell him to back off too even though he was at a lot more profes-sional distance.

The sickly feeling in my gut is because I'm looking out for Denver's career. *That's all.* Because I know what it's like to lose one, and I don't want the same for him. He's too precious for this industry.

When I hear the sliding door to the guesthouse slide open, I raise my head. Denver's tall but slim frame fills the space.

"Don't tell me," I whisper, "you found a naked contestant in your bed and you need me to rescue you." I'm only half-joking.

"Nope, but all the bullshit you put in my head about it made me too conscious of every single sound in that house. I couldn't sleep in case I did wake up to someone trying to climb into bed with me."

"Like you're doing to me right now?"

"Hey, you offered, and it wouldn't be the first time this has happened."

"True." I shuffle over. "Get in here, then."

The bed dips as he crawls into the spot next to me.

I'm suddenly aware of this only being a double bed, and I'm a lot bigger than I used to be. Denver's body heat warms my side, and my cock twitches in my sleep pants.

Huh. That's new.

Although, not all that surprising. I haven't shared a bed with someone in … eighteen months? Somewhere around there. Right before everything blew up and I ran home to Momma.

All those years of only wanting temporary fun and treating women like they were disposable made moving home so much lonelier. It felt like every hookup was a waste. Even the fleeting highs I got from it didn't make them worth it.

"You were really good today," Denver says, his voice quiet and unsure. "You helped them out more in one session than I have the entire show."

"It's because you're too nice."

Denver laughs. "Fucking am not."

"Okay, I'll rephrase. All those advisors and managers and PR specialists the label gave us got too much into your head. You always think about what you're going to say publicly before you say it because you know anything could come back to bite you in the ass. Therefore, you don't know how to be honest with the contestants without feeling guilty they might take it the wrong way."

"Mm, that sounds more like it."

I roll onto my side to face him. "It's admirable that you want to help them, but like you said, you don't really get a say in this, do you? If the producers are all behind who's going through to the next round, you may as well educate them on the things you know about the industry instead of trying to teach them how to win. Prepare them for all the bullshit coming their way if they get picked up outside of the show."

"It wasn't all bullshit, was it? You talk about it like you never had fun." His eyes shine in the dark, the faint glow from the pool lights the only thing keeping the room from being pitch-black.

"If I had to pick the best thing I got out of it … well, yeah, it would've been you once upon a time."

He leans up on his elbow and stares down at me. "But not anymore?"

My lips curve at the sides. "I'm slowly coming around."

"How against being on film are you?"

I frown. "Why do you ask?"

"I want to get what you did today on the show. It could put you back in the public eye in a positive light. You, taking time to help up-and-coming acts? I'm sure the producers would go for it because no one has seen you in, like, forever. No one knows where you've been."

"Yes, they do, thanks to those photos. And I'm not …" I almost say I'm not back to where I was physically, but just like walking in on Denver and Blondie, I get that overly sick feeling in my gut. It's an *I hate this industry* feeling, and I tell myself I should fight against the body shaming.

Things will be said online—things always are. If it's not about my weight, then it will be about how I've aged ten years instead of eighteen months.

"You're not what?" Denver asks.

"Never mind."

"I really hope you weren't talking about this again." His hand skims my stomach over my tank top, and I flinch. Not because he's touching me, but because of *how* he's touching me.

It's soft but confident, and while I thought it would make me feel self-conscious, it has the opposite effect. It makes me feel like the sexiest man alive. It's a glimpse of how he sees me, and I really like that image.

And apparently my dick feels the same way. My sleep pants tent so fast I have to hope he doesn't notice. I want him to keep going, but he pulls his hand back when he realizes I haven't responded.

"Sorry," he says.

"It's okay." More than okay, but I don't say that.

"For a moment I forgot we're not that close anymore. I shouldn't be touching you."

I shouldn't be liking it.

He stares at me, and our eyes lock. There's this electric charge between us that started last night when we touched, and it's been in my head all day. It's warm and all-encompassing. It's years of regret and longing mixed with forgiveness and a new beginning.

"So that song of Reggie's …" I swallow and try to get my breathing under control because I'm overly aware of how quickly my chest is rising and falling.

"Producers chose it. When it airs, they'll tell the world we picked the songs for our contestants, but it's a lie."

"Why …" I want to ask why the song upset him and if it touched him the same way it did me.

It was as if Reggie was singing *my* life. No matter how angry I was, I couldn't help keeping tabs on everyone from Eleven. Especially Denver. Seeing him in the limelight made me jealous, but not because he was succeeding and I wasn't. It was that he was doing it without me. He had this whole other life, and I was jealous of anyone who got to share it with him.

Since being back here, things are different between us, but that deep, raw connection we had while touring is still there. It's slowly evolving and turning into something else. It makes me question every single moment of our past and the way I used to look at him.

Lying next to him, my dick hard from a brief brush of his hand against my stomach, that friendship I thought was *brotherly* ... maybe ... it wasn't?

Maybe the urge to kick his contestants out had nothing to do with protecting his career. In that moment all I could think was they need to get away from him. If my feelings toward him have always been *friendly* and *brotherly*, why did the emotion swirling in my gut feel a hell of a lot like the words of that Jealous song?

Denver chuckles. "You kinda trailed off there."

I really did. I don't even know what I was going to say. "Sorry. I'm tired." Yes. Tired. That's why I'm having an existential crisis over my ex-best friend.

I've never reacted that way to Denver before, and the only thing I can think that's changed is our time apart.

"That song kind of slapped me in the face," Denver says. "It's exactly how I felt that first year after Eleven split. I constantly thought about what you were doing. If you were as miserable as I was." He sure as fuck didn't look miserable. Then again, none of them realized how close I was to running home until I did it.

"I thought I was happy," I say. "But ... I missed you." The admission feels heavier than it should, but that's probably because it's weighted with inexplicable urges. Like the urge to reach for him. To hold him.

"I missed you too," he murmurs.

The air between us is thick, and I almost cave in to the temptation to touch him, but then he breaks away and rolls over the other way. "We should get some sleep."

Disappointment sears through me because I'm on the cusp of some big revelation here, I can feel it.

I just don't know what it is.

CHAPTER 13
DENVER

WAKING up next to Mason and sneaking out of his room is surreal.

It's like a dream come true, apart from the no-sex thing. In my fantasies, I would've liked to have gotten off instead of falling asleep with a raging hard-on I couldn't do anything about.

After last night, I'm one step closer to gaining Mason's full forgiveness and getting things back to how they were, but I have to keep reminding myself that's the only goal.

I get my best friend back. Nothing else could ever happen.

Even if I let my hand linger on his stomach that little bit too long and he didn't swat it away. He tensed, and that was enough to tell me I crossed a line. I just wish I could kick this hold Mason Nash has over me.

It's early, so I don't expect to find anyone inside, but as I enter the house, I see Henry at my kitchen table eating cereal. This is why house guests aren't supposed to stay for long. They eat my food and are awake when I'm trying to be sneaky. Although, it's technically not my food. Craft services stacked my house with groceries for the contestants to eat. But that's not the point.

I nod to Henry as I turn on the coffee machine. "Morning."

He eyes me and the direction I came from. Ah, shit.

"Mason asked me to wake him up before production got here so he could come in and have breakfast, but he told me to fuck off because he's still sleeping."

Henry laughs. "Man, I wish I could sleep. I'm too nervous and keyed up."

He runs a hand over his blond hair. His eyes look a little tired, and not for the first time, I contemplate what this type of show does psychologically to everyone competing. They all have so much on the line.

I feel sorry for the guy. "You've come this far, and that's an amazing achievement. Winning isn't everything. In fact, most people who win these types of shows get overshadowed by the acts who get picked up by other labels."

"Are you saying I should throw the competition?"

"No. I'm saying don't worry about winning. Only worry about showing your best."

"Thanks. I take it Mason isn't joining us today, then? I liked working with him yesterday. He really helped me."

I asked him, but he didn't really give me an answer, so I'm guessing that's a no. As I go to say that, Mason steps through the back sliding door wearing his usual black tank top, but instead of sweats, he's wearing jeans, and on top he has an unbuttoned flannel with the sleeves rolled up to his elbows.

I have to swallow my tongue.

I face the coffee machine which is still warming up so it's not obvious drool is about to come out of my mouth. *Come on, come on, come on.*

"Morning, Henry." Mason steps up behind me and reaches above my head, pulling down two coffee cups. "Denver."

His warmth at my back sends a shock straight to my groin. I shouldn't have slept in the same bed as him last night. I knew that, but I did it anyway. This is where my trouble lies. I miss being close to him, but when I am that close, my brain and heart are at war with each other. One searches for him while the other likes to remind me it will never happen.

I get pulled in two different directions, and it sucks because it's like my heart gets torn in two over and over and over again. Soon it's going to be shards of shattered pieces inside my chest.

"I just asked Denver if you were going to be helping today," Henry says.

The girls make their entrance next before Mason can answer. They sit at the table and choose their cereal, while Mason leans in even closer than he already is. And he's fucking close.

Personal space means not being able to feel someone else's body heat, damn it.

"Is your offer still good?" His deep voice rumbles low in my ear, and I hold back a shiver.

"You want to go on camera?" I was totally expecting him to bail.

"I put on my good flannel and everything." The smartass toys with the hem of his shirt.

"Thank you."

"You were right. We should help them. If Joystar hadn't given us our big break and taught us everything we know, I would've been home years ago living in Mom's tiny cottage."

"We never would've met."

Mason's lips disappear between his beard and mustache as he takes in that notion. "It's hard to remember a time you weren't in my life. It feels like we've known each other since we were kids."

Yeah, I know. Because you see me like a brother. Got it.

The alert for my front gate sounds, so I leave Mason to the coffees while I go greet the production team outside.

"Hey, guys."

Camera crew pull their equipment along, and I let them pass, but I pull up one of the producers and step in front of her.

"Hi." I put on as much charm as I can. "I need to talk to one of the execs. Someone who's willing to cut a giant check."

She cocks her head. "Why?"

I gesture for her to come inside the house. "I have a guest staying with me who's willing to help me with my contestants."

She looks intrigued and follows me inside. The second she lays eyes on Mason, she pauses. "I'll get you a giant check within ten minutes."

Mason might not even accept it. I don't think he decided to do this for the money. But screw doing it for free.

The production team sets up in my music room where my piano is, and today is going to be the same as yesterday except they're going to film it. All of today's footage will probably become three minutes of actual screen time where they show the contestants practicing and getting vocal coaching.

By the time they're done with the right lighting, the set designer has filled the space with some of the ornate crap I have lying around the house so the room looks lived-in. I always need a clean and neat space to think, and all those horrendous art pieces I bought distract me, so my music room is the barest of them all. Or, was. Now it looks like some futuristic alien threw up on the place.

The worst part is they moved Bill, and he's not happy. I can tell. Duck statue or not, he belongs in my main room where he can watch all my party guests and pass judgment. Before I can go move him back, the producer from earlier approaches and taps my shoulder while holding up a signed check they had couriered over.

"Oh, and get him to sign this." She shoves a release form into my hands.

"On it."

Mason's in the kitchen, clearing away the dishes the contestants left lying around.

"There are production assistants for that," I say.

He looks at me over his broad shoulder. "It's okay. I needed something to do with my hands. I've been waiting for the network execs to say they don't want me for the show."

"You'd be wrong." I hold up the check for him.

He pulls back and then does a double take at the figure. "For one appearance?"

"I should take a cut. Like I'm your manager."

"I'm not doing it for the money. You can keep all of it."

"I was joking. And you're not turning it down." I fold it up and put it in his shirt pocket and then pat his chest. Unlike last night, I don't let my hand linger.

We have a group meeting before we start filming, and the producer tells everyone in the room they have to pretend to be meeting Mason for the first time. Oh, the joys of "reality" TV.

It's a bit ridiculous introducing Mason to them again as if they didn't spend all yesterday with him, but we move through the first few people quickly. They saved Isla for last, and I have to say, she's a good little actress. She fangirls all over Mason and screams with more enthusiasm than she showed when she actually met him.

I get the sinking impression the show is setting her up for the win.

She has some talent, there's no questioning that, but she needs so much training. It's possible for her to get there with time, but I fear if she takes out this competition, they'll slap Auto-Tune on all her albums and not care so much about quality.

Not that we can talk. Hello, boy band.

Like she did yesterday, she fumbles through the song, which is "More Than Words" by Extreme. Mason gives the same advice he gave her yesterday, and she tries again but stops halfway through.

"I can't relate to the song," she complains.

Shocking. Does she really think we related to every Eleven song?

"It's by old dudes singing about wanting sex instead of the words I love you," she says.

Wow. Umm. Okay. "That's, uh … an interesting interpretation, but it's not actually accurate *at all*. It's saying actions speak louder than words. Small gestures of affection. A warm smile. Doing something for the other person to show them you care about them."

Just like Mason always does for me. Like covering me with a blanket when I fall asleep on the couch. Wanting to protect me. He's done it the whole time I've known him.

It's my fault for confusing that for real love.

Isla stares blankly at me.

Mason steps in. "You don't need to relate to a song to sing the crap out of it." He pauses and turns to a producer. "Shit, am I allowed to say crap? *Fuck.*"

Everyone snickers.

"I'll try that again." Mason walks across the room and drags two stools out from behind the bar and moves them over to where the microphone is. "Denver, join me?" He picks up a nearby guitar and then turns to Isla. "Don't relate to the lyrics. Relate to the *music.*"

"What are you doing?" I ask when Isla steps aside so only he can hear.

"Figured I need to earn my keep." He strums the guitar a couple of times and then looks at me.

My heart's in my throat because even though I've performed with Mason countless times, this is different. This is just me and him.

He smiles at me. "Ready?"

I nod. I know how to follow his lead. Those first few years of performing together where we were all still green, I always looked at what Mason was doing because he was confident but not conceited like, uh, other high-maintenance members might have been. Not mentioning anyone by a name that starts with an *H*.

As soon as Mason starts playing, I get goose bumps before he even opens his mouth to sing. It's like it was years ago, us doing our thing and the rest of the world barely existing.

He sings the opening verse, and I join in harmonies at the right spots. I don't take my eyes off him. He's concentrating on the guitar, but then when he sings about needing more than words, he looks up at me, and our gazes lock.

In my peripheral, I see a producer bring the other contestants to gather behind the cameras so they can witness this also. This will probably go viral once it airs.

We're in sync. We sound amazing, if I do say myself, but the words cut deep.

It makes me realize saying sorry to Mason will never be enough after what I did to him. I shouldn't have let my embarrassment and confusion get to me the way it did. I neglected him when he really needed me.

Sorry will never be enough.

Maybe a big fat check from the show will help, but I still need to give him more.

I want to give him *everything*. I just don't know how to go about it without getting heartbroken again when he ultimately only wants to be friends.

CHAPTER 14
MASON

I'M STARTING to think the universe is playing a sick joke on me. Either that or the producers for this show are choosing songs for their contestants to purposefully hit me in the gut.

From "Jealous" to "More Than Words," all I can say is thank fuck the other three are singing Tracy Chapman, Coldplay, and ironically James Blunt, which is being performed by the guy who doesn't look like him. Go figure.

Yesterday when Isla was trying to sing "More Than Words," it didn't hit me the way it did today, and that's because of one glaring difference: I wasn't performing it or looking into Denver's eyes while words about love were floating around the room.

While singing, all I could think about was the number of times the lyrics to that song have applied to Denver and me. It's no secret between us that we love each other. I've never questioned it. What I'm trying to understand now is if those actions ever meant more than platonic love.

Did I lead him on? Am I being an oblivious dumbass here?

"Tomorrow's your actual performance," Denver says to everyone around the dinner table while I'm still stuck on my almost revelation.

It's been gnawing at me since last night when for the first time in years I've been that close to Denver, and my body reacted in a way it never has to him before.

Denver continues. "I want you all to know that no matter what happens tomorrow, you're all talented and have the potential to make it if you work hard enough."

"Have they told you how many of us are going to the live performances in the studio?" Declan asks—the James Blunt lookalike.

I hate to say it, but I don't think he'll be one of them. He's talented, but he's missing that oomph. That … spark.

My gaze travels to Denver. Performing with him today set my body on fire, and there was that definite spark. But the song made me question everything. Every motive, everything I've ever done for Denver, and everything I get from making him happy.

Instead of explaining it all away like I usually would, I saw it for what it actually was.

We're *connected.*

I don't know when that formed.

The hurt he left behind when he walked out of my life was so intense, I know I've never felt that way about anyone else before. It hurt less losing my fiancée than it did losing Denver.

And I've been blind this whole time. Friends come and go— especially in this industry—but what we have? I understand all the confusion he went through years ago because I can recognize it in myself right now. There's this emotional attachment I don't want to lose, but physically …

We've always had a certain level of affection that's probably more than the average friend, but thinking back to when we kissed … if it were to happen again, maybe I wouldn't be so quick to dismiss it.

Reggie turns to me. "I know this is, umm, probably crossing a line and everything, but, uh, I've been wanting to ask, and uh, we leave tomorrow after filming, so I'll never get this chance again—"

"Ask it." That's a risk. This could be anything. From asking who my fiancée cheated with—I know better than to rat out another famous person, so I would never answer in fear of starting a Twitter war—to why I ran away from Hollywood. I'll have no problem answering that one.

"What went wrong with your solo album? It had some great songs."

Ouch. Okay, that stings a little, but it's fair.

Denver eyes me across the table, and it's as if I can read his mind. *I can get you out of this. Just say the word.*

I take a sip of my water and give everyone at the table a valuable lesson. "When Eleven split, I was determined to have my own sound. I got a whole new team. A new manager, producers, assistants, songwriters. I told them, 'This is what I want,' and they happily complied. That's where I messed up."

Each and every face contorts into confusion.

Cece asks, "Having supportive people is bad?"

"Not at all. But there's a difference between telling people what to do and collaborating with your team. You need an amazing support system to survive in this industry, but when you only have *yes people*, that's where the problem lies. I had no one to pull me aside and say, 'Hey, I think this song is great, but it's not right for this project.' I didn't have enough mainstream pop to carry the album. I was so focused on sounding completely different to Eleven that I overshot it, and none of the fans carried over. Music is a great creative outlet, but you need to find the right balance between what you want to put out there and what will sell. If you're only in it for the music, you might be disappointed when sales are lackluster and your label drops you. You need to go into everything viewing it as a business. For every personal song, you need five mainstream ones."

"That's really good advice," Reggie says. "Thank you."

"Though, keep in mind, it's annoying and frustrating when your team can't see the vision you have, and there will be disagreements, but that's a good thing sometimes." I turn to Denver. "Remember how many fights we used to get into with Harley and Ryder over what they'd written for us to sing?"

Denver chuckles. "Epic yelling matches."

"I'd choose fighting with Harley Valentine over being placated and finding out later from the masses that I suck any day of the week."

Everyone laughs, but I realize something. I actually miss fighting with Harley Valentine.

I talk more with Denver's contestants and then excuse myself after dinner. As I get to the sliding door, I look over my shoulder at Denver—a clear invitation for him to come to my room later—but he subtly shakes his head that he won't be joining me again.

I want to make the argument that I have no doubt his contestants still want him, but he's a big boy, and I'm sure he can handle them.

Just like last night, though, I can't get comfortable because all I can think about is what's happening inside that house and why I don't like it so much. I try to get my thoughts together, but they're all a jumbled mess.

And now, as he surprises me by sliding open the door and falling into bed next to me, my cock again hardens. He's practically plastered himself against my side. I'm on my back, but my right arm is covered in his body heat.

"I thought you weren't coming tonight," I say.

"Changed my mind."

I want to ask what changed it, but maybe I don't want to know. I don't want to hear him say someone made a pass at him. And how ridiculous is that?

When I should have been a jealous person with my fiancée, I wasn't. Now, when I have no right to be …

"For what it's worth," Denver says, "regarding your solo

album, if I had been on your new team, I would've been helpless too. I loved every single song."

I turn my head. "You were one of the thirty thousand people who bought it?"

"Of course I bought it. I was practically in love with you."

Wait, what? "Really? *Love*?" My voice cracks on the word. Two years ago, that word would've scared me, but I've had a lot of time to think about that kiss.

I've made excuses, dismissed it for an emotional weak moment on Denver's part, but being in his house, being back here with him the way it used to be, my denial can't be ignored any longer. I think I've had deeper feelings for him for a long time. I was just never in a position to acknowledge them until after he kissed me and fled my life like his ass was on fire.

"Mase, what do you think I meant when I said my feelings for you were *confusing*?"

"That you were attracted to me for a split second and it confused you for a while." That's what I've been telling myself for *years*.

Denver huffs and sits up, running a hand through his unstyled hair. Without the product in it, it's longer than I thought. Still not the shaggy mop of hair he used to have, but I get a little glimpse of the old him sitting in front of me. "I told you that kiss didn't come out of nowhere for me."

"Come here." I open my arms for him, and he only hesitates for a second or two before he comes willingly. I roll onto my side so we're flush up against each other.

It's not like we've never cuddled before, but this is definitely closer than it would've been back in the day. I have my right arm under his neck, while my left rests over him. My hands aren't touching him even though I want them to. I want to run my hands over him like he did to me last night for the briefest of moments.

"Why didn't you stay that night and talk to me about it?"

I ask.

A frown line appears above Denver's brow. "After you rejected me, you mean?"

"I didn't mean to reject you. No, wait, I did, but I didn't mean for you to feel rejected. I saw you like a brother, and it was weird that you were kissing me. But maybe ..."

Maybe, what, Mason?

What would that night have looked like if Denver hadn't run out of there?

"Maybe if you'd stayed and talked it out, I could've seen it from a different perspective."

"What perspective?" Denver asks. "You're straight. I'm ... whatever. There's not much more perspective than that."

"What if it's not that simple?"

"How is any of this *simple*?"

He's right. It's not. Not even a little bit. But the more I think about it, the more I realize we've always been in this limbo state between friends and more than friends. I thought it was a familial feeling. But maybe ...

Am I sexually attracted to Denver? My cock says yes. My brain says I can't be. Because he's *Denny.*

Yet, my eyes keep glancing at his lips while my tongue feels the need to wet my own in anticipation of having Denver's mouth on mine again. Only, this time I'm not going to push him away.

"I'm curious what would've happened if you hadn't taken me off guard and gave me a chance to process—"

"What, you might have kissed me back? Doubt it."

"I could see it happening."

Denver falters. His face is so expressive. He still wants it. He's hoping what I'm saying is real. "W-what?"

"Maybe you would've kissed me properly and gone 'Oh, wow, I was so misguided in my confusion. Never mind. Seriously not in love with you. That was like kissing my brother.'"

"So you would've kissed me back in the hopes I wouldn't

like it?"

"No, I'm saying I think that night would've happened differently if you hadn't run away. And now, with so much missed time between us, I want ..." What do I want? "I want to set the record straight."

Denver snorts. "Pun intended?"

"There's this weird vibe between us. I don't know if it's because we hurt each other or if it's new, but I don't want us to run away from it like last time. I ... I need to know."

"Need to know what?"

I lean in closer, just a tiny bit, and lower my voice to a whisper. "If I should've kissed you back."

Denver sucks in a sharp breath. "Are you hoping I'll feel nothing? Because if we're doing this honesty thing, I have to say, I'm ninety-nine percent sure that won't happen."

My lips twitch in anticipation as I move in even closer. "Did you lie to me? Do you still have a thing for your ex-best friend?" The teasing in my voice is supposed to be playful. I might not pull it off.

Denver's eyes fill with anger. "You better not be fucking with me."

I shake my head. "I'm not. I want something to break this weird haze I have when it comes to you so we can move past it or explore it."

"What weird haze?"

"I can't ... I can't stop trying to make sense of you. Of us. It's like I've always felt more but still not enough. And I know I make absolutely no sense right now, but that's why I want to try that kiss again. Maybe this time I will get some clarity."

"What happens if you kiss me, then I want more, and you still feel nothing?"

I pause. He makes a good point, damn it. I don't want to make this worse.

What happens when it's impossible to go back to being best

friends but moving forward risks everything?

"We can work through it," I say.

"Easy as that? What if—"

"Denny." I give him my *no bullshit* look. "I'm asking you to kiss me."

He hesitates. "I'm scared."

"Of what?"

"What if I lose you again? I just got you back."

"I'm not going anywhere. I never did. You're the one who ran away. I'm here for you no matter what. I always have been, and I always will be."

And if I'm right about my theory, this kiss will be different. I'm prepared for it. I'm going into this with an open mind.

I *want* this.

I think.

"Kiss me," I demand.

Denver's eyes flutter shut as he surges forward and touches his lips to mine.

Unlike last time, I welcome it. My heart thumps hard, and I'm sure he can hear it. I feel it everywhere. In my ears, in my cock. My whole body thrums.

I can't say the answers come all at once because he's not letting me sink into it. His mouth is warm but tentative, and I can't say I blame him. His body is stiff, his lips hesitant.

I cup his head, my hand finally touching him, and I bring my other one around to hold him close to me. I flick my tongue against his lips, and Denver parts for me, letting me lick my way inside. Then he groans.

My cock responds, and I pull him closer. I have the urge to roll on top of him and pin him down, but ... kissing. This is supposed to be about kissing.

Denver's hands trail down my chest, and just like last night, I'm not self-conscious of my body like I thought I'd be. His fingers wander over my shirt like they want to explore every inch of my torso. I'm close to sitting up to take my shirt off because I want to feel his hands on my skin, but to do that, I'd have to stop kissing him, and I'm not ready to do that yet.

I want to keep going until I've found a definitive result. I want a damn epiphany. But I don't think that's how this works in real life.

I'm loving kissing him. I'm enjoying being pressed against his body. It's bigger and more masculine than I'm used to, but that only makes me hold tighter. I run my hand down his back, exploring and taking him all in.

My body trembles, my cock aches, and while that should be proof enough, I want to keep feeling good without overthinking it.

The basics of it are simple: Denver means the world to me. He's the only person I've ever cried over, other than when my dad passed away, but living without him sucked, and I never want to do it again.

At the same time, I don't want to sit back and analyze my sexuality and dissect it or struggle with it, and maybe that's what has been making me put all that raw emotion in a box labeled *Doesn't Make Sense So Don't Even Try*.

Out of nowhere, Denver breaks his mouth from mine.

"No." I follow after him, trying to get him to kiss me again, but he holds firm.

"Mase …" He sounds so tortured. "If you're going to freak out, I need to know now."

"I'm not freaking out. I want more."

"More what?"

Damn, I don't know the answer to that. It's like I'm a teenager again, back when kissing was everything and the thought of sex was alluring, but the thought of going below the belt made me nervous as fuck.

"Keep kissing me? Please?"

"Not enough data to find an answer?"

"Exactly."

Denver pulls away completely now. "Instead of more kissing, I think maybe you should try to wrap your head around what we just did because at some point, I need to protect myself."

I want to protest, but can I? Here, in this moment, there are so many things I want to do to him, but when it comes to tomorrow and how I'll be feeling then, I have no idea what's going to happen, and it's unfair of me to ask him to do anything more when I can't give him a clear answer.

"That's fair," I say.

He flops back onto his pillow and then rolls away from me. A coldness fills the gap between our bodies, and our breathing is the only sound in the dark room.

I want to say something, but I don't have the right words. No words in the English language could adequately describe what that was.

My cock aches, but telling him I have a major case of blue balls could either help this situation or make things worse. This isn't really about sex.

Denny's breathing is uneven, and there's this tension rolling off him, letting me know he's not asleep.

"Denny?"

"Mm?"

"I …" I what? *I really liked kissing you. I wasn't expecting to like it so much. I want to do it again.*

All of the above.

I went into that half expecting Denver to realize he was wrong, not the other way around. I'm glad to be wrong, but at the same time I'm not. Because I'm no closer to working out what has changed between us.

I can only accept that something has.

"Uh, goodnight," I mutter.

"Night."

Yep. I'm definitely not getting any sleep.

CHAPTER 15
DENVER

I HAD no idea my self-preservation instincts were stronger than my need to get off, but apparently, they are.

I shouldn't have even kissed him, and I know I'll regret it come daylight. Which will be soon because there's no way I can sleep after *that*, and I've been staring at the bathroom door ever since. Without a doubt, if I rolled over, I wouldn't be able to stop myself from touching him.

Kissing him.

Heartache be damned.

Mason's mouth is as strong and confident as he is. His touch is as warm as his heart.

If I was confused years ago, I'm not now.

I've been in love with Mason Nash for close to ten years. Nothing compares to being with him even if we're just hanging out. And that's why I had to stop kissing him. Because as desperate as I am to be closer to him, to explore his body with my tongue, and do many, many things I've only ever fantasized about, I know if I didn't stop it, I'd be in so deep I'd never recover from it if he walked away.

If it had gone any further, everything would've become *real*.

My hopes would get too high. I'd be devastated beyond measure when he inevitably says he can't love me like that.

Everything inside me wants to take the only chance I might get to be with Mason, but there's the tiny piece of my heart that knows the truth. He kissed me because he was hoping I'd hate it and have some big revelation. That suddenly, I'd pull back and say, *Huh, I do only see you as a brother.*

News flash and no shock here: it only made me want him more.

I should get a medal for pulling away.

When the breaking light of dawn filters in through the small gap in the curtains, I slip out of bed to make a break for the house.

"You didn't get any sleep either?" Mason's groggy voice makes me pause.

I turn to find him slowly sitting up and running a hand over his beard.

"You've been awake this whole time?" I ask.

"Yeah ... been thinking. Trying to organize the jumbled thoughts in my head." That hand runs over his black hair now, and while it's trendier how he's cut it, I kinda miss the longer hair. It suited him.

"I'll go make us two really big cups of coffee," I say.

Mason's mouth tips upward on one side, giving a sexy half-smile.

My heart gallops and then skips a beat because I'm picturing things I shouldn't be. Like waking up next to him every day. Making coffee for both of us indefinitely.

But like I told him last night, he needs to process it first.

Ironically, it's all *I* can think about. All. Fucking. Day.

Today should've been the shortest shoot of them all seeing as the contestants get one chance to perform their song for me and Mason. But, again, they blindside me by saying that's what we're telling the audience. We're actually going to do as many takes as we can until we get the perfect performance out of each and every act.

By the fifth artist, I'm about ready to bullshit my way out of it and tell them they are perfect even if they're not.

I swear production is doing it because they know I'm impatient for everyone to get out of my house.

And then? When we finally wrap for the day? A production assistant guides us all inside where craft services has organized a goodbye thing. Even though we're all back in the studio on Monday.

I'm supposed to be the nice one, but I'm thinking my manufactured persona is wrong. I'm about to become the homicidal one.

I catch Mason's eyes across the room, just like I've been doing all day. From watching my reactions to the contestants' songs to smiling at me right now … I'm eager to ask him how he feels after he's had time to think about last night. At the same time, I'm dreading it because as hopeful as I am that he has the sudden urge to switch teams, reality doesn't work like that.

Even if I catch his heated gaze more than once.

Focus on the contestants. Get through this goodbye party. Try not to stare at Mason.

I distract myself with food, shoving a cracker and all the camembert cheese as I can manage down my throat.

Mason's distinctive chuckle rings out, and when I swallow, I find him standing a few feet away, watching me. Mmm, I'm sure the attractive sight of stuffing my face will have him falling at my feet and offering to blow me as soon as everyone leaves.

Considering I thought they'd all be gone by midafternoon, when the sun begins to set over the horizon, I'm about ready to throw them all out.

After no sleep and hours of having Mason's intense dark gaze on me all day, I'm exhausted, horny, and I can't decide what I need more: a drink, a fuck, or three days of sleep.

A fuck is out of the question. I know I *shouldn't* drink because since Vegas and the impromptu trip to Montana, I haven't touched a drop. I've stayed strong even though I've desperately wanted to drink just so I could dim all the emotions Mason's presence has dredged up. So that means it looks like passing out is the option I'm gonna have to take.

Hurrrrrry up and leave.

I even start doing dishes as a massive hint, and I *never* do dishes—that's what hired cleaners are for—but at least it's quiet in the kitchen.

Turns out parties full of people you hardly know are boring when you're sober. Who knew?

I'm almost done rinsing the dishes to go into the dishwasher when a presence behind me makes me flinch. I'm so tired I didn't hear Mason come in, but now that he's practically pressed against me, I need all my strength not to lean back against his big body.

"You know, I've heard detergent washes dishes better than just water."

"Ha, ha, smartass. I'm only rinsing them all before putting them in the dishwasher."

"They have production assistants for that."

I spin, and Mason takes a step forward, boxing me in. It's a brave move considering I can still hear everyone out in the main area of the house.

"Are you hiding from me or from everyone?" His low voice goes straight to my cock.

I clear my throat and look Mason in the eyes. "Haven't I peopled enough for four days?"

He has me locked in place, and I'm fighting every urge to lean in and kiss him again. That has to come from him.

"I thought today was a good day," he rumbles.

I got to spend it with him by my side, so yeah, I guess it was good. Exhausting and long, but he's all that matters.

Mason licks his lips as his gaze drifts down to mine. I mirror his movements.

For the briefest of moments, I think he is going to kiss me.

Kiss me, kiss me, kiss me, I silently beg.

He doesn't. Mason steps away. "You always were a bit of a loner."

No, come back. I'm not a loner. I just want to be alone with you.

"I guess we have that in common," I point out. "You ran away to Montana ..."

"There's a difference, though. I didn't have much of a choice. You surround yourself with people, but you don't enjoy it. You've always been like that. And one day, you're not going to be able to pull off the nice-guy act anymore. No one is as happy as the person you are on camera twenty-four hours a day. You need an outlet." He moves to the dishwasher and starts stacking plates.

He's right, of course, but I don't want to go there.

"In your words, they have production assistants for that." I nod toward the dishwasher.

"I'm being helpful."

"Mm. Helpful or torturous?"

Mason's deep brown eyes crinkle at the edges like he's trying not to smile. "Me doing your dishes is torturous?"

It's sexy is what it is.

I don't have the balls to say that. "It's scary. You ... doing something so domestic? Never would've happened back in the day."

"You know I've been living alone for over a year, right? Who do you think did the dishes?"

I narrow my gaze. "Your mom?"

"I do have the ability to look after myself, thank you very much."

"But you still can't cook."

"You can't either!"

"I can cook more than you."

"A turtle can cook more than me. That isn't an accomplishment."

I grab the closest dish towel and whip him with it, laughing when his whole body tenses.

"I know you didn't just do that. There is no possible way Denver Smith threw down that challenge."

"Why wouldn't I?"

"Because he knows he will lose."

"Do I, though? I mean … really?"

"Oh, it's on." Mason steps closer to the counter where there's another dish towel, but I step in front of him and whip at him again.

It makes a satisfying thwack against his arm.

"Son of a—" He reaches around me, pinning me against the counter again. "You're going down, Denny."

"I wish." I really do wish.

Mason pauses, and I waggle my eyebrows at him. His mouth drops open, and I take the opportunity to use his distraction to my advantage. I steal the other dish towel, so now I have both.

"Oh, so you're going to play dirty," Mason says. "Good to know."

We struggle and wrestle, Mason's hips still pinning me against the counter as he tries to get a towel from one of my hands.

Damn, he's stronger than he used to be.

I spin so I'm facing the counter, and I clutch the towels to my chest, but holy fuck, that's the wrong move. Because now Mason's big body is pressed against my ass, and if I'm not mistaken, that very big, very hard thing digging into my back isn't his leg.

He's … hard? For me?

I look at him over my shoulder. His expression is so lustful it makes my dick ache. His dark eyes are fiery and focused on my lips.

It's difficult not to push back and rut against him, but I hold firm because I think he's going to kiss me again.

His pink tongue darts out the tiniest bit, and then—

He steps back and turns toward the dishwasher.

I blink.

What just happened?

Did he chicken out? Is he trying to drive me fucking crazy?

I startle at a feminine voice. "People are starting to leave." The production assistant stands near the entrance to the kitchen, her gaze ping-ponging back and forth between Mason and me, and suddenly it makes sense.

We were too careless.

"Thanks," I say to her with a casual smile. "I'll be right out."

As soon as she leaves, Mason's entire body relaxes.

I snap the towel at his ass one last time. "You have the ears of a dog."

"Luckily."

Yeah, if she'd have walked in a second or two later, we'd be having a very different conversation.

"I'll go say bye to everyone."

"I'll be here." He still hasn't turned around or looked at me, but I know what I saw.

I know what I *felt*.

Mason wants more of last night, and I'm not strong enough to hold back.

These people can't get out of here fast enough.

CHAPTER 16
MASON

WHAT IS GOING on with me?

If that same scene had happened years ago, Denver and I would've play fought, wrestled, had fun, and it would've ended when one of us gave in or accidentally got a towel to the eye.

It's all fun and games until someone gets hurt.

This time, though, messing around, being pressed against him, I've never been more turned on in my life. I don't think I've ever been so hard that a few thrusts through layers of clothes could've sent me over the edge.

I wanted to kiss him. Since last night, I haven't been able to get his mouth out of my head. All day, I've been reliving it. Hearing his moan every time he speaks. I was two seconds away from closing the gap so I could hear it again when I heard the PA coming.

She could've seen anything. I'm still not entirely convinced she didn't see something. I'm not sure I was quick enough to move away. I made sure not to turn around because she would've seen the massive bulge in my jeans, and that wouldn't look suspicious at all.

My insides are still buzzing, though.

Reggie comes to find me to thank me for all my help which is touching, but I scare the poor guy by jumping a mile high when he simply says, "Hey."

I'm on edge, and I need to get a grip.

I haven't even begun to find clarity in my feelings for Denver beyond not wanting to lose him and trying to hide my permanent hard-on around him today.

Seriously, he tells a contestant they did a good job, bam, my dick responds. He smiles at me from across the room, my dick gets happy. Worst of all—or is it best of all?—when we were messing around, all I could think about was holding him close while I came all over him.

That's definitely not best-friend feels.

There's that old saying, absence makes the heart grow fonder. Can absence make your dick grow fonder too?

I walk Reggie out after he's done thanking me and notice aside from one more production assistant, Reggie's the last to leave. When they're both gone, I turn and shut the front door and lock it behind me.

I find Denver standing in the middle of his informal sitting area where he'd fallen asleep nearly every night last week, and our eyes lock.

My feet take tentative steps toward him as I approach cautiously. I'm waiting for him to ask me my thoughts on last night, but all he does is watch me with his stunning eyes. I'm thankful because all I could probably answer with is *"I don't know, but I want more of it."*

"They're finally gone," I say, stopping a few feet away from him. Any closer, I might not be able to contain myself.

"Finally," Denver growls. Without warning, he grips my shirt and pulls me against him, slamming his mouth against mine.

I guess *he's* the one who can't contain himself. Unlike last night where he was hesitant, he's all in now. He's forceful and confident, and fuck if that doesn't turn me on.

I've been wanting to do this all day. When I haven't been watching Denver, I've been thinking about last night's kiss and how much I wanted to pin him down.

My hands run down his back and grip his ass, pulling him against me so he can feel how hard I am already. If that doesn't give him his answer to if I want this or not, I don't know what will. You know, apart from me saying the actual words, but I'm not there yet. Doing this and admitting aloud what it means are two very different things.

Denver's tongue tangles with mine, but it's not enough. I want to push him against the wall or down on the floor. I want to get closer even though I'm already pressed against him.

He works his hands inside my flannel shirt and slips it off my shoulders, leaving me in my tight tank top. I want to lose more clothing, but I'm nervous.

This is different than I'm used to. Because he's closer to my size? Because his mouth is forceful and takes the lead? Or is it that this is my best friend in the whole world and everyone I've been with for the last decade are women who only wanted me for my fame.

Denver and I, we know everything there is to possibly know about one another, but now … this is learning something new. I'm learning if I grip the back of Denver's head, a little whimper leaves his mouth. If I kiss him harder and try to take control, he doesn't back down. He trembles in my arms like he wants more but doesn't have the courage to go for it.

I want to tell him to do whatever he wants with me, but I might not be ready for that. I have no fucking clue what I'm doing.

Denver backs us up so slowly I don't even realize he's pushing me down on the couch until I'm on my back and he's on top of me. His plush couch is wide enough to hold us both and long enough our feet don't hang off the end.

His erection digs into my hip, and it's … different … empowering maybe, to know that I'm doing that to him. That he's doing that to *me*. I'm just as hard and needy as he is.

I try to take in the new sensations, the heavy weight on top of me, and the strong mouth on mine, but he doesn't give me the chance.

Denver breaks away from me, putting his hand next to my head so he can hover above me, and I want to pull him back down. I want to keep kissing him.

But then he says, "I want to touch you," and I get a chance to catch my breath and think this through.

My entire body is screaming *yes*, but his voice is so small I can't stand it. I don't think it has anything to do with lack of confidence. The wariness in his tone matches the doubt in his eyes and makes me think it's fear holding him back. He's worried I'm going to say no or change my mind.

I need to reassure him that I don't plan on pushing him away.

"Touch me," I beg.

My cock throbs as I anticipate Denver's hand on me. His hesitance is gone as he rises and lifts my shirt up to my pecs with one hand while he flicks the button on my jeans with the other. And then? His head dips as he kisses along my stomach.

A shudder rolls through me. I should be self-conscious. I should hate that he's focusing his mouth *there*, but as his hot breath ghosts my skin, and his hands lower the zipper on my jeans, he glances up at me through thick lashes with a look of awe filling those hypnotic eyes, and I'm no longer body-conscious because he stares at me like I'm the most attractive person he's ever seen.

His mouth moves up, trailing hot, wet kisses up my chest, and then it's back on mine, his tongue pushing past my lips as he shoves his hand inside the waistband of my pants and wraps his hand around my aching cock.

Denver's warm palm on my tight skin, his firm grip, and his

callused fingers get me to the edge faster than I thought possible. It's intense, it's explosive, but fuck, I can't come too fast.

Sure, I could blame no one touching my cock in a really long time—including myself—but that would be a cop-out. I'm teetering on the brink of orgasm because of the same reason I was crushed when Denver left me. There's something between us that I've been blind to but not anymore.

I want to figure it out with him. I can't go home again.

Back in Montana, I went through some dark shit. I was feeling worthless and like a failure, and if it weren't for my mom and sister and her family, I don't even want to contemplate the news headlines that people would've been reading about me. Because without their support, there was nothing stopping me from walking out into the snowy forest and never coming home.

I thought my depression was over my career, but being back here, being with Denver, it's shown me it was so much more than that.

I lost the best friend I've ever had, and I never realized how much light he brought to my life until I didn't have it anymore.

He strokes me with an expert hand, making me question if he lied when he told me he's never been with a man. Then again, I guess it's not any different giving a handjob than jerking off, and I perfected that when I was a teenager.

Denver's thumb swipes over the head of my leaking cock, and every muscle in my entire body contracts. I try to thrust up into his hand, but he's big and strong, boxing me in. I can barely move.

"More," I say into his mouth, but it comes out all muffled. He keeps going, only now he's grinding on top of me, using my body to get himself off.

I try to reach between us because we're both still clothed. His pants are zipped up, mine only undone. I want to even the playing field a bit, but he shakes his head, and his mouth breaks away from mine.

"Let me do this. Let me show you how much you turn me on."

"I want you to feel good too."

"I'm so close to coming, any more and this will all be over way too fast. I want this to last a little while longer." His words send a tingling sensation down my spine.

Denver takes my hand and pins it above my head and then asks me to do the same with my other one.

I let him hold me down while he keeps jerking me and rubbing his cock over my hip.

He stares down at me with this blissed-out expression that's so fucking beautiful. His cheeks are flushed, his hair is sweaty, but it's the look in his eyes that does me in. It's as if he doesn't want to break his gaze in fear I'll disappear. That this isn't real.

I want to cup his cheek, and I want to hold him close, but I can't.

"Denny ..." I whisper.

That's all it takes. His hand jerking my cock doesn't slow down as he trembles and makes a grunting noise that turns me on like no other sex noise ever has. It's a deep rumble and sounds completely involuntary.

It sends me over the edge too. Red-hot lust shoots through me, while my cock erupts and my body tries to ride out the orgasm. I writhe beneath him, lost in lust and pleasure.

He thrusts a couple more times, but his hand doesn't let up until I melt into the couch.

Denver uncoils and relaxes, and his heavy body collapses on top of me. I expect it to get uncomfortable really fast, but the opposite happens. My arms wrap around him, and he molds to me like we fit perfectly together.

I could stay here the rest of the night. Or my life.

His head is buried in my neck, and our breathing syncs so our chests rise and fall as one.

"Sorry," he says. "I know I said I didn't want to do that, but ..."

"You couldn't resist me. I get it."

"Wow. You could rival Harley with that ego."

"No one can rival Harley in the ego department."

Denver laughs, but then it dies off quickly. "We didn't just ruin everything, did we?"

"Not even close."

He lifts his head. "You're not freaking out?"

"Not about this." I lean up and touch my lips to his. We kiss in a lazy postorgasmic haze, but then he asks the one thing I can't answer.

"What *are* you freaking out about?"

Everything, nothing, our lives, what a future looks like, walking away from this and losing him again, making past mistakes, making future ones … you know, nothing major.

"I might have developed a touch of anxiety over the last couple of years, so I kind of worry about everything," I say vaguely.

"So it is about me." Denver finally moves to sit up, and I do the same, tucking myself away in my cum-covered pants.

"It's not about what we just did. That … that came more naturally than I thought it would."

He cocks his eyebrow at me. He's either mocking the accidental innuendo or calling me out for sounding somewhat judgmental.

"Not that it's *not* natural," I'm quick to add. "It's like when you get a new pair of shoes and they feel weird at first … no, wait, that's a bad analogy because it implies I didn't like that. I did. Uh, obviously." I gesture to where my cum is all over my jeans and his shirt from where he wiped his hand. "I thought it would feel *weird*, and it didn't. That's what I meant."

Denver breaks into a small smile. "You should shave your beard."

"What? Where did that come from?"

His finger trails over my cheek, the part above my beard. "I don't think I've ever seen you blush before, and I want to see it all." His hand moves to my neck where it feels hot.

I swat his hand away. "I'm not blushing."

"You're so blushing."

"Do you have plans for your weekend away from your contestants?" Yes, Mason, change the subject. That's a surefire way to make sure he never brings it up again. Moron.

"Not much. Work out, sleep ..." He leans in, dipping his mouth next to my ear. "Maybe try to entice you for a repeat."

"Wouldn't need much enticing. Research, maybe, but not enticing."

"Mm, research sounds fun. Can I add that to my list of things to do this weekend?"

"Are you telling me you've never watched gay porn? Even when you had those confusing feelings back in the day?"

It's Denver's turn for his cheeks to turn pink, but unlike the asshole he is, I'm not going to call him on it. "I might have," he says cautiously. "But total honesty here, it didn't really do anything for me unless ..."

"Unless, what?"

He looks unsure but doesn't break eye contact as he says, "Unless I was picturing *you*."

CHAPTER 17
DENVER

MASON DOESN'T REPLY for a long time, and I think I may have broken him. I thought the handjob might have been pushing it, but apparently, no. Telling him I've watched gay porn and thought of him, implying I've jerked off to him *many* times, is the thing that crosses a line.

"Mase?" I wave my hand in front of him to make sure he's not stroking out.

"Is it weird I find that oddly romantic?"

I blink at him. He finds *that* romantic? "Yes, it's weird."

"Okay. I'll stop, then."

"Stop what?"

He stands. "I'll stop picturing what that would've looked like. I should get cleaned up anyway."

I'm left staring after him as he ducks out the sliding door to the backyard and runs down the steps to get to the guesthouse.

I should really get up and shower, but I can't bring myself to move yet. I lean back on the couch and blink at the roof. Did that just happen?

The evidence of it is in my underwear and on my shirt. My face still stings from beard rash.

Did I really jerk off Mason Nash? How am I even thinking these words right now?

Mason.

Mason Nash.

His mouth on mine, my hand on his dick …

But now he's gone, and I realize he didn't even think to suggest we clean up together.

I mean, of course he didn't.

Mason hasn't exactly given me anything to cling to. A handjob isn't going to flip a switch.

I should've forced myself to hold back, but after messing around with him in the kitchen, and with him staring at me all day, I couldn't help myself.

Oh, Denny, you naïve fuckhead.

I head to the bar and pour myself my usual even if I'm in dire need of a change of pants. This calls for a drink or ten.

The amber liquid swirls in the bottom of the glass, but as I go to take a sip, I pause.

My hand shakes.

I can't seem to bring it to my lips.

I've been sober for twenty-eight days. Four whole weeks. I know because I counted. Ever since we turned up on Mason's doorstep after I went and blurted shit I shouldn't have to Harley and Blake. It's unheard of for me to go that long, but ratting out Mason's location like that, and then seeing him, it made me reevaluate some things.

While I don't think I have a drinking problem, I have a problem with drinking. There is a difference even if it's only slight.

There's no doubt with my biological parents being the delightful people that they were, I'm prone to addiction, but I don't crave alcohol when it's not there. I crave it when I have issues to face that I really don't want to. Temptation and addiction go hand in hand, and maybe I'm in a little bit of denial, but as I stand here, drink in hand, I realize I don't want to handle this Mason situation the same way I do my other problems.

There technically isn't even a problem right now. All my fantasies from the last few years just came true. I should be happy, not staring down a glass of whiskey.

I have no idea what's going on in Mason's head which makes me insecure, which makes me want to drink.

It's not healthy.

With my last ounce of willpower, I pour the drink down the sink and practically run to my bedroom to shower.

I finally have my house back, and the last three nights, while they've brought Mason and me closer than we've ever been, they've also exhausted me beyond words.

If everything sticks to the schedule, we should only have two more weeks of shoots until the show is wrapped up. At least until the live finale in a few months after all this lead-up is aired.

The high from my first ever shared orgasm with a guy doesn't last long as I wash all the cum off me. I take my time, trying to hold on to any last shred of satisfaction, but it's no use. When the high is stripped away, all that's left is doubt.

I rinse and get out, drying off with my towel and then shoving my legs into sweats. I don't bother with a shirt, and I wonder if Mason will reappear for dinner or if he'll hide away in his room for the rest of the night.

Is that why bitterness is clawing at me?

Because he went to his room? Or is it because he didn't ask me to go with him?

Welcome to Overthinking, LA. It's my permanent residence when it comes to Mason Nash.

The sound of manly grunts fills my ears as I make my way back to the informal living area, and I'm confused as fuck. Right up until I see Mason's dark head of hair poking up over the top of the couch, and as I get closer, his laptop comes into view.

He's watching porn … *Gay porn.*

"What are you doing?" I ask.

He turns his head and looks back at me with a smile. "Research. I'm getting a head start."

"Porn research. Looking for a new career? Think you'll go gay for pay?" I have to joke about this because every negative thought I had two minutes ago, they're all gone. Because he's watching porn. Yep, that's how easy it is for poor Denny Mariano to forget all the reasons to protect his heart.

"Research for us, dumbass."

My heart skips a beat, but I tell it to calm down and not get ahead of itself. "Us …"

"Hey, you might've fantasized about being with guys—"

"You," my stupid mouth says. "It's only ever been you."

His dark gaze holds mine for a beat before he turns back to the obnoxiously loud sex noises coming from his laptop. "Anyway, my point is, you know how there's like all these sex acts you've never done, so you're nervous to try them? I have no clue what guys do to get off with each other. I've never really thought about it. I actively tried *not* to think of Ryder's and Harley's sex lives because that'd be like thinking about my sister having sex, and *eww*." He shudders.

I thought about ways I could get off with Mason every damn day for … well, *years*. I try to think back to when my view of him really started changing. It wasn't an overnight thing. It was gradual until one day I realized I'd been checking out Mason's ass for the fiftieth time that week, and I'd get butterflies whenever he so much as looked my way.

I clear my throat. "Getting off with a guy is not all that different than with a woman, and if you can't think of the logistics on how to do that, I feel sorry for all the women you've been with."

He snorts. "So do I, actually. You know what boy band sex was like. Wait, that sounds kinkier than it should."

"Yeah, it was all pretty vanilla. It had to be."

"Could you imagine what Vivian would've said if it leaked into the tabloids that one of us was a full-on Dom? Oh, the outcry!"

Vivian was our own personal PR tyrant. The one responsible for our manufactured personas and our good boy reputations.

"Yeah, the NDAs she handed out like candy were fun," I say.

"Out of curiosity, if one of us was a Dom, who would it be?"

"I'm not touching that with a fifty-foot pole."

"Who'd be a sub?" Mason asks but then as if he realizes his question is a no-brainer says with me, "Blake."

Blake's the type of guy who'll go along with anything. I'm sure he was hooking up with just as many women as we were back in the day, but he was smarter about it. Never got photographed leaving with them, would never kiss and tell.

Mason goes back to the porn, watching intently, and I cannot make sense of anything that is happening. The sound of bodies slapping together weirds me out.

I go to the bar and pour myself a Coke. "Can you at least mute that?"

"Not doing it for you?"

I don't think anything would do it for me right now. I can't remember a time I've come so hard or without being touched since I almost lost my virginity on tour that first year. "Almost" being the key word in that sentence because I blew it. *Literally.*

Probably for the best anyway. It was with a fan, and I can't even remember her name now. The Disney Channel's *it* girl at the time wasn't much better a month later, but at least I can say I know the person I lost my virginity to.

"Do you want a drink?" I ask. And yes, I'm avoiding his question. I've already said too much when it comes to my porn preferences.

"Sure, whatever you're having."

"Uh, I'm drinking Coke."

"And whiskey?"

I sigh. "No."

"Oh, so rum, then."

"Are you being a dick on purpose?"

His face falls when he sees I'm being serious. "Wait, really? No alcohol?"

"None. I didn't …" I take a deep breath. "I didn't want to numb my feelings after … that."

Never in a million years would I ever admit something like that to anyone. Except for Mason.

He stands from the couch and approaches me. He's in sweats like me but is wearing one of his loose tank tops, and my gaze gets stuck on his muscular arms. I stay still, unsure what he's going to say or do, but then his hand finds my hip, and his lips land on my cheek. "I'll have Coke, then, too."

"You're allowed to drink in front of me. I'm not going to be upset if you do."

"Are you sure?"

Mason's always had this low-key disapproval when it comes to my issues with drinking, and I guess he has a right. I use it as a crutch, and he's been there from when it started, but sometimes I get the impression he thinks I need rehab or some shit.

"I know you worry I'm some huge alcoholic and I'm always drunk, but I didn't touch a drop while the contestants were here. I haven't had any since the night before we turned up on your doorstep in Montana."

He holds up his hands. "Okay, okay. You don't need to get defensive. I want to support you, and if you're deciding to be sober, then I'm proud of you. It threw me is all because I've never heard you turn down a drink."

I shrink back. "Oh."

A warm hand grips my shoulder. "Are you sure you're okay?"

No! This is weird. And he's acting normal. Like watching gay porn on my couch is perfectly average for us.

Apparently one orgasm is enough to send me, the one who

knows he's not entirely straight, into a downward spiral of doubt, and it hasn't even affected Mason.

"I'm waiting," I say.

"For what?"

"That's the hard part. I'm waiting to wake up from this dream, I'm waiting for you to realize your ex-best friend jerked you off and to freak out, I'm waiting …" I suck in a breath. "I'm waiting for the moment you break my heart." *Again.*

"Oh, Denny." Mason says this in a tone that suggests I'm either too dumb to live or that he's truly sorry. Maybe it's both. But as he pulls me against him and holds me tight, he says in my ear, "I don't want to break your heart."

He doesn't want to. That doesn't mean he *won't.*

"I wish I had answers for you. I wish I could tell you exactly where my head is at, but I don't know. I'm trying to figure it out. Maybe that's unfair—"

I shake my head. "It's fair. I never thought you'd forgive me let alone ever want to kiss me."

"If I'm being honest, me too. I was ready to hate you forever, but after I got over the shock of seeing you again … I realized I could never hate you. You're important to me in ways I never knew until you turned up in Montana. It was the kick in my ass I needed to realize you had valid reasons for disappearing on me."

I pull back and look into his eyes, and when Mason brings his mouth to meet mine, I believe every word he says. Easy as that.

"Let's try not to think about everything this isn't and focus on what we know," Mason says. "We care about each other, and I want to make you happy."

"That's the problem. I don't want you to compromise your happiness for my sake. We will end up hating each other."

"Eh. I've been there, done that, and I don't want to go back. I hated hating you. Maybe I want to try this instead."

He kisses me again, the type of kiss that sends tingles all over my body.

He's trying to reassure me, but after so long apart, all I can think about is what it was like to live without him and constantly analyze if risking our friendship is worth it. I can probably live without his touch, without his lips on mine.

I can't live without *him*.

Then his tongue enters my mouth, and I realize, no, now that I've kissed him, now that we've crossed this line, there's no way I can go back to being friends.

Mason's a "see what happens" kind of guy, and I'm the "all or nothing" type.

We're a recipe for disaster, and yet I can't bring myself to walk away.

"Stay with me tonight?" I murmur.

"I'm not going anywhere."

CHAPTER 18
MASON

"COME ON. How am I more in shape than you?" I run a circle around Denver and slap his ass as I do—in the totally straight, jock kind of way that no one would blink at if they saw it. And there's a good chance people can see it. These trails are popular this time of morning.

"You know, when you woke me up and told me we were going for that workout I wanted, this is definitely not what I had in mind."

The sun rising over LA is breathtaking, by evidence of Denver struggling to breathe. Surely that's the reason. It couldn't be that I'm making him hike almost three miles in the Santa Monica hills. Nope. Not at all. He bends at the waist and puts his hands on his knees. Okay, maybe it is this hiking thing. Hiking, running … totally the same thing.

We're both covered in sweat, and my heart pounds. It kinda feels like I need to vomit, but Denver? He looks like he's ready to collapse right here in the dirt.

"I think I worked out our problem," I say, panting now that we're apparently taking a break.

"That you're an evil bastard and are making me run? Uphill? What is wrong with you? Who hurt you as a child?"

"Our problem," I continue, "is that we haven't been onstage for-fucking-ever. Those boy band dance moves were lame, but damn, they burned calories and gave us some muscle definition. You're skinny fit now."

He glances up at me, his face all red and splotchy. "Like the jeans?"

"Nooo. One would think you're deliriously dehydrated. I mean you look fit, but you're just skinny. Me, I look lazy and overweight, but I have muscles hidden under the padding from my time on the tree farm."

Denver finally stands up straight. "You're not overweight, for fuck's sake."

"By Hollywood standards—"

"Hollywood standards are ridiculous and impossible to maintain. Seriously, after dating actresses, I can't be with another person who counts calories and yells at me when they eat a whole chocolate pie to themselves like it was my fault for not stopping them."

"That was totally that Heather chick, right?"

"You know about her? She and I only broke up …" He looks like he's trying to remember the last time he saw her. According to the tabloids, right or not, they broke up right before she flew to Atlanta to shoot her next teenage action flick. She's thirty and still plays a sixteen-year-old.

"It's been about four months," I say for him. "I followed that story. She seemed …" I purse my lips, trying to think of the politest way to say it.

"Batshit," Denver says. "Never trust a Heather."

"She does seem like the type of erratic actress who lets her crazy flow so she can 'feel the rainbow of emotions at the drop of a hat.'"

Denver cocks his head. "Did you date her too?"

I laugh. "Nah. Dated one back in the day, though. Remember Beth?"

"Oooh, yeah. She hated me."

"She hated everyone."

"Probably because she was constantly dieting and starving. I'd yell a hell of a lot more if I was hangry too." Denver steps into my space now and lowers his voice. "Which is why you shouldn't be pushing so hard at this. Exercise is healthy, and that's great, but please don't become obsessive over it. I love your body."

"To be fair, I'm pretty sure you loved it back when I was scrawny like you too."

He scowls. "Can we stop with the body shaming, please? For both of us?"

An elderly couple pushes past us, and I step closer to him to let them through. It's a good excuse to press against him. "Just so you know, I'm messing with you, but I'll stop. I'll try to stop calling myself names too, but it's hard when online haters are still claiming I ate the guy who used to be Mason Nash."

"Fuck them, Mase. They don't matter. They also need to come up with something more original."

"What I'm going through is nothing compared to what women get in the industry, but you know what it's like when something is said about you so many times that you start to believe it. And if Eleven is getting back together—"

Denver throws his hand over my mouth. "Shh, the trees have ears."

I try to talk, but it comes out all muffled. "We don't live in Narnia."

He ignores me. "They'll tell Harley you're contemplating coming back, and then he will literally camp on our doorstep until the end of time. Or until we relent and sign to his new label."

"Okay." My voice is still muffled, but then he removes his hand. "My point was I will try to stop being so hard on myself."

"Thank you. Because you deserve better."

I lean in. "And for the record, I love your body the way it is too."

There's the look I wanted. The awe of *Mason said something seriously not-straight sounding.*

"If we weren't in public, I'd show you how much," I mutter. "But we are. So come on. Those sixty-year-olds are beating us."

"We passed them like two minutes before we stopped for a break. It's not like they're going the same speed as us."

"We're almost at the turnaround where we'll start going back downhill."

Denver whines. "Can't we turn around now?"

"Nope. One-way track. Sorry."

He starts stomping his way up the hill. "Note to self. Never ever, ever, ask Mason to work out again."

"Shower and then meet back in the kitchen for breakfast?" I ask when we get back to the house.

Denver pauses, or maybe it's a small flinch. "O ... okay."

"Something wrong?"

"Nope." He tries to make a break for it down the hall, but I follow him. He doesn't stop, and we end up in his bedroom.

"What is it? What did I say?"

"Nothing. I'm being stupid. Overreacting."

"This isn't going to work if you don't tell me when I fuck up. Which I will. A lot. I've never ..." I wave my hand between us. "With a guy."

"Neither have I," he exclaims. "This isn't about gender, this is about ..."

"About ..."

"Showers."

I frown. "I'm confused."

"Last night after we … you know—"

"Made each other come?"

Denver's cheeks pinken. How is it that he's had years of coming to terms with this, yet I'm the one comfortable saying it out loud?

"Yeah, after that, you disappeared to your room, and now you're running off again to the guesthouse, and—"

"You wanted to shower with me? Is that what you're saying?"

It's subtle, but he nods.

"You know you could ask."

"I don't want to push."

I step toward him and bring him against me, sweaty and all. "The worst I'm ever going to say is 'Hey, I might not be comfortable with that yet.' And then you would say …"

"No problem."

"Great. I'm so glad we had this chat. Now, I'm going to go out to the guesthouse—"

His mouth drops open to say something, but I cut him off.

"But it's only to get fresh clothes. Then I'll come right back and join you in your big-ass shower. Together."

I love that he tries to cover his smile but can't. "Okay."

As I'm walking to the guesthouse, though, nerves start to make me uneasy.

It's not like we used to walk around each other naked all the time or anything, but on tour, you see stuff. I've seen Denver's dick countless times, and even though this will be different— closer—I'm not nervous about his body. I am nervous about how he will see *me*. I promised him I wouldn't be so hard on myself and my image, that I won't obsess over it, but when I know I'm going to be completely naked in front of him for the first time in years, it's scary. I'll be conscious about him mentally comparing my new body to the old me.

I want to do this for him. And we're going to see each other naked at some point if we want to get off again. Though we managed last night without peeling our clothes off.

No, I can do this. Denver says he likes how I look, and I have to keep reminding myself of that. It's what gives me the courage to go back into the house and make my way into Denver's bedroom.

He's already in the shower when I get there, which helps with my nerves as I strip down and step in behind him.

His bare ass is right there, and I can't help staring.

I've never taken notice of his body before. Not like I am now. I've always seen from an abstract kind of way how masculinity can be considered sexy, but similar to Denver, it has never turned me on. Him, however—his narrow shoulders, the muscles in his back, the curve of his ass—Denny definitely does it for me.

What that means in terms of my sexuality, I'm not sure. There's a label for it out there somewhere, but I don't want to have to wrestle with an identity while I work out what this draw is. I want to work on us more than myself.

Denver glances at me over his shoulder. "Getting a good look?"

"Dunno," I croak. "I might need to get closer."

He spins to face me, and I try not to drop my eyes to his cock. It doesn't work.

I take it back. I've seen Denver's cock countless times, but I've never seen it hard and standing at attention. Not gonna lie, it's a little daunting, but when my gaze travels up to his face, my hesitance wanes. My heart warms and fills with the familiar feeling of solidarity. Denver and me against the world.

I step closer. I push him against the tiled shower wall and box him in.

"Mm, if this is where working out leads, I'll exercise with you whenever you want." His hands roam my chest, and my insecurities over my body diminish a little more.

"If you only shower after you work out, we might have bigger problems. Like basic hygiene."

Then his aqua eyes flicker up to my face. "If you insist we need to shower together all the time to make sure I'm clean, it's a sacrifice I'm willing to make." He cups the back of my neck to pull me closer and press our lips together.

For whatever reason, when his mouth is on mine, everything else fades away. We're not Denver Smith and Mason Nash. We're not two parts of a boy band. We're not about publicity or fame or anything remotely Hollywood.

We're just two people with a connection I'm desperate to understand.

I want to pull Denver close and not let him go until I figure everything out.

His hard cock digs into my side, and I roll my hips. The thought of his hand on me again makes me desperate for it. I want to touch him this time too, but I hesitate. I know what I like, but that doesn't mean I'm an expert at getting other guys off.

Denver breaks the kiss and leans back, resting his head against the wall.

The water runs hot between us, beating down on mostly my back, and I have to say Denver wet is all kinds of hot. I could take a photo right now and put it in any editorial magazine.

"You're nervous," he says, not asks.

"I want to make you feel good like you did for me last night."

"Then don't overthink it. Follow my lead." He skims his hand down my stomach, and his long fingers wrap around my cock. It only takes one slow stroke for me to lower my head on his shoulder and shudder.

"Oh, fuck. Are you sure you've never—"

"No man but you. No one even came close to giving me what you do."

I lift my head and thrust into his hand. "What do I give you?"

"Butterflies."

A swarm of them let loose inside me. "I'm familiar with that feeling."

His wet lips skim my cheek. "Someone to belong to."

I grip his shoulders as I thrust again. A little harder this time. "I get that. You've been on your own for most of your life."

"But not with you. Never with you. You took me in as one of your family. You looked out for me. I knew if I ever needed anyone, you wouldn't have hesitated. You were my first and only stop."

"You've always been mine to protect like that."

This time, Denver shudders against me.

"Let me touch you," I say. "I want you to feel as amazing as I do."

"Touch me," Denver rasps. "Please. I need your hand, Mase."

I reach between us, tentatively skimming my fingers down his hard cock that twitches in my hand.

"You don't need to be gentle." Denver's sex voice turns me on even more.

I can do this. With direction and a little faked confidence, I can totally make my best friend come. It's not weird, not weird at all. Okay, it's a little weird, but that doesn't mean I don't want it.

Denver deserves to be cherished and taken care of for once. He needs to not feel so alone.

I might've been lonely back in Montana, but I wasn't alone. My family is my biggest support system. Denver has no one.

I'm dying to be that person for him, and that's why I'm willing to put my nerves aside while I focus on his needs.

It's how I can block out potential repercussions of us doing this, and there are many. Namely, Harley, Ryder, and Blake. Tabloids. The whole world would have something to say about this.

They think my weight was a big change for me? Wait until they find out how much I'm enjoying having Denver's hand on my cock, or how much I love his body against mine. How much I want to suck on Denver's tongue.

If anyone found out, it could be all over for both of us.

For me, it's not a big deal. I know what it's like to lose a career, and even though I want back in the game, I know I can live without fame. I can live without Hollywood.

I can't live without Denver.

Not again.

Denver's hips thrust, pushing his cock through my fist, while his grip on mine tightens, and he holds his breath while he strokes me from base to tip. The look on his face as he grits his teeth and fuses his eyes shut is hard to look away from. Veins in his neck pop out.

I can't wait to watch him fall apart, but his hand is distracting me. He jerks me expertly just like he did last night, and it's hard to concentrate let alone copy his movements, but I try.

It's probably the sloppiest handjob known to man, but he doesn't seem to care. He keeps whispering my name as if he can't believe I'm actually here and this is happening. The breathy way he says "Mason" will be etched into my memory.

I glance down between us at our hands wrapped around each other's cocks. The head of his dick is red and needy-looking, so I run my thumb over his slit and lick my lips, wondering what Denver would taste like.

Before I can build up the courage to ask or drop to my knees, he sucks in a sharp breath, his body stiffens, and then his cock erupts. I'm torn between lifting my head to see his face and watching as ropes of cum release from his dick.

His grip on me has become lazy and distracted, so I take over for him, moving my hips and fucking into his hand. My orgasm builds and builds, and my balls ache and tighten.

As soon as he stops convulsing, I release him and lift my fingers to my mouth. Denver watches me as I suck the heady, salty flavor down. It's not as bad as I'm expecting, and if it makes

Denver look at me like he is now—his eyes wide, his cheeks flushed—I'd happily drink him all up.

Then he pushes forward and crushes his mouth to mine, his tongue licking into my mouth, and I realize he can taste himself. That's all it takes for me to spill into his hand.

My release hits me full force, and it takes all my strength to hold myself up.

Denver wraps his free arm around me and holds me close.

"Definitely going to shower more if that's what's going to happen," he says.

"Your water bill is going to be insane."

"Worth it."

CHAPTER 19
DENVER

HOW IS THIS REAL LIFE? No really. How?

Mason Nash is on my couch, tablet in hand, just ... sitting there and reading after an entire day and night of orgasms and spooning. His legs are casually crossed at the ankles like he's made himself at home. In my house. With me.

I close my eyes and pinch myself, but when I open up again, Mason's still there.

I'm going to take advantage of this while I can. I throw myself on top of him. He lets out an *oomph* but doesn't take his eyes off the screen.

"You better not be looking at Hollywood gossip sites again. They're toxic."

"They're everywhere." He turns the tablet toward me, and there on *LA Life* are photos of us during our hike yesterday.

There are several shots of us smiling. One of me scowling at Mason, and one where we're standing a little too close to each other. The good thing about that shot is it looks like we're having a serious conversation, instead of what it really was—Mason telling me he loves my body.

My cock twitches at the memory. I wanted to kiss him right

then and there even though I was mad at him for making me exercise to the point of dying. Not being melodramatic or anything.

"The trees might not have ears, but they have cameras," Mason says.

"How did we not see the paparazzi? Instead of being in our faces, they're hiding in bushes now? Wannabe ninjas."

"Maybe it was a fan, and they were taken with a cell phone."

"Doubtful. They're too far away and too high-quality." I take the tablet off him and blow up one of the photos. "I have to say, this one?" I show him. He's wearing a hat in the photo, we both are, but Mason's breathtaking smile, all white teeth among a trimmed beard, stands out. "You look genuinely happy."

"I was mocking you for being unfit. I *was* happy."

I want to say I think it's more than that, but I'm trying desperately to tone down those claimy feelings. It's hard for me because I didn't realize that hooking up with Mason wouldn't be like hooking up with other people.

I've done the casual thing for nearly my whole career. I've dated actresses and fans, knowing things would never last in the long run. I didn't have real feelings for any of them, so it was easy to fool around for a while and then call it quits when we needed to.

With Mason, it's so different that a few shared orgasms and sleeping wrapped around him has made me want a future and happiness and forever with my best friend.

I have to stop desperately needing him to fall in love with me and make him want to.

"Let's not look at that crap." I reach over and put his tablet on the coffee table and then adjust how I'm lying on him so it's more comfortable. And by comfortable, I mean so our cocks are lined up and the smallest amount of friction will drive him crazy.

His arms wrap around me and hold me close so our noses are almost touching. "What were you thinking of looking at instead?"

"Mm, I wouldn't mind seeing your O face again."

"Right back at you." Mason's hand moves down my back and grips my ass.

I love that he's not shy about exploring with me sexually. He's nervous, that's obvious, but so am I. The only thing that makes it seem like I know what I'm doing on the outside is how long I've wanted this to happen. It far outweighs everything else.

I lean in and kiss him hard, but we don't even have time to add tongues when my damn buzzer for the front of the house goes off.

Motherfucker.

"Expecting someone?" Mason pants.

"Nope."

I give him three seconds to figure it out. He only needs one.

He closes his eyes, and his body goes slack underneath me. "We were in the tabloids. Harley knows I'm in LA."

"Bingo. And he knows you're with me." I climb off him. "How do you want to play this? You can hide, and I'll tell him you're not here."

"Nah. I'm willing to hear him out now. As long as he knows I'm not signing anything anytime soon."

I laugh. "Good luck with that." The door buzzes again. "I'll go get him."

When I answer my door, I'm surprised by who's standing at the outer gate. Or rather, isn't. "Blake? What are you doing here?"

Blake Monroe stands there with his blond hair and trademark half-smile that his character does in his movies. He's also wearing jeans and a leather jacket, and he's holding a motorcycle helmet. I buzz the gate to let him in.

"Hey." He doesn't wait for me to step aside. He just pushes his way past me. "You got Mason to LA? Where is he? Is he here?"

"Hello to you too. Does the studio let you ride your bike? After visiting you on set, I thought you weren't allowed to do anything dangerous."

"Oh, we're wrapped. It's okay if I die now."

"Fun."

"So, Mason?"

"Uh, yeah, in my living room."

"Cool." He leads the way because I've owned this house since nearly the beginning of Eleven, so everyone knows where everything is.

On his way past, Blake rubs my statue duck's jewel-encrusted wings. "Hey, Bill."

Unlike some people who will remain nameless, Blake understands why I love the gaudy duck so much.

Mason stands when we enter the room.

Blake puts his hands up in surrender. "Don't shoot."

"Ha, ha." Mason moves toward him and hugs him. "How are you, man?"

"Good. Busy. Only got back to LA yesterday and woke up to find you guys splashed all over TMZ."

"Shit, it's there too?" I ask.

"We thought you were Harley," Mason says. "Now he knows where I am, we know he's going to try again."

"Oh, for sure, he's on his way here. I wanted to beat him to it." Blake sits in the spot where I just tried to maul Mason on the couch.

Don't think about that. There's no big queer secret hanging over our heads. Nope. *None.* Not at all. Pretend it's not there.

"Beat him?" Mason asks as he takes the seat next to Blake.

I sit in the armchair. At least this far away, I won't be reaching for Mason.

Blake runs a hand through his blond hair. "I'm having second thoughts about this whole getting back together thing. I drunkenly agreed to it if all of us were on board, but then I remembered what it was really like going on tour and recording and learning all those horrible dance moves. Aren't we past all that?"

"From what I understand, Harley wants us to evolve and do

our own thing," I say. "We make our own rules. Sing what we want. And the schedule will be light."

Blake glances between us. "Can we believe him?"

It's hard to trust people in this industry. Contracts are ironclad and usually go in a production company or label's favor, but the alternative to signing is don't be famous.

Back then, we wanted to do anything to get us to the top. We had no control. Now we do.

"I know his heart would be in the right place …" I say.

"Hand up if you've been screwed over by good intentions in this industry." Mason throws his hand up.

"I want there to be a band again," Blake says. "But I want us to get the kind of contract we all want. Be up-front about it."

I'm surprised, but only because Blake has acting to fall back on. Mason and I don't have that. "You really want to come back?"

"I've finished the last Coby Godspeed movie contracted, and I need something to fill my time before I get any more acting roles. I can only do it if it fits around my schedule, though. It would be for fun."

"Sticking with the acting, huh?" Mason asks.

"Think so. There's talk of more in the franchise, but I think they're waiting on how this new one does first before they green-light it. I'm looking for kind of serious roles in between."

I know he has a half-finished album floating around out there somewhere, but I have no idea what happened to it. "No plans to release your solo album?"

"Nah. You guys know I loved being part of Eleven, but I did it more for the fame than the music. All the glamor called to me. I don't care if it's acting or singing."

"And how's it working out for you?" I ask.

Blake thinks about that a little longer than he probably should. "I love it. Don't get me wrong. But do you ever feel like it's … empty?"

"Yes," Mason and I both say at the same time.

"I thought there'd be more ..." Blake can't think of the word.

"Shine," Mason and I say in unison again.

"Whoa," Blake says and turns to Mason. "Stay with Denver for a few weeks and now you share one brain?"

We share one bed, does that count?

Mason locks eyes with me, and my face heats.

Blake's gaze lands on Mason. "Are you really coming back?"

"I only came here to get away from all the paparazzi who found me after you guys visited."

"Fuck. Sorry."

Mason shrugs. "Maybe it was time anyway." He looks at me. "Get things back on track. I keep flip-flopping over the Eleven thing, though."

"So you two have kissed and made up, then?" Blake asks.

In many, many ways.

I stand. "Who wants a drink?"

Mason frowns because we only had the sober conversation two days ago. "It's two in the afternoon."

"Okay, I meant, like, coffee or soda. Calm your tits."

"You guys haven't changed at all," Blake says.

There are ways we could argue we've changed a lot, but I won't. "How do you mean?"

"You drinking. Mason glaring at you and telling you not to. You giving him attitude. I swear you two were always like a married couple."

Blake could sense that shit?

"Whatever, dude." Mason shoves him. "It's not my fault some of us partied a lot harder than the rest of us." He smirks my way.

I lift my chin. "I am an innocent and delicate flower. Ask the fans." Both of them crack up at that. "It wasn't *that* funny. Just for that, you fuckers can get your own drinks." I throw myself back on the armchair.

"Okay, what's our game plan with Harley?" Blake asks.

Mason tilts his head. "How do we feel about sending him on a wild goose chase?"

Blake and I look at each other. Easy answer.

"We're in," I say.

"You don't even want to know the details?" Mason snickers.

Blake stands. "Nope. Let's do this."

Before we can formulate a plan, the buzzer for the front sounds again.

The three of us freeze, like that could make us invisible, and then my phone dings.

"It's him, isn't it?" Blake asks.

I check my phone. "Yep." I flip it to show them the screen.

I know you're in there.

Mason shivers. "Creepy. Has Harley been taking notes from his stalker?"

"You know about that?" I ask.

"Only what was in the media."

"Do I reply, or do we sneak into the garage and flip him off as we drive out?" I ask.

Mason takes my phone and types away.

"What are you saying?" Blake reads over his shoulder. "*New number. Who dis?* Original, dude."

Now I get in there too. Harley's message pops up immediately.

Ha, ha, open the door.

Mason replies: *What door?*

I know Mason's been staying with you.

Mason types: *What makes you think it's Mason?*

I snort at his reply. "You're better at playing dumb than I thought."

Who else would it be in the tabloids with you?

"Ooh, I know how to handle this." I take my phone back.

Oh, that guy. That's some random mountain man I found. He's now my life coach. He says Eleven getting back together is a bad idea. It will mess with my juju.

"Mess with your juju?" Blake laughs.

"My juju is a very serious matter," I say solemnly.

"How are we gonna get out of here without him seeing?" Blake asks.

"We should let him see for my plan to work." Mason turns to me. "Where are your car keys?"

"You want to take the Maserati?" My heart thumps at the thought. "Harley will have his ex-military, special ops boyfriend with him. He'd probably be able to chase us down and kick our asses before we even hit Sunset."

"Not if we have your car," Mason points out.

"Let's do this," Blake says.

The garage has an interior door to the house, so we don't have to go outside to get into the car and back out.

Mason asks for the keys.

"Not on your life," I grumble.

"You know," Blake says, "I've had stunt driver training for the Coby Godspeed movies. I could—"

"Not on your fucking life either. My car. My baby."

"You don't even know where we're going," Mason says.

"Tell me."

"Actually, I might need help with that. A year ago, the Q was popular. We need somewhere there'll definitely be paparazzi."

"Oh, so when you say wild goose chase, you literally mean it. You want to leave a trail of paparazzi photos in our wake for Harley to follow?"

"Yep."

I shake my head. "You're evil, but I love it."

We get into my car, Blake in the back and Mason in the passenger seat, and I rev the engine.

My finger pauses on the garage remote. "Are we ready?"

As they smile at me, I realize I can't remember the last time I used my celebrity status to have actual fun. I can't remember ever going to the paparazzi-filled places for anything other than needing publicity.

Right now, I don't care about the exposure. I'm only interested in one thing.

Messing with Harley Valentine.

CHAPTER 20
MASON

WHEN WE PULL out of Denver's driveway, all three of us wave to Harley, laying down the challenge. His pretty-boy features turn to a scowl, but then at the last second, his lips quirk. Because he realizes what this is.

If he can track us down, there's no doubt his prize will be our signatures on a recording contract. We just want to make him work for it first.

I thought I'd be self-conscious about being photographed, but the idea of making Harley chase us all the way around LA has all the tabloid drama and body weight issues leave my mind. Maybe that will change in a few hours when my photo is splashed all over the internet, but I've already filmed for *Fandom*. I'm in the tabloids because of our hike. This is the same shit, different day, but I get something out of this.

Denver weaves in and out of traffic expertly, and I didn't know it could look as sexy as it does. He's hyperfocused on the road, and the concentration line on his forehead is adorable.

I'm only mildly regretful Blake is along for the ride with us, or I'd reach over and … Well, I don't know what I'd do. I want to jerk him off again, but I also want to get ahead of Harley. It would be a difficult choice.

The first place we plan to go to is somewhere Blake suggests. It's an outdoor restaurant in West Hollywood famous for celebrity sightings. According to him, he has nearly all his Coby Godspeed meetings there with directors and other stars to give the movie media buzz.

We only stay at the restaurant long enough to have coffee and be photographed before we move on to the next thing.

"How do we feel about going to the Chinese Theater and taking photos with fans on the street?" I ask.

Denver's eyes widen. "Without … like, bodyguards?"

"It'll be fine," I say. "We'll park illegally and stay right near the car so we can all jump back in. We'll be fifteen minutes tops. We only need to light up social media. Harley will hate it."

"Ooh, we should tell them to all post it with the hashtag *come find us*. They'll think it's a challenge for the fans, but it'll actually be for Harley," Denver says.

"Perfect."

Blake leans in between our seats. "One thing, though. Do you think people will start talking about a reunion if we do all this?"

"They definitely will," I say. "Technically, we're doing Harley a favor, but …" I turn to him. "We should probably face it. You know this reunion is going to happen. I think at this point Harley would move mountains for it. Do you know he called me every single week for almost six months before you guys turned up at my door?"

Blake nods. "He showed up on set many times for me too."

"Me too," Denver says.

"I say we go for it." I put that out there. "But, like we've agreed, we stay firm on what we want. If Harley wants it to happen, he's going to be our new label head, and we can't let him walk all over us like Joystar did."

"Agreed," Blake says.

"I think Harley will make it work," Denver says. "You know, if he can catch us."

We pull to a stop and park illegally right outside the theater, which already turns some heads, but when we get out of the car, the screaming starts.

"Can you believe it's been over two years, and this is still the reaction we get?" Denver says before he's promptly hugged by an overenthusiastic fan.

A small crowd gathers quickly, and as much as it is overwhelming because it's been a while since I've experienced this kind of horde, it's also intoxicating hearing how much people still love us.

There are the aggressive types who'll cut a bitch to get to us, but like I always used to do, I find the one who's hanging toward the back, patiently waiting their turn even if it means they'll miss out.

I make my way through the people shoving their phones in my direction and find a girl with bright red hair, freckles, and oversized glasses and who's looking down at the ground. "Hey."

Her gaze flies to mine, and her eyes widen.

I smile. "Selfie?"

She nods and fumbles for her phone, almost dropping it in the process.

This is why I used to love what we did. It's what made the bullshit worth it.

"You were always my favorite," she says quietly, and I chuckle.

"Thanks."

She runs off like I just made her day, and it makes my heart feel so full.

The three of us hang around for a bit, we all take selfies, I'm only asked a couple of times why I look so different, and each of us deflect when asked, "When is a reunion going to happen?"

About the tenth time we're asked, Denver finally gives them

an answer. "I dunno. Ryder says it'll happen when we're forty." Denver looks over at me. "That's in, what, only three years for you, isn't it?"

I give him the finger. I'm allowed to do shit like that in public with me being the "bad boy." Imagine what these people would do if they found out I'm a small-town family man who grew up on a failing tree farm in nowhere Montana instead of what they think I am.

Then again, I don't even know what the media thinks of me anymore. Running home to Momma doesn't scream bad boy. Neither does being nice to shy people in a crowd, but that's different. Bad-boy attitudes must only be against the system, the man, or other famous people. Attack the fans and it's a good way to lose a career.

"Can I get a kiss?" someone asks Denver.

His eyes flick over to mine before he smiles awkwardly. "Uh, sure." He goes to kiss her cheek when she pulls away.

"Wait. I need to get it on camera."

I was about two seconds away from having to deal with that ugly feeling known as jealousy, but then she went and said that.

The fastest way to ensure someone famous will never want to kiss you again is by asking for it to be photographed.

Denver kisses her cheek while I sign an autograph.

It doesn't take us long to get swarmed by a huge group, and Blake checks his phone. "We've been here almost half an hour. Might need to make a break for it?"

I feel bad for those who got here too late, but any longer and Harley will be marching down the street. Or maybe he's already here in his car, waiting for us to make a move.

"We've gotta go," I say loudly so the group surrounding us can hear.

We all step back and wave to everyone, and as Denver gets in the car, he yells, "Don't forget to hashtag *come find us!*"

We leave just in time too. News crews turn up as Denver pulls out onto the street.

"That was fun," Blake says. "It's weird to me how movie fans act compared to Eleven fans. My movie fans are pretty hard-core, calling me Coby instead of Blake, but Eleven fandom? I'd almost forgotten how intoxicating it is."

I have to agree. That did feel good.

Toward the end of Eleven, where we were all tired and burned out, fans approaching us began to feel like an intrusion. Their questions grated on us. It wasn't because we didn't appreciate them, though. It was because we were so damn tired.

"Where to now?" Denver asks.

"Dinner and then a club," Blake says. "I can get us into Scarlet. I'm there all the time these days when I'm not on set."

"I know where we can go for dinner." Denver takes us to Soho House, an exclusive club where you need to be a member to even get in.

"You can't take photos in here, right? Isn't the point of this to be seen?" I ask him.

"Inside there's a photo booth. I say we eat, then get our picture taken in the booth, and then tag Soho House and use the *come find us* hashtag before making our escape. People will think we're doing a publicity stunt. Harley will be taunted."

"Who knew you were an evil PR genius?" Blake playfully slaps Denver's arm.

Denver shakes his head. "The things my manager has made me do to try to stay relevant will make your heads spin."

"Was it really that bad?" I ask.

He's mentioned briefly that his career is in trouble, but he hasn't exactly told me how much other than this reality show has to do well or he's basically toast.

I'm starting to think he needs this Eleven reunion maybe even more than I do. I didn't like being at home, but I could handle it.

I'm not sure if Denver's strong enough to handle the industry rejecting him.

His phone dings in his pants as we get out of the car to enter Soho House, but I can't resist shoving my hand in his pocket to steal it off him. To the outside, we look like friends messing around, but deep down, I just want to fucking touch him.

I unlock his phone—his passcode has always been his grandmother's birthday—and laugh at what's on the screen. "Harley is calling us assholes, in case you wanted to know."

Denver grins. "Plan's working, then."

Okay, this might be the longest I've gone without kissing Denver for two days. I didn't realize how addictive his mouth was until I couldn't have it.

Dinner is the longest dinner in the history of all dinners, even if it's delicious. I'm close to pulling the plug on the whole ploy so we can go home, but Denver's being smiley and happy and genuinely seems excited to go to Scarlet.

I have no idea what Scarlet is, but I'm assuming it's a hot new club only important people know about. Eighteen months at home has ruined LA for me. I realize I don't give a shit about that kind of stuff.

What I do care about is getting Denver off. And as paparazzi take our photo outside the club, I realize we won't be able to stay here long without Harley finding us, and I'm totally okay with that.

Inside, we're offered free bottle service in the VIP area if we let them take a photo of us for their website.

"I'm on there all the time," Blake says to us.

We take the photo and then are led upstairs to our own booth on a VIP balcony overlooking the dance floor. Denver and I take one side, while Blake sits across from us.

The booths are scarlet red, and I'm starting to see where the name comes from.

Denver asks for Coke and then points at me and says, "He'll have a single malt scotch. Whichever one you have. On the rocks and with a twist."

Blake orders tequila for all three of us, but Denver turns it down.

"What's up with that?" Blake asks over the music.

"I have to be on set tomorrow at 6:00 a.m. I am not dealing with the show while hungover. It's driving me nuts."

Blake leans in closer. "Are you sure that's all it is?"

"I'm kinda sick of being known by you guys as the drunk one. And I want to prove to myself that I can do this. I can go out and not drink."

Blake's eyebrows shoot up, but he nods. "Fair enough." He turns his attention away from us.

I subtly grip Denver's thigh under the table. "You okay?"

"Honestly?" He glances around us, but it's not like anyone would be able to hear us. I can barely hear him. "I'm starting to worry it might not be possible. I really want to fucking drink, okay? So much it scares me."

Good for him for seeing it in himself and stepping back, but at the same time, I wish I couldn't see the hurt in his eyes.

That hurt suddenly turns to fire before he leans in and whispers in my ear. "Besides, when we get home, I want to be completely sober for all the things I want to do to you."

My eyes flutter shut. "You're mean, Denver Smith."

"Don't you know it." He pulls away and winks.

The server either didn't hear Denver reject the tequila or ignored him, so Denver slides it over to me.

"Oh, so you can't drink, but I can get drunk?"

"Mmhmm. Well, not drunk drunk, but tipsy Mason is fun. From memory." His eyes shine in that mischievous way of his.

I think if I drink, all that's going to do is turn me on more. I get horny when I'm drinking, and considering I've been wanting to jump Denver's body all day, I don't know if I'm going to be able to hold out.

"What's going on with you two?" Blake asks.

We both freeze and turn to him.

"What?" I act innocent, but maybe I can't pull it off like Denver can.

"You guys are a lot friendlier than the last time I was in the same space as you."

Denver casually does the bro up-nod thing he does. "We're making up for lost time after our fight."

Blake leans in. "And what was that fight about again?"

I bite my lip. "Not staying in contact after the band split." It was so much more than that, but I really don't want to get into it.

A man, a security guard by the look of it, approaches the table and leans over to say something to Blake.

Blake's gaze darts toward the other side of the VIP lounge, and he gives a half-smile before standing. "I'll be right back. There's a director over there I've been dying to meet with." We both go to turn, but Blake stops us. "Nuh-uh. Don't look and fuck this up for me. It's Benjamin Randt."

I let out a whistle, but in the noise of the club it gets drowned out. "Damn, he's a serious movie guy."

"I know. I've been trying to land one of his movies, but he keeps rebuffing my agent because I only do brainless action flicks."

"Go say hi!" Denver says.

"I am. I am."

As soon as Blake leaves us, I turn my head to look. "Who's that he's with?"

Denver looks and narrows his eyes. "He's that actor, isn't he? The gay one. Uh …"

"Well, that narrows it down," I snark.

"Jordan someone."

Ah, that's it. "Brooks."

"Yeah, him!"

Blake is invited to sit with them, and Denver and I watch for a while, but there's no way to tell if it's going well or not. Then again, if it was going badly, I guess Blake would be back already.

I inch closer to Denver and lean in to say in his ear, "I've been wanting to touch you all day. Just so you know."

"Is this payback for telling you what I want to do to you when we get home or what?"

"I don't think I can wait until we get home," I murmur.

Denver shifts, and I bet all the money I have that if I were to reach for his lap, I'd find an uncomfortably hard cock behind the zipper of his pants. He looks around the small VIP area, but no one's paying attention to us. We're not the biggest celebrities in here. No one can take photos up here either—it's against the rules.

"I'm going to go to the bathroom," he says. "In a few minutes, get up and follow me."

I watch as he walks away, and then I wait the torturous couple of minutes before I get up too.

CHAPTER 21
DENVER

AS SOON AS Mason's through the door to the small VIP bathroom, I cage him in against the door and flick the lock.

"Fuck, I've wanted to do this all day." I don't give Mason a chance to respond before I slam my mouth on his.

He moans, loud and long, and if it weren't for the deafening music out there, I'd worry someone would hear.

I break away from his lips and kiss down his neck.

"Do you think this is really a good idea?" he breathes.

"We'll be fast. There are no cameras. No phones. If people find it weird we locked ourselves in the bathroom, we'll just sniff a lot and say we were doing cocaine. No one would bat an eye."

True.

"Handjobs?" Mason asks. "You're suspiciously good at getting me off fast with those."

I pull back and lock on his dark eyes that are filled with heat. "I was thinking something else." I reach for his jeans and pop the button and then undo the zipper.

Mason leans against the door, his mouth dropped open, his eyes hooded.

He's so sexy when he's turned on.

Then? I drop to my knees.

Mason's strong hand grips my shoulder. "Are you sure?"

Am I sure I want to give my first blowjob ever on the floor of a nightclub? No. Is that going to stop me?

No fucking way.

"I might be terrible at it," I say, "but I always have my hand for backup if I need it."

Mason's grip loosens on my shoulder, and it's enough of an encouragement for me.

I don't remove his pants, just lower them a little and tuck the waistband of his boxers under his balls. My mouth waters, and I think of all the times I imagined doing this. His tip is swollen and leaking, and as I stroke him with my hand, more precum dribbles out.

I run my tongue over it and get a hit of saltiness.

When he licked my cum off his hand in the shower and then I kissed him, I could faintly taste my cum, but this? There's no comparison.

Mason shudders, and I've barely even had my mouth on him yet. "I don't think we'll have to worry about you being bad at it. You're already driving me crazy. I want to come."

He runs a hand through my hair, but it's gentle and affectionate.

"I want you to come in my mouth," I say.

His hips thrust, and his cock hits me in the chin. I grab the base with my hand, but before I wrap my lips around him, I glance up into his lust-filled eyes.

"I'll take that as a yes?"

A feral look crosses his face—his bad-boy persona coming out to play—and I am so here for it.

No more fucking around. I want his dick in my mouth more than I need my next breath.

As much as I want to dive on that thing and suck him down, I know I should ease myself into this. Slowly, I run my tongue along the underside to the tip and suck just his head.

The sounds Mason makes when he's getting off are hotter than any grunting, panting, or moans that I've ever heard before. In real life or in porn. Here, in this moment, Mason is barely hanging on, and when he makes those same noises, I know it's because he's trying to regain control.

Moving my mouth over his dick is all a blur. Sucking him becomes a mission on trying to get him to keep groaning, but then my own cock protests.

It aches to the point I have to do something. I release my hand from him, and he lets out a tortured sound this time. It's still hot. I want to tell him my hand will be right back, but I don't need to, because the second he sees me struggle with my pants, he says, "Fuck yes. Touch yourself, Denny. Get off with me."

That's the plan.

With my cock free, I'm able to stroke myself while I use my other hand to help my mouth on Mason's dick.

I suck, I stroke, and I jerk myself so fast the edge comes creeping up. And when Mason starts thrusting into my mouth and losing control, my orgasm only builds faster.

Mason's hand in my hair that was gentle and caressing changes in an instant. His fingers tighten, and my scalp stings. The shock of it sends an electric current right to my dick.

And when Mason gasps, "Denny," it's all over.

For both of us.

I want to swallow him all, but it's hard to breathe when his cock is near the back of my tongue and his cum is shooting down my throat.

I continue to convulse in my hand while his load dribbles out the side of my mouth. But then our wrung-out bodies relax, and as I pull off him, he runs his thumb over my lips and wipes away the evidence of him from my chin.

"That was hot."

I can barely catch my breath. "So hot."

"Let's quickly clean up, go back out there, and find any excuse to leave Blake here and go home."

I wipe my mouth on the back of my hand. "Is there really any point to that? I don't think I'm going to come again anytime soon." I stand and make my way to the sink, plucking hand towels from the dispenser to finish cleaning myself up.

Mason steps up behind me. "After that, I want to hold you while we sleep." He lowers his head and kisses my shoulder.

Yesterday I was worried he didn't even want to shower with me.

I turn. "I still can't believe this is happening."

"Me too. But I don't want it to stop."

"Neither do I."

He pulls away from me. "If it didn't look super suspicious, I'd hold your hand, but I don't think straight guys do that."

"Hey, affection between guy best friends should be normalized." But I pull open the bathroom door and let him go first.

"I agree," he yells over the music, but then he moves in closer. "But we're not only best friends anymore, are we?"

My heart gallops a million miles a second. I guess he's not expecting an answer to that because he goes back to our table where Blake has returned with the actor beside him.

When we take our seats, Blake cuts off his conversation with him and looks at us. "You two go to the bathroom together now?"

"Safety in numbers?" I croak.

With anyone else, we'd be able to do the whole, oh we were doing coke, but not with Blake. Blake knows I don't go near drugs. Ironically, because I didn't want to develop an addiction. Now I'm sitting here wishing I could reach for Mason's glass of scotch and down it.

I won't, but I want to.

"Exactly. What if there was some fan lurking in the bathrooms ready to attack us?" Mason asks.

The actor laughs. "I'm Jordan." He holds out his hand for me to shake and then Mason.

"Jordan Brooks. We know," Mason says.

He's midthirties, has brown hair with golden highlights, and his smile screams Hollywood actor. Blake has a similar one. Acting lessons 101: teaching good-looking guys how to smile properly.

"Man, that never gets old," he says.

"What doesn't?" Mason asks.

"When people know who I am. When *celebrities* know who I am."

I remember what that's like. That first year of hitting big is crazy. Jordan has been in a lot of small roles over the years—namely, he played the gay brother of a main character in some TV show I can't remember the name of now—but he recently hit it big with a lead role in a rom-com.

"I've been in this town for fifteen years," Jordan says. "Finally, I'm getting my big break. You guys need to convince Blake to do my movie. He's reluctant because he'd have to kiss me, and apparently I'm not selling it when I tell him I'm a really good kiss-er." He grins.

Blake rolls his eyes. "That's not why I'm reluctant."

"What's the movie?" Mason asks.

"It's a gay rom-com slash family drama," Jordan says. "Think *Brokeback Mountain* but less depressing and more snarky. It's going to be a mainstream, big-budget thing."

I look at Blake, who downs what's left of his drink. "Well, it will definitely be different to Coby Godspeed," I point out.

"It might be *too* different," Blake says. "Plus, a straight guy playing a gay dude? People are going to hate it. Why don't they ask Matt Bomer?"

Jordan smirks. "Went with the only other gay actor you could think of, huh? Two gay leads would be ideal, I agree, but there's no way Ben will allow it."

"Why not?" I ask.

"He'd prefer it if I couldn't fall for my co-star."

Is he implying they're … together?

"He never learned to share his toys." He turns to Blake. "Just think about it. Ben's gonna call your agent either way, and I know from experience that if you get in with Ben and make a good impression, he'll look at you for casting in any of his other movies. I had a small role on *Mercenary of Honor*, and since then, my career has exploded. I'm getting offers across all genres."

Blake's lips purse in contemplation. "I'll talk to my agent, but I think this could create more backlash than promote my career. I think it should go to a gay actor. Or bi. Or, just, someone who's not another cis, straight white guy."

Jordan seems unfazed by that. "It wouldn't be completely horrible to show that straight guys can be comfortable in their sexuality. Think of what it could do for your bandmates who are totally hooking up but are still in the closet."

Mason drops his drink, and it spills all over the table, but the glass doesn't break.

"W-what?" He glares at Jordan.

"Ryley4Ever? Harley and Ryder are a thing?"

I let out a loud breath of relief. "Total fabrication."

"No way? Really? I thought for sure those rumors were true. I have a weird six degrees of separation from Harley's ex, Jay. So I thought …"

Wow, okay, so he really is in the Hollywood loop if he knows about Harley and Jay.

"Harley and Ryder were never a thing," I say.

"Ah." Jordan nods. "That rumor isn't true, but the others about their sexuality are. Got it."

"Did I say that?"

"Not in so many words." Jordan stands. "Anyway, this was fun, but I should go. Nice to meet you two." He turns to Blake. "Your people will hear from my people."

He exits, and Blake watches him as he leaves.

"Maybe you should do the film," I say to him.

"We'll see what my agent says."

I take out my phone to check the time and find a message from Harley. "Okay, I think we can call it a night."

I turn the phone around so they can see:

You win this round, but this is far from over.

CHAPTER 22
MASON

I PULL down my cap and adjust my sunglasses as I slink my way inside the restaurant and head for Cameron's usual table.

He's there waiting for me and stands to hug me as I approach. He's in his early fifties, but after two and a half years of not seeing him, he looks a hell of a lot older than I remember.

"What was so important I had to put on a clean shirt for?" I take a seat across from him and slide off my poor disguise.

It usually works so long as you're not in one place for very long, but after our little *come find us* stunt, everyone's on the lookout for any of us.

The hashtag was trending before we'd even got home from the club. Photos were posted all over Instagram and Twitter, and I have to admit, as a publicity stunt, it worked amazingly well even though that wasn't our intention.

Someone recognized me as soon as I parked my truck and had their phone in my face. I took a quick photo with them so I could get to this "very important business meeting I can't miss."

"You're back," Cameron says.

"I am."

"You didn't tell me."

"To be fair, I didn't tell anyone. The only reason anyone but Denver found out was because of stupid paparazzi."

"All right, then." He nods to my menu. "Choose what you want for lunch. My treat."

It would have to be his treat. This is the kind of place where they don't have prices on the menu. If you have to ask, you can't afford it.

I order a steak, Cameron orders his usual duck, and once the orders are in, he starts in on me.

"When are we getting you in a recording studio?"

I hold up my hand. "Whoa, slow down there. I'm … testing things out. I filmed a couple of days for Denver's reality show, and I'm writing some, but I don't want to jump in headfirst like when Eleven first got together."

"Have you met with Harley yet to see what he has to offer?"

"From the millions of voicemails, I know what he wants, but …"

"You're hesitant. I understand that after your solo album." Cameron sighs. "I wish you'd come to me when all that went down."

In hindsight, I should have asked his opinion before releasing my album. He would've told me like it is. "I wanted to prove I could do it myself, and I didn't need you to hold my hand anymore. You were there for me when I needed."

"I don't like to see any of my boys fail."

"I know." Yet, the word failure still cuts me. Probably even more so when it's said out loud. By someone else.

"Not all is lost," Cameron says. "It's no secret I want Eleven back together, but if you want to try the solo thing again, I'm here for you. We can find a label who'll run a comeback tour and album."

I take a sip from my water glass. "Aren't I too young for a comeback tour?" I want to cringe just at the words.

"A redo? We can call it The Album It Should Have Been."

"Catchy," I say dryly.

Cameron leans in. "Just promise me something."

Cameron's the only person in this world I could say this too without questions first. "Anything ... wait, unless it's to sign something right now."

He laughs. "I wouldn't do that to you. Just, whatever you decide, fill me in? If you have questions, reservations, anything, I'm here, okay? You did the hard part already."

"What was the hard part?"

"You showed your face in a town that was an asshole to you. After that, the rest should be easy."

"Hmm, maybe."

Until Hollywood turns its back on me again.

"I'm happy you found your way back and you're enjoying your time there," Mom says into the phone.

"Me too."

After lunch with Cameron, I realized he wasn't the only one I haven't updated about what's going on, and I called her as soon as I got home.

I haven't gone into details about what's been happening with Denver, just that we're working on rebuilding what was lost, and it's going well.

Really well. I don't emphasize that, though.

I doubt Mom would have an issue with me being with a man—especially not Denver because she loves him—but I do know she will worry about us in the same way she worried about the label shaping us into manufactured pod people for seven years.

There will be hate comments. There will be the same ignorant comments there have been when rumors of Ryder and Harley were going around like *I so hope they're not gay! What a waste!*

Every single reason Ryder and Harley have chosen to stay closeted now applies to us, which is hard to comprehend. They have had to worry about this their whole careers, and maybe that's why they're so strong in remaining silent, but for me, absolutely nothing has changed between me and Denver except for the sex. *The mind-blowing, amazing sex.* And even Hollywood doesn't ask for specifics on that kind of thing. The world is fascinated by who celebrities sleep with for whatever fucked-up reason, but no interviewer anywhere is going to ask, "So who's the hot dog and who's the bun, so to speak."

Our personal lives have been splashed over the covers of tabloids for years—some of the stories true, most fake, but if this got out, it would be ten times worse.

I can see why Harley and Ryder keep quiet.

"Do you have any plans to get back with the band?" Mom asks. "The news is saying—"

"The news picked up on a story where Denver, Blake, and I were messing with Harley. They think it's a big PR stunt and we'll announce the reunion soon, but we haven't really discussed it as a group yet."

"Where do you go from here? Are you staying in LA for a while? Everything has died down here now they know you're back in California."

That's good. I hate that they think they have the right to harass my family. My sister has young kids, and it's not fair to scare them like that.

"I think I'll stay. At least for a few months. Denver's doing this reality TV show, and I've been writing some songs while he's at work. I'm not sure about Eleven yet, but the plan is to see if we can all be in the same room without wanting to kill each other first."

"And can you? Or is this phone call about to take a dark turn? Oh God, you didn't kill poor Denver, did you?"

"Did I ever tell you you're not funny?"

"My child would never do such a mean thing."

"I don't know if I want to go back to Eleven," I say.

After the other night, we've agreed to at least give it a try and meet with Harley, but there's a part of me that thinks going back to Eleven is almost selling out. Or admitting failure. Then again, when you have hardly any money and moved home to be with Mommy, I guess I can't really say I've been even remotely successful on my own.

"As long as you're happy," Mom says. "Follow your heart."

My heart is only leaning in one direction, and that's toward Denver. If any of the songs I've been writing are anything to go by anyway.

When Eleven was together, Harley and Ryder wrote most of the songs because the label wanted poppy and light. They wanted happy songs. A lot of what I'd try to write back then would be too angsty with an angry tone to it. There are breakup songs that make you sad, payback breakup songs that are empowering, but mine were … a little dark. Too depressing.

The lyrics I'm coming out with now make heartache feel like love, and Denver is my muse.

I hear the front door open, and Denver walks into his living room looking happy. "Mom, I have to go, but talk soon?"

"Love you!"

No sooner have I hit the red button to end the call than Denver's pressed against me.

"You're home early," I say.

He inches his mouth closer to mine. "I have some news."

"Yeah?" My phone beeps, and when I look down, I see a missed call and a voicemail message from Cameron.

"What does Cameron want?" Denver asks.

I snort. "I had lunch with him today, and he's full of ideas on how to get my career back off the ground. Big hint—it involves you and the other guys from Eleven."

"You didn't tell me you were meeting with him."

"I didn't know. He called me this morning after you'd left, telling me I just had to go to lunch with him because I've been back in LA for how long and didn't tell him?"

Denver laughs. "Oh, guilt trip for the win! That's so him."

"What's your news?"

"How would you like another big fat check from *Fandom*?"

"Depends on what I'd have to do. If it's become a contestant, I might have a conflict of interest. I'm kind of sleeping with one of the judges."

"Are you now?"

"Yep. Alondra Casey has moves for a woman who's almost fifty."

He playfully shoves me.

I grip his shirt and pull him back against me. "Nuh-huh, you're not getting away that easily." I bring our lips together, and he tastes like Coke.

Our tongues tangle, and before I know it, we're panting into each other's mouths and pawing at each other's clothes.

The wild ride we've had over the last week where we've been fooling around only gets better and better each time we're together. Granted we're still on handjobs and blowjobs—well, more accurately, I'm still on handjobs—but Denver's mouth on my cock is my new favorite thing. I haven't gone there yet even though I really want to. I want to make him feel good, but there's so much pressure to be good at it that I'm worried I'll choke and gag and yeah, that's not sexy at all. I'm worried I won't like it, and I don't want to hurt Denver's feelings by being all "Yeah, no thank you." Then I think of other things we could do, and I half think I'd rather have his cock in my ass than in my mouth.

Denver gets his shirt off and then comes straight back to

kissing me, but when I reach for the button on his pants, he steps away again. "Wait, wait, wait."

His lips are puffy and swollen, his chest rising and falling heavily, and I can't help running my gaze over his naked torso.

"What's wrong?"

"I got to come home early so I could ask you about making another appearance at the live finale. I told them I'd have to ask in person because you can't say no to this face." He pouts.

He's definitely right about that, but I'm not sure if I want to do the finale. I did the home visit filming fine, but I really think I have developed a mild case of stage fright in the time I was gone.

"They want us to sing 'More Than Words' again because they're gagging over what we did while they were shooting here."

"When's the finale happening?"

"Eight weeks from the last day of filming, which is next Friday."

"Hmm, can I think about it?"

A frown line appears above his brow. "What do you need to think about?"

"Well, it's live, right? That's daunting. They can't edit when I swear."

"It's just been too long since you've been onstage in a live setting. I guarantee once you're out there, the old you will come out."

"Maybe." I'm not as confident as he is.

Denver's eyes catch on the coffee table where I've scribbled some lyrics. "Oh, you've been writing?"

Shit. The last few days I've stashed my stuff away before Denver's gotten home.

"It's nothing. Just ... trying to find my muse." I take the papers and shove them in the drawer of the coffee table. "How did you get out of filming to come home early? Are they going to CGI you onto the judging panel?"

"Nah, it's cut day. I told them if they want me to ask you, they have to film my team first."

"Oh, who'd they cut?"

Denver scoffs. "Cece and Declan."

"Noooo. Cece was so good."

"I know." He sounds so defeated.

"Come here." I reach for his hand and pull him against me. "Where were we?"

A small smile breaks through on Denver's face. "I was trying to convince you to say yes to being on the show again."

"Mm, that's right." I lean in and kiss his cheek. "How were you planning on doing that?" I move to the other side and kiss his other cheek. Then I move my mouth closer to his but stop shy of pressing our lips together.

"I could get on my knees for you," he rumbles.

"Definite possibility."

"Or … I could do something else?" He pulls back the tiniest bit to look me in the eye. "Is there something you were thinking of?"

I shrug. "I don't really care. I just want to be with you."

"Want to watch a movie and cuddle on the couch?"

"Not really what I was thinking, but I'm good with that too."

Denver throws himself on the couch but then opens his arms. "Cuddle first. Then embarrassing sex talk."

"Embarrassing sex talk?" I lie down next to him, pressing our bodies together on our sides. Whatever he's going to say next has my stomach fluttering in anticipation. Or is it dread?

Denver traces over the curve of my cheek with his finger, stroking my beard. My eyes flutter shut at the touch, and then he leans in and kisses the tip of my nose.

The soft humming sound of contentment that leaves his lips makes my heart feel full.

"Umm, the sex … stuff," Denver says.

Oh, shit. He's going to tell me I'm terrible at it. Or that he expects me to return the favor and get on my knees. Not that I'm opposed. Just nervous.

"Is that what we're calling jizz these days? Sex stuff? Give me all your sex stuff." I have to joke about this because I'm worried about saying the wrong thing. My mouth scrambles to explain. "I want … I want to make you feel good, but being with a guy is still weird for me. Even though it's you, and I'm comfortable with you, but, uh, yeah. I don't know what I'm saying. I want to do more stuff, and I want to explore, but also? I'm terrified I won't like it. Or I'll be bad at it. What if I bite your dick off while trying to suck it?"

"Okay, maybe we put that one on the list of things not to do for a while because I kind of like my dick attached to me."

"But you go down on me, and—"

Denver cuts me off with a kiss. "You know why I do it? Because I like it. Because it makes me feel amazing, and I like seeing you come. I like being the one who does it. I don't do it because I expect it in return, and I'm not expecting you to ever do something you don't like or you don't want to do. I wanted to talk to you because I think I'm ready for more. Like I want you to fuck me."

I suck in a sharp breath because I want that. Fuck, I want that.

Denver continues. "But if we never try another thing, I'm happy with what we're doing now. Because you turn me on like fucking crazy, and there's nothing that has made me happier in the last few years than when your hand is on my dick and your tongue is in my mouth. And if that's all you could ever give me physically, I'm okay with that. You being here for me is more than enough."

"Damn it, Denny." I move closer, resting my forehead against his.

"What?"

"Why did we waste so much time apart?"

Why did I spend so long hating him when I should've realized why I was so upset at him? I have feelings for him. Like, *wake up and smell the bisexuality in the air* kind of feelings.

"Neither of us were really ready to face this back then," Denver says. "You were blindsided by my feelings for you, I was still trying to convince myself that I was forming an unhealthy psychological attachment to you and what I thought was attraction wasn't real, and then we both had to focus on our solo careers. Maybe our time apart was longer than we needed, but it gave us both some perspective that I'm grateful for. I don't want to have to live without you again."

I swallow hard. "Me neither. Since being with you, I've realized those deeper feelings for you have been there a while—maybe for years—but I associated those emotions with you being my best friend. I didn't analyze it too hard because until you kissed me, I didn't know. Hell, I still didn't know until you turned up on my doorstep wanting forgiveness. The kind of hurt I've been carrying around isn't because I lost my career. It's because I lost *you*. And ... you're kind of the most important person in my life."

"Mase ..." Denver's raspy tone makes my cock harden, and suddenly, all the sex stuff doesn't matter.

If he's willing to be patient with me, then I'm willing to go outside my comfort zone for him.

Starting now.

CHAPTER 23
DENVER

THE MOMENT MASON moves down my body, I'm keyed up and ready for it, but I don't want to pressure him.

I lean up on my elbows while he gets to work on undoing my pants. "You don't have to—"

"I know. I want to try."

And try he does. Not that he has to try hard.

Being with Mason is unlike any of the hookups I've ever had. Every touch. Every sensation. I've never experienced that kind of intensity. My body yearns for it. It craves it.

I lie back on the couch and try to be as still as possible while he takes out my cock and gives a tentative stroke. I don't want to thrust or move and scare him off. His breath is hot on my skin, his mouth not even an inch away from my dick.

When he finally lowers his head, it takes an insane amount of control not to come immediately. Mason starts soft and slow. He's not so much teasing but testing it out.

With his mouth on me, it fills me with a weird sense of reassurance that he's in this for real. Which is absurd because anyone can suck a dick. It doesn't mean anything. But with Mason, it does.

It's been obvious in the way we've been hooking up that he's not one hundred percent comfortable with it yet. I give him a blowjob, and he jerks me off. I seem to be the one to take things to the next level.

But with this ... Mason closes his mouth over the tip of my cock and runs his tongue over my slit. I leak precum into his mouth, and he moans.

"Is that a good moan or a bad moan?" I ask.

He pulls off me with a chuckle. "So good. I want to taste more."

"Keep going," I encourage. "I don't think it will take long."

Mason takes his time, only driving me closer and closer to the edge. His eagerness to please with his nervous energy somehow turns me on even more.

I resist the urge to thread my fingers through Mason's hair while he works me over with his mouth. Instead, I grip onto the couch cushion for something to hold on to.

The wet slurps, the sight of his dark head bobbing up and down on my dick.

It's too much.

I grunt in warning because I can't seem to make my mouth form words.

If anything, that only spurs him on.

He sucks deeper, draws it out longer, and then does it again.

I grit my teeth, and my knuckles turn white as I tighten my hold on the couch cushion, and then all at once, my orgasm hits.

I shudder and gasp while I spill into Mason's mouth. It's impossible to rein it in. I let go, and my hips writhe.

Mason can only take so much before he pulls off me and strokes me through the rest of my release.

Cum hits my clothes, and I'm thankful for the *Fandom* wardrobe department making me change my on-air clothes each day before I leave the set. I do not want to be explaining that stain to the producers.

When my dick finally stops erupting, I sink back into the couch.

Then I hear a faint chuckle.

I can barely lift my head, but when I do, I lock eyes with Mason, and his laughter dies. "Something funny?"

He shakes his head. "Not at all. I was just wondering what I was so nervous about. That was … I know I could use some practice but—"

"That was perfect." I crook my finger to get him to climb up my body.

When we're face-to-face, I smile and reach for his beard, rubbing away some of my cum. "Oops."

"Yeah … you really got it in there."

"Your fault."

"It's so not my fault I couldn't swallow your entire load. There was a lot. Like a tidal wave of cum."

"A cum-tsunami? A … cumnami?"

Mason laughs, but I cup the back of his head and bring his mouth down on mine. I don't care if his mouth is covered in *me*. I don't care if I can taste myself on his tongue. After that, I want to kiss him and hold him.

We stay like that for a while, kissing softly, taking each other in, until an impatient Mini-Mason is grinding against me. I reach between us, pushing my hand into the waistband of his sweats, and wrap my fingers around him.

He doesn't stop kissing me, and it only takes a minute for him to lose himself.

Now we're both covered in cum, our clothes too, but we don't move to get up. I'm in no rush, and Mason doesn't seem to be either.

I run my hand down his back and then back up again.

"We're really bad at removing clothes," he murmurs.

"We really are. We might need to do this over and over and

over again until we finally learn. Ditch clothes first. Then come all over each other."

"Sounds like a plan." Mason finally rolls off me and stands. "Shower? We have to get rid of our clothes for that."

"I'm in." I force my wrung-out body to stand and then follow him down the hallway toward my room where he has a stash of his clothes. He still has half his crap in the guesthouse and half in here, but he's in my bed every night without fail.

We strip down and throw our clothes in my hamper.

While we wait for the water to heat up, I remember something. "Oh, by the way, guess who messaged me today."

"The Pope."

"Harley wishes he was the Pope," I mutter.

Mason spins and pins me with a confused look. "Message? No showing up unannounced, no following you?"

"I was shocked too. But no, Lyric … I don't think you've met him yet. He's Ryder's partner and Harley's first act on his label. Anyway, his single is dropping, so Harley's busy with that seeing as he's his manager. The text basically said the chasing has been put on hold for a while, but, in his words, it's still happening."

"Only a small reprieve? We can work with that."

I step closer and run my hand down Mason's wide chest. Dark hair covers his chest, and not for the first time since he's been back, I take in the differences between now and when we were on tour. He's manlier now, and it's sexy as fuck. Where the label used to send him to have his chest waxed, he's let that go. He's unkempt, and I didn't know that could be a turn-on. Living in Hollywood, everyone is superficial and materialistic. Stripped down to his bare personality, Mason is simple and … average, but it's the thing I love about the new him the most. Because he's raw. He's genuine. He's truly himself for the first time in ten years. I'm both envious and happy for him.

I can't really wrap my head around a lot of things when it comes to my sexuality—why Mason's the only guy I've ever been into, why I'm turned on by him even more now that he's physically more masculine than he was—but I do know my feelings toward him haven't wavered. They've only grown stronger.

He's my Mason. My rock. My best friend.

My hand keeps traveling down his stomach, which I'm noticing has changed since he's been back.

"You've lost weight." My voice is laced with slight disappointment.

"I've toned up. A tiny bit. It's from working out while you've been on set. There's still plenty of me to love."

My gaze flicks up to his, but his head is turned as he reaches for the water to test it. I don't think he realizes what he said or he didn't mean it the way I heard it.

"It's hot." Mason pulls me into the shower.

He's completely oblivious to what the word *love* does to me. We've said I love you to each other plenty of times, but that was before. When we were friends. When he saw me as a brother.

Now, that one simple word has implications I don't think he's ready for. Hell, I'm not ready even though I'm desperate for it.

"You okay?" Mason asks.

I've been standing under the water while he's been soaping up, and I haven't moved.

I shake my thoughts free. "All good. I was just thinking."

"About what?"

Yeah, Denny, about what? We're so not ready for this conversation. "Uh, I'm wondering if you're going to show me your songs anytime soon."

"That would be a hell no."

I nod. "I suspected as much."

We might not be ready for love, but try telling my heart that.

There're only nine contestants left in the competition, three on each team, and this last week has been filled with a studio audience for the first time since the initial auditions. And tonight is it. The end. At least until the live finale in two months after everything airs.

Gone are the horrible singers only brought on for comedic effect. The ones that are left have talent. Well, some more than others, but the core elements to make a pop star are there with each and every one of them.

Before we go to the live finale, we have to whittle that number from nine to six, and the audience gets to do that by voting with little keypads attached to their seats. *Supposedly.*

At least the hard work for the judges is done. We no longer have to mentor or give advice on their songs, and we no longer have to pretend like the decision was ever in our hands.

If it were up to me, I'd have a very different top three up onstage for my team.

Isla is up first, and she performs well. Surprisingly well for her. All the sessions we've had leading up to these last few qualifying performances were as bad as the home visits. She's proven she performs well under pressure, so maybe she's been saving it all up for the shows that count. Hell, maybe this is a strategy she's been told to use by one of the production crew—pretend to struggle, pretend to be pitchy, and then *look how much you've grown over the course of the whole show!*

She's still a little pitchy, but her stage presence makes up for it, and the crowd goes crazy for her.

"She has improved so much," Alondra says to me.

"She has." I still think she could do with some professional training, but I get the impression the show is setting her up for the win. Hopefully, she'll take my advice and hire vocal coaches and a team to help her really succeed in this business.

The cameras focus in on us then, and because Isla's on my team, I'm up first to deliver her critiques. "Where has that been?"

I say into my microphone with a small laugh. "You've come a long way, Isla. I'm proud of you."

I want to keep things short and sweet because I'm ready for this to be over.

We're so close to the end.

So close to getting a break.

Well, not a total break because we have to do promo for the show in between now and leading up to the finale, but I won't be in a studio for twelve hours a day.

I'll actually get to spend time at home with Mason.

Our *sexploration* is going addictively well. I can't get enough of him, and each night, Mason's becoming increasingly eager to figure out all the ways to make me come.

Something I wasn't aware of until just last night, but the prostate is apparently a whole other ball game when it comes to getting off. And if his fingers alone can do amazing things, I've been thinking all day about what his cock could do.

Alondra nudges me, and I realize I've spaced out. One of Brian's contestants is up there waiting for my comments.

Okay, no more thinking about Mason's cock at work.

I lean closer to the microphone. "Good job." At least, I think he did a good job. "Ah, nice pitch, great sound. Yeah ..." Great feedback, Denver, really.

When Brian calls for a bathroom break, we're given ten minutes to freshen up.

Alondra turns to me. "You're distracted today."

I smile. "What gave that away?"

"Your answers are short."

"I want to go home." I laugh.

"Oh? Shacking up with another actress?"

"No. And don't believe anything you read. You should know that. I've lived on my own forever."

"Then why the rush to get out of here? I find the house so empty when I'm not working."

I realize she's right. When we started filming this show, I was always eager to get out of here but not necessarily excited about going home to an empty space. Now, I get to go home to my best friend.

I stand. "I'm going to go to the bathroom and then to get coffee. You want one?"

"Thanks, honey, but I have an assistant for that type of thing."

"I can get it."

She looks up at me. "You're such a sweet boy."

"I don't think someone my age is allowed to be called sweet. Or a boy."

"Oh, honey, you're half my age. You're a boy."

I don't fight her on it. "I'll be back soon."

As soon as I step out of the lights and go offstage, someone in the wings grabs my arm and pulls me against them. I'm so out of it, I have no idea what's going on. Then I smell that piney smell of Mason's, and my heart flutters.

"Hey," he says.

I glance behind me. There are crew mulling about, and the audience can't see us, but as much as I want to lean in and kiss him, it's too risky. I go for an awkward as fuck man-hug with the back patting and "*Hey, bro*" masculine approach.

He whispers low. "I missed you too."

I pull back. "What are you doing here?"

"Got a call from someone in production. They asked me to come in and sign a contract for the finale appearance and then said I can stay and watch if I wanted. And I definitely wanted. What's up with you out there? You seem ..." He licks his lips suggestively. "Distracted."

"You know exactly why I'm distracted. I can't stop thinking about you."

He grins.

"But right now I'm on a mission to piss and then get me and Alondra some coffee."

"You go to the bathroom; I'll get you coffee from craft services."

"Ooh, are you going to be my bitch boy? I like that idea."

Mason shoves me away. "Go."

Knowing Mason is here watching, the rest of the taping goes smoothly, and I'm more focused than before. Though I still keep my feedback short because I do want to get out of here and finish what Mason started last night with his fingers.

Only, it seems Mason has other ideas.

"Ready to go home?" I ask when I meet him backstage after we're done.

"Nope. I was thinking of doing something drastic."

"Shaving off your beard? Getting a tattoo? Ooh, Botox!"

He mockingly gasps. "I do not need Botox."

"You might if you shave off your beard. Who knows what kind of loose skin you got all under here." I rub his cheek in a condescending way that wouldn't look suspicious to any of the crew around us.

"You're way off base. Harley's act. The one with the song."

"Lyric."

"Yeah, him. They're having a party to celebrate the single making the Billboard charts. I figured we could kill two birds with one stone. We have our own celebration to do. Filming is wrapped, which means more time in your bed."

"You're voluntarily going into Harley's territory? Oh, you sweet summer child, we'll have contracts signed before he'll let us out of there."

"We're not signing anything, but I figure extending an olive branch and expressing our interest without cementing anything is a step in the right direction."

"There will be signatures," I declare.

"No signatures."

"Mmhmm, we'll see."

CHAPTER 24
MASON

AS WEIRD AS IT IS, I'm nervous to come face-to-face with Harley again. The last time, I was pointing a rifle at him, so yeah, there's that.

When we walk into the bar on Sunset, more than a few heads turn, but it's not because we're famous. It's because we're together. With Lyric being Ryder's partner, and Harley being Lyric's manager, Denver and me showing up means at least four out of five of us are here. If Blake got the same invite we did, this might be the reunion everyone's been hoping for. Even without performing, it will be the first time the five of us will be in the one room since that last night on tour years ago.

We're approached by a few industry people who know better than to ask questions, but they're like eager puppies all the same. We both respond politely but try not to get held up.

Lyric's single plays through the speakers, and while I pretend to listen to whatever the producer in front of me is saying, I pay attention to the song. I have to admit, it's pretty good. It's catchy, but the lyrics are deep. The bopping beat behind it might diminish the impact of the emotion, but it's a decent debut and doing amazing things. It's still climbing the charts and making news. It might not make number one, but it's a great start.

Am I bitter it's selling better than my debut solo single? A little. But that's the business, and I won't hold it against him.

We find Ryder tucked away in a corner talking to Cameron, and as soon as Cameron sees us, his face lights up, and he hugs me.

"You've been ignoring my calls."

"That's the first thing out of your mouth?" I snark. He's been calling since our lunch date last week, just checking in, "not pushing" apparently.

As annoying as it is, he's the only one who has actually cared, so I appreciate him making the effort. I might not know where my head's at, but I know he'll be there when I make up my mind. I won't be so proud this time to ask for his help or opinion.

"It's almost happening." He rubs his hands together. "Four of my boys in the one room. I'll see you all together again yet."

"Oh, Blake's not here?" Denver asks.

"Apparently he needed to do reshoots for his film," Ryder says. "Cameron is Team Harley, so prepare to have your ears talked off about signing to Valentine Records."

Denver laughs. "Yeah, we knew that coming in here."

My eyes lock on Ryder's, and his lips tip up in a tentative smile. We haven't seen each other since that last night on tour either because he's spent the last two and a half years trying to disappear. It was easy for me, not so much for him. Paparazzi still want his story because he has a baby momma scandal and an illegitimate child. Ryder refuses to get into the story with the media, which means the vultures think it's something huge when it's not.

Maybe that's what my career needed. Mystery. Damn it, I should've knocked someone up years ago. Because you know, having a child as a publicity stunt is a perfectly normal thing to do. That child wouldn't grow up to need intense therapy or anything.

There's this tense vibe between Ryder and me, but he breaks first and steps forward to hug me. "I've missed you, man. Where have you been?"

I hold on just a little bit longer than would be considered normal because I've missed him too. I've missed all of them. "Went home for a bit, but I'm back."

Denver's gaze flicks to mine. "For good?"

I pull away from Ryder. "For the foreseeable future."

"I can practically smell the ink drying," Cameron says.

I hold up my hand. "No. No business talk tonight. We came to support Harley and his new act. That's it."

"Mmhmm," Cameron taunts.

I turn to Denver. "Why does no one believe me?"

"Because the rest of us have already given in," Ryder says.

"Blake hasn't yet, has he?" Last we talked, we were going to fight for what we wanted out of it, and I'm still waiting for that final thing to click into place. Something to tell me it's the right move. After my horrible career choices since Eleven broke up, I'm reluctant to pull the trigger even though I want back in this life.

I do think it's inevitable, but something's saying *not yet, not yet, not yet*.

It's probably a mix of stage fright, anxiety, and imposter syndrome. I'm not the guy I used to be. I can't go back to being the Mason Nash everyone knows because that guy was only ever a front.

"We're gonna go say hi to Harley and Lyric," Denver says.

"And not promise to sign anything." Cameron winks. "Got it."

Denver pulls me away and into the throng of people. "Doesn't Cameron realize goading you will only make you dig your stubborn heels in further?"

"Me? Stubborn? Never." Okay, I'm a little stubborn.

Harley's Cheshire grin as he sees us approach makes me wonder if he'll whip a contract out from behind his back.

Lyric, the blond guy beside him, looks at ease as he talks to a new fan, but when they're interrupted at our arrival, his easy demeanor slips away, and he actually looks … nervous?

Harley's and my arms wrap around each other reflexively. The animosity that was there in Montana has dissipated, probably because my biggest issues were with Denver, not the others. When I forgave him, my anger over falling out of touch with all of the Eleven guys disappeared. Do I wish we had been there for each other? Of course. But we all had to do our own thing.

"Well, this is a better welcome than the last one," Harley says.

I squeeze him just that bit tighter before releasing him. "They're checking people for weapons at the door, so …"

He laughs. "Lyric, you know Denver, but this is Mason." He pulls Lyric closer, and I shake his hand.

"My sister was obsessed with you," he blurts. "Can I please get a selfie to taunt her?"

I rub the back of my neck. "I guess? If she'll even recognize me now."

"Oh, she will. She cried when you got—" He cuts himself off, and I know what he was going to say. *Engaged.*

"Lucky that never panned out, then, huh? Is your sister here?" I force a smile I don't feel, and this is weird, because I can sense Denver's glare too.

Dude, I'm not going to hit on Lyric's sister, but this is awkward. I've forgotten what it's like to be in these situations. The other day, running around LA, it was fast. Selfie here, signature there. This is a proper conversation. Apparently, I don't know how to talk to someone new anymore.

"Nah, she lives in Fresno."

"Okay. Uh, pic, then?"

We take a quick photo.

"You must be special," Harley says. "Lyric here hates Eleven. Says we're all cliché and lazy."

Lyric's mouth drops open, and he looks terrified. "I said that before I knew any of you."

Well, that I can respect, but I don't say that. I'm enjoying Lyric's torment a little too much.

"And he has never lived it down since," Harley says. Then, as if sensing the smallest gap in conversation, he turns on me. "So, the contract."

I cover my ears. "Lalalalala. Nope. No. No. Not tonight."

"When?"

That's a heavy question.

"Why don't we all talk after *Fandom* has wrapped?" Denver says.

"When's that?"

"The live finale is in eight weeks."

"Two months? Okay. I can focus on Lyric and writing new songs for the album until then." As if forgetting something, Harley clicks. "Oh, also, I want solo songs on the album, so you two need to get writing. Unless you want Ryder or me to write for you."

"Mason's actually—"

I cut Denver off. "You guys can do it. You always did."

Harley's face turns smug. "And I just got you to agree. Verbal contract is still a contract. It's happening. It's all happening!"

I turn to Denver. "Whose idea was it to come here again?"

"*Yours.*"

Well, shit.

Lyric's song kicks in again over the speakers, and he groans. "Is it possible to be sick of yourself this early in your career?"

The three of us laugh because he's in for a rude awakening.

"Okay, I'm taking him to go meet with more 'important' people," Harley says.

"You know everyone can see your air quotes, right?" I point out.

Harley slaps my shoulder. "But they can't hear me, so they don't know who I'm talking about."

I smile as I watch them walk away, and then I feel Denver's voice in my ear.

"You know, we can always leave if you want. I had big plans before you decided to make an appearance."

I cock my head and eye him. "Plans?"

He licks his lips. "They involve a lot more of what we did last night."

I flash back to being between Denver's legs, with my mouth wrapped around his cock and my fingers lodged inside him.

It wasn't the plan to do that with him, but this exploration thing is fun and has a mind of its own. Plus, when he was writhing beneath me, begging me to use my fingers, it's not like I was going to deny him of it.

"Ready to go?" he rasps.

"Definitely." My cock more so than me.

This time as we make our way through the crowd and people try to stop us to talk to us, I practically bowl through them like they're bowling pins.

Sorry, not sorry.

I have somewhere to be.

An hour later, I have Denver where I did last night. Naked, legs spread, and my fingers moving in and out of his tight hole. I lick my way up the underside of his cock, and he trembles.

He's on the edge of the bed, feet flat against the mattress while my knees dig into the carpet. My cock is heavy and hard, but I'm neglecting it for now because seeing Denver like this is worth holding out for.

As I look up at him, this wild look of need crosses his face, and I would do anything to keep him staring at me like that.

He's resting on his elbows, watching me as I move my mouth up and down his hard cock. Every time I take him deeper, which admittedly still isn't very deep, his eyes do this glazed fluttery thing that makes my cock ache.

I pull my mouth off his dick and replace it with my free hand while I watch my fingers move inside him. I can only imagine what it will feel like to slide my cock in and out of his body. I want to be inside him so bad, but we haven't had another discussion about it other than when he said last week that he's thought about it and could be ready for more. We've been preoccupied with exploring in other ways.

As if reading my mind, Denver's voice breaks my concentration. "I want your dick."

I stall, my hand unmoving around his cock, my fingers still inside him. "A-are you sure?"

All those nerves come rushing back, but it's mixed with excitement. If sucking Denver's cock can do it for me, I'm willing to try anything new. It's just … daunting. Because I want to make it good for him. I want to take care of him.

"Please."

Damn, it's hard to say no to that.

Before I can think too hard or give myself the chance to back out, I pull away from him and stand. "Condom?"

"Don't need it." He blindly reaches for the lube and throws it at me.

"We don't?"

He shakes his head. "Not with us. Not with you."

With anyone else I would insist, but I trust Denver more than I trust even myself. I haven't been with anyone since I went home, and when your childhood doctor insists on a full STD workup because "All those years with Hollywood types, you're bound to catch something," you don't argue with him. And yes, it was awkward as fuck.

I squeeze lube into my hand and cover my cock.

Denver lies where he is, splayed out for me and ready, watching as I work myself over. The sight of him with his legs spread, his cock standing tall and hard, and the pure want on his flushed cheeks builds need inside me. A few more strokes and this could all be over before it's really begun.

Denver squirms. "Mase ..."

I know that tone. That's a hurry the fuck up tone. Apparently, it doesn't matter if it's in a dressing room because we're running late or in the middle of sex, his impatience sounds the same.

I push two fingers inside him once more, just to be sure he's ready. The way his body trembles and his hand flies to his dick, gripping it at the base, I'm confident he's more than ready to take me. We're both dangerously close to the edge, and this might end up being the quickest sex known to man.

"Roll over for me," I say.

Denver's mattress is high off the ground, so when he gets onto his hands and knees and rests on his elbows so his ass pushes into the air, my cock perfectly lines up with his hole as I stand at the foot of the bed.

I want to dive right in, and I want to take his body hard, but I know I need to start slow.

My cock sits in between his ass cheeks while I run my hands over his slim but toned build. The muscles in his back contract under my fingers.

I trail my hands down to grip his hips, taking in the sight of his round ass while I refrain from leaning down and biting it. He's completely smooth, unlike me. I'm not covered in a blanket of hair by any means, but Denver's all white, creamy skin.

"Hurry up." Denver pants.

I let out a small laugh. "Sorry. I'll stop admiring your sexy body."

"You can admire it while you're fucking me."

I snort. "Your bossy when you're horny."

"I'm not bossy. I'm *needy*. There's a difference, and I fucking need you."

Holy hell. There's a reason it's so hard for me to say no to Denver: I like feeling needed, and when he says those words, I melt inside. All that time I was gone, all that time he was ignoring my calls, all he ever had to do was say those three little words, *I need you*, and I would've come running.

I finally put him out of his misery but then enter a world of my own, because as I line my cock up with his hole and push through his tight ring, he tenses, and I know I have to go slow so he can get used to having more than my fingers inside him.

I don't like seeing him in pain, but even worse is the pressure surrounding the tip of my cock. It's hard not to slam inside him like I want to.

I reach for the lube without pulling out of him which is probably a mistake because it makes me move inside him a bit more, and he grunts. It's definitely not a happy kind of grunt.

"Sorry." I go to pull out, but he blindly reaches behind him.

"No, don't. Not yet. Give me a second."

"I'm still here," I reassure him and dribble more lube into his crack and on my hand.

While he adjusts to the tip, I stroke the rest of my cock, trying to stop the urge to move inside him.

Denver stares at me over his shoulder, watching me as my slick hand moves over my hard shaft. "Fuck, that's hot."

"Feels good too," I rasp. "I could come like this."

"Don't. I need you completely inside me when you come."

That thought alone is enough to get me close.

A new determination crosses Denver's face before he hangs his head. As if summoning the courage to try, he pushes back, taking my cock deeper. His breathing is sharp and fast.

I hold myself strong, making sure I stay as still as possible while he works himself onto my dick. I have to grit my teeth, and I tense nearly every muscle in my damn body to keep control, but I manage.

When I'm all the way inside him, he starts to relax, but the second I try to move, he tenses again.

"And here I thought I wasn't going to last long," I say.

"Shut up," he mumbles. "Just wait until it's your turn. I'd like to see how easy you can take it."

"My turn?"

After weeks of exploring with Denver, I'm learning really quickly that *never* shouldn't be a word in my vocabulary. The way we've been exploring, discovering new things, I wouldn't say no to anything anymore.

"Turnabout is fair play and all that." Denver pushes himself back on my dick again, and this time, the sound that leaves him is much more pleasurable.

"Oh, yeah? Is that a warning to go easy on you?"

He doesn't answer, only trembles beneath me.

I like him like this—at my mercy and handing over all his trust. The shaking mess of need is a bonus.

"I can take it," he says. "I'm good now."

"Are you sure?" I rotate my hips slowly to test it out. I move easier now, but holy fuck, it feels way too good. His ass is warm and tight, and— "Fuck."

Tingles shoot down my spine as I thrust in and out of him. I watch as my dick disappears between his ass cheeks.

"Yes. Keep going," Denver says in between moans and grunts.

Our bodies meet, coming together over and over again, and I'm mesmerized. The desperate sounds he makes frays the last cord of control I have left.

I want to let go and fuck him hard. I've never needed to come so bad in my life.

Denver's breaths are rapid now. "Mase … I need … I need you to touch me."

I reach around him, his cock hard and heavy in my hand as I jerk him off.

As I ride that edge between holding back and letting go,

Denver pants my name over and over in a way that makes me think he's trying to convince himself it's me he's with.

I can't hold out anymore. My orgasm rocks through me so hard I have to grip Denver's hips with both hands as I spill inside him. He whimpers when I release his cock, but I can't help it. I'm about to collapse on top of him.

He's quick to take over, stroking in earnest, jerking off so fast that by the time I stop trembling, his ass contracts around my dick, and he falls apart. It draws out my orgasm a little longer.

I didn't know sex could be like this. Sex has always been great, fun, sometimes awkward, but the payoff has always been worth it.

This? This wasn't sex. It was an *experience*.

Denver's body relaxes, losing all the tension, but I still hold his hips in place. "Uh, Mase? I'm gonna need my ass back sometime soon."

"Uh, right. Umm. Yes." I pull out of him slowly, and he flops onto his back with satisfaction written all over his gorgeous face.

"That was …"

I don't have words for it either. "Yeah. It was. But, umm, now we're all messy."

Denver holds out his arms. "Cuddle now. Clean up later."

I crawl onto the bed, and we wrap ourselves around each other.

He lets out a sigh that screams contentment. "We're so doing that again."

I kiss the top of his head. "I can never say no to you."

He pulls back and looks into my eyes. "I mean, you're allowed to say no if you want to."

I shake my head. "Not what I meant. I want to do that again. What I meant to say was I'll do anything you ask me to if it will make you happy."

"Mean it?"

"Of course."

CHAPTER 25
DENVER

MASON in my bed shirtless is becoming my everything. I love him in my space. In my home.

I've performed to sold-out arenas. I've lived the life of a celebrity.

But this moment, right here with my best friend, it's all I've ever wanted for a long time. It's happiness wrapped up in a shiny bubble.

Annnnd, I'm about to fuck it up. Because of course I am.

"I did something," I say hesitantly with my hand firmly behind my back, hiding exactly what I did.

Mason sits up in bed and rests against the headboard while eyeing me playfully. He thinks I'm playing a game, and I wish I were. I almost don't want to disappoint him, but I can't let this go.

"What is it?" he asks.

"You're not going to like it."

"Let me be the judge of that."

"I, uh …" I pull out the sheets of paper with lyrics scrawled all over them.

Mason's face falls. "Are those …"

"Your lyrics? Yep. I couldn't not look, and I know I should be sorry, but I'm not, and they're really great songs. You should send these to Harley to put some of them on the new Eleven album."

He stands and approaches, but I can't tell his demeanor.

Is he pissed off? Of course he's pissed off. He didn't want me reading them, but I did it anyway.

If they were bad, I could easily pretend I didn't see them, but they're amazing. He shouldn't keep them in a drawer.

He takes the papers off me. "They're not good. Harley won't like them."

"Is that what you really think, or are your solo album sales clouding your objective creativity?"

Mason cocks his head. "Do you really like them, or is my dick clouding your objective creativity?"

"Your dick is amazing, but I'm not sure it's *that* amazing."

"You said yourself you loved my album, but you were one of the only few, so I can't really trust your opinion on this."

"Hmm, no, you can, because it's true that I do love your album, but I can also see why it didn't sell. It wasn't mainstream. These songs … with the right melody, these could be our next number one hits."

Mason places the papers on the bed and then inches toward me. "Did I ever tell you that you believing in me is superhot?"

"Lies. If you thought that, we would've been sleeping together years ago."

He's close now, only a few inches away. Mason wraps his big arms around my back and pulls me against him.

Our breaths mingle as his mouth moves closer to mine.

He lowers his voice. "If I hadn't been so blinded by what I thought were platonic feelings for you, maybe we would've been sleeping together back then."

My head snaps back, and I level him with my gaze. Does he mean that? I can't tell. His deep brown eyes tell me he's serious. His lips tell me they're just words to get me to kiss him. Then again, he doesn't need lies to do that.

"I love all the guys like brothers," Mason says. "But you … you've always been different than them. I thought it was because you were also my best friend. I didn't realize … I didn't know it could be like this. We might be famous, but it was only recently I began to believe the whole world revolved around us. It feels like the entire reason you and I exist is so we can be together."

Mason saying these things to me after all this time … I was sure kissing him in my hotel room years ago was the biggest mistake of my life. Now I'm realizing running away from him was.

We could've had this.

We could've been together.

"You're not saying anything." Mason's tone is more amused than anything.

"I'm trying to make sense of it. I'm trying to work out if this is real."

Mason trails his hands down my back and grips my ass, bringing me against him. "Does that feel real to you?" He's so hard. "Do you feel what you do to me?"

"Fuck," I breathe.

He lowers his head, his lips capturing mine in a slow, gentle kiss. "I want this. I want us."

"I've never wanted anything more."

This feels like a momentous occasion, something to celebrate with our closest friends, but that notion brings a whole slew of questions we probably aren't ready for.

"You seem to be thinking awfully hard when you should be kissing me." Mason's big hands cup my face and hold me to him while he pushes his tongue into my mouth.

I groan because no matter how many times Mason does it, no matter how many kisses we've shared over the last few weeks, I cannot, and will not, ever get used to the way Mason kisses me.

It's not only the beard and the sensation it leaves on my skin. It's not that he's a man. It's everything Mason. The way he has always tried to protect me and take care of me. The way he has always loved me in his own way.

I break away for just enough time to grit out, "Bed."

Then we're back at it. He reaches for my jeans, but he's only wearing sweats. He's easy to get naked.

Before I can get them down his legs, though, right as I dig my fingers into the waistband, his phone rings on my bedside table.

He turns his head to look at the notification.

"Ignore it," I say.

"It's Cameron. I'll call him back later."

Thank fuck. I need Mason more now than I ever have.

His phone stops, and I tackle Mason to the mattress, totally forgetting I still haven't taken off his damn pants.

"We're wearing too many clothes," he says.

Then his phone starts up again.

"What now?" Mason glances at his phone again. "Harley this time."

"Ugh. They're probably trying to gang up on us over the Eleven deal. We'll call them back."

But they don't let up, and we don't get any further.

When Cameron calls again, I decide to answer it for him.

"This better be good, old man, we're kind of busy here."

Mason's eyes widen, but I wave him off and hold the microphone part of the phone so Cameron can't hear when I say, "I'm not going to tell him doing what, geez."

He laughs, but then the voice in my ear isn't what I'm expecting.

"Mason? Is that you?" It's a woman.

"Uh, sorry, it's Denver. I took Mason's phone. Who's this?"

"This is Cameron's assistant, Evelyn."

Ah, right. "I remember you." She's a sweet lady. Honestly, I always thought Cameron had a thing for her, but she's his age. His wife is younger than us. Evelyn always used to joke that Cameron likes her *too* much to make her his next divorce.

"I figured he'd want me to call you boys first. Before you found out in the media." There's a crack in her voice, and I know it can't be anything good.

Suddenly, I'm wondering why his assistant is calling Mason and not himself. Cameron has always made time for us and never palmed us off to his employees.

"Why?" My tone sounds like I'm five years old again and I didn't know why I was being taken away from my mother.

"I really don't want to be the one to tell you all, but …"

"Tell us what?" A heavy weight crushes my chest, anticipating bad news.

"Cameron wasn't feeling well today. He …"

Oh God, are those tears I can hear? I don't want her to say the next thing that's going to come out of her mouth. I really don't.

"I told him to go to a doctor, you know? It wasn't normal. His skin was kind of ashen and pasty, and he didn't look well. I thought he might've been coming down with a flu."

Mason stares up at me, all playfulness gone.

"He collapsed an hour ago and was rushed to the hospital."

"Which hospital?" I climb off Mason as fast as humanly possible. I pace the room, looking for clothes. Wait, I'm wearing clothes.

We need to go to him. We'll wait by his side. We'll—

"He's gone, hon. Massive heart attack. I'm so sorry."

It's like a punch through my rib cage, right to my heart.

"G-gone …"

"He'd passed away before the ambulance reached the ER."

With each word, the pressure on my chest gets heavier and heavier, but no, they can't be the right words. She's mistaken. I can't have heard that right.

"I'm so sorry," she whispers, but I can't answer her.

I drop the phone, and it hits the carpet with a soft *thump*.

This is not happening. This can't be happening.

"He was only fifty-two," I say. "That's too young."

Mason stands and picks up the phone, muttering words I can't hear. Or maybe I'm drowning them out. I'm in a fog of disbelief, and nothing can pull me out of it.

"Denny." Mason gets in my way to stop the pacing.

I look at him. "He … He's …" I choke on the truth.

"I know."

Tears fall freely down my face. "What are we supposed to do with that?"

Mason swallows hard. His eyes are glassy, but he's holding strong. "I don't know."

I sink back onto the bed and hang my head in my hands.

I think back to when my grandmother died. We were on tour at the time. I was sixteen. It was a sad time, but I remember being so busy I barely had time to process her death let alone grieve over it.

Then we had the court issues of proving I didn't need a guardian because I could look after myself. Cameron was the one who was there for me through all that. Who's going to be there for me to get through this?

"Mase?" I sniff, but when I look up, he's gone.

I guess my answer is *not him*.

I'm too consumed in my initial shock and then grief to notice how hard Mason takes the news, but it becomes obvious in the days following the call. He's withdrawn, depressed, and he moves on autopilot. He barely knows I'm here half the time, and the other half I'm met with subtle nods and single-word answers. I'm trying to hold it together for him, but we're both as lost as each other.

Grief is a weird thing. I want to break down. I want to give up.

Hell, I want to fucking drink just so I can numb the sadness. But at the same time, I've been through this before with my nanna, so I know the pain will dim. I know it will get easier.

Mason doesn't have that same mentality. His dad is the only person he has lost in his life, and it was when he was young. He's not sleeping, he's barely eating, and I think he has said all of two words to me since we got the news.

When my phone rings with Harley's name on the display, I leave Mason sleeping on the couch and slip out onto the balcony but keep the door open.

"Hey," I say quietly.

"How are you holding up?" Surprisingly, Harley's voice is a calming presence. He's always so together, and I trust he'll know what to do.

"I'm worried about Mason," I say.

"I'm worried about both of you. How are *you* handling it?"

Not great. "I'm better than Mason. He's barely even spoken to me, and we're—" Shit, I can't say what was about to fall out my mouth. We're supposed to be in this together, but it's as if his grief has broken him. "We were back on track to being … us. And now …"

I have no idea where his head is at. This is testing us at a time we're not ready to be tested. I don't know what to say to him or how to make either of us feel better. Anytime I've tried to initiate sex to try to get out of my head and forget, he's shot me down.

The only other option I have is drinking, but I want to prove to myself that I can get through something major without turning to the bottle.

I lick my lips and taste whiskey on them even though I haven't touched a drop. That's how desperate I am for a drink.

"Evelyn wants to know if either you or Mason want to talk at the funeral," Harley says.

"Are you doing it?"

"Haven't decided."

"I can ask Mason later. He's asleep." I turn to where he sleeps on the couch. I don't want to wake him, but apparently I'm wrong anyway. And he's been listening.

"I'm awake." He sits up. "What do you need to ask me?" He looks horrible. With bags under his eyes, messy hair, and he hasn't changed his clothes in days, so they're all wrinkled.

"If you'll speak at the funeral," I say.

"I don't even know if I'm going, so you can put me down as a hell no."

"Did … did he say what I think he said?" Harley says in my ear.

"You're not going?" I ask Mason.

"I … I, uh …" He lies back on the couch again and throws his arm over his eyes. "I don't know, okay?"

"Harley, I've gotta go."

"Look after yourselves. Talk soon, okay?"

I end the call and approach Mason, dropping to my knees next to him, but my phone starts buzzing again. This time it's Keith, my manager. Just the sight of his name reminds me that he's terrible compared to Cameron. He wants me to make a public statement and turn Cameron's death into another publicity grab, but I can't bring myself to do it.

I posted a heartfelt statement the night it happened, expressed my sadness at the news, but I didn't want to step outside the generic condolences. I didn't want to make it about *me*. Mason had said similar, so I made a statement for him on his social medias because he refused to.

He doesn't have a manager to tell him that even though he's going through a rough time, there are still expectations he should meet. Even if it's the minimum. I'm trying to be that voice of reason for him.

I ignore the call. "Mason." I lift his arm off his face, and his cheeks are wet.

He pulls away and stands. "I'm going to go shower." He tries to leave, but I stop him with the only words I can find that won't break us.

"You're allowed to be upset, but please don't shut me out."

Mason pauses and turns back to me. He approaches slowly, and I honestly don't know what to expect. When he reaches for me and pulls me off the ground, he wraps his big arms around me and holds me the way I crave it.

Other than a kiss on the back of my head at night and spooning me to sleep, it's the most affection he's shown me in days.

"We're good, okay?" he says softly into my neck. "I don't want you to doubt that."

This is reassuring, protective Mason. The guy who made me believe he'd be there for me always. It tempts me into letting go and breaking down because I know he'll hold me and make me feel like everything is okay. I'm on the brink of losing it, but I can't do that to him. He needs to grieve too, and he can't do that if he's worried about me.

Mason pulls back and cups my head. "Hey. I'm here, okay? I'm here for you, but … I also need to be there for myself. Cameron's death … it's brought up a lot of shit I don't want to deal with."

"It's hard on me too."

"I know it is. I need to … I need to breathe. I can't breathe here."

"With me?" I croak.

"In LA."

My breath gets stuck in my throat. "You're leaving again?"

"I don't … I …. maybe. The thought of going to Cameron's funeral makes me want to hurl. It would be easier if I wasn't there. Or here … or just … anywhere." Mason winces. "I'm not even making sense. I'm thinking of going back to my mom for a while."

"You'll regret not saying goodbye. This is *Cameron,* not some random person you barely know."

Mason pulls out of my arms. "Don't you get it? I can't face saying goodbye because I don't want to believe it's actually happening. He …" His throat bobs as he swallows hard. "He was the only one who never gave up on me. He can't be gone. He can't."

If one thing could be learned from all of this—from Mason coming back to LA, to us hooking up and realizing we've always had more than platonic feelings for each other, and now Cameron's death—it's that denial can be a powerful thing.

I want to yell at him that he can't run back to Montana again. He can't leave *me.*

But is it really fair of me to ask that when it's exactly what I did to him two years ago?

CHAPTER 26
MASON

EVERYTHING IS EMPTY.

Each day blurs together with the last. Death has a weird way of cloaking time, which is why I don't realize it's the day of Cameron's funeral until Denver's standing above me in a black suit with a black shirt, trying to wake me.

I don't want to face today. I'm still trying to convince myself it didn't happen and that Cameron is still here.

"Where's the service again?" I ask.

"Hollywood Forever, but we're supposed to be going from Harley's place. Show a united front."

Sure, united front. Fuck, that pisses me off. "Use this opportunity as a PR stunt to get us back together, you mean?"

Denver frowns. "You don't actually believe that, do you? Harley's a workaholic and obsessive to the point I worry about his mental health, but he wouldn't use Cameron like that. No way."

Deep down, I know what Denver says is true, but all the toxicity from this industry is bleeding into real-life issues—serious ones—and I'm not okay with that. It's maddening enough that instead of Cameron being in the headlines, we are. He's the one who died, and everyone is speculating about the Eleven boys and whether or not this will bring us back together. It's disgusting.

"I'll meet you there. I … I need to do this alone." If I do it at all.

"I'll call Harley and tell him to save us seats at the service."

"That's not exactly the definition of *alone*."

Denver flinches back. "What?"

"Sorry. That came out harsher than I intended it to. I really need to process this separate from us. From Eleven. And from everything Hollywood."

Denver kneels by the bed, and his lips form into a thin line. "I have a bad feeling that if I walk out of here, I'm not going to see you at all today. Everyone is allowed to grieve in their own way, but I guarantee if you miss out on saying goodbye, you're going to regret it for the rest of your life."

I lean up on my elbows. "What's the difference between saying goodbye to him when I'm alone without the media and saying goodbye to a casket? It's not like his soul will be there. It's his body in a wooden case being covered by dirt. I don't need to see that."

Denver takes my hand. "It might make you finally accept that he's gone."

I want to say I've still got four more stages of grief to get through before I'm anywhere near acceptance, but maybe he's right. It might be a step.

I just don't know if I can face it. "Maybe I can come late and stand at the back. I don't want the attention. I don't want to have to keep it together in front of the media."

"It's being held in the gardens. I really hope you make it. For your sake." Denver leans in and kisses my forehead as he stands. "Call me if you need anything, okay?"

What I need is to forget, but I don't think even Denver has that kind of power over me.

When Denver leaves, I force myself to get up and shower in

case I get the sudden urge to go, but like I said to Denver, I can say goodbye to Cameron wherever I am. I don't need to be where he is.

I'm not exactly a spiritual person—I don't believe in God, I don't have *faith*—but I believe once someone is passed, their soul is no longer here. Where it goes? I have no idea. I like the idea of an afterlife, but it's hard to believe in one.

Cameron wouldn't give a flying fuck if I was at his funeral service. He'd tell me to toast to him, say a prayer because he *was* the faithful type, and get my ass back to work.

And it's there, under the warm spray of Denver's shower, that I finally let myself break down and cry for the first time since it happened. I've shed tears, but I haven't full-on bawled until now.

Thinking back over the last eighteen months, of him turning up in Montana, of calling me, him constantly trying to get me to come back, it reminds me of the voicemail he left a few weeks ago after our business lunch. I listened to the message but didn't delete it.

I rush to get out of the shower and find my phone. Only wearing a towel, I step onto Denver's balcony overlooking his view of Malibu, the water in the short distance, a view not dissimilar to what I used to have in Palos Verdes. It may be a different beach, a different area, but it's the same damn ocean, and I have the same alone feeling.

Sucking in a deep breath, I put my phone to my ear and listen to what Cameron had to say.

"Just calling to say it was good seeing you today."

Oh, shit, maybe I'm not in the right space to listen to this. A sob falls from me.

"I'm so happy you're back in LA. You guys were always my pride and joy to watch. It might not have been all smooth sailing, but I think if you give Harley a chance, you can fix all that was wrong. You just need to give him a chance."

The last thing on my mind right now is getting back together with Eleven. Do I owe it to Harley? Owe it to *Cameron*? I try to think of what I actually want from life, but listening to a dead man's voice, all I really want is to stop hurting.

"Don't forget to make more time for the old man while you're here. I miss all you kids, and I'm determined to get you all in the same room. I just know the magic will spark once again."

Damn it. I don't think I owe Eleven or its fandom anything when they all turned their backs on me, but I do owe it to Cameron to go and see him one last time. Even if I don't believe he's there in spirit or whatever.

I need to go and say goodbye.

Denver's guitar I've been using to write songs calls to me, and I know exactly how to give Cameron the type of send-off that he'd want.

Fucking Cameron Verikas.

Always having the last word, even when he's dead.

I'm late, but there are so many industry people here that it's standing room only at the back of the gardens. It's easy to slip into the crowd, and hardly anyone notices me as I arrive.

It's perfect sunny LA weather, and that old song pops into my head. The one about expecting it to rain on such a depressing day.

Guests are seated each side of a reflecting pool that's lined with purple, yellow, and orange flowers. All the seats are taken, and I spot the other four Eleven guys down the front near the altar.

I get a few side-eyes as I make my way past people, but are they looking at me weird because I'm late, because I'm Mason Nash, or because I barely look like the old me anymore? It could be any one of those reasons or all of them. What I'm wearing probably doesn't help. It doesn't scream funeral service. I'm in black jeans, a tight T-shirt, and a blazer from a suit Denver had organized for me while I've been in my grief-induced trance. It doesn't exactly fit because I mumbled a guess at the size I thought I was. Apparently, I haven't lost as much weight as I thought I had. Playing guitar will be interesting. If I don't rip seams in the thing and hulk out, I'll be surprised.

Right now, though, I don't care. I don't care what anyone here thinks of me. All I care about is fulfilling one wish of Cameron Verikas's. It seems I arrive at exactly the right moment.

The person running the service asks for Harley to come forward to talk.

My feet work fast to move past all the guests and get to the front where Harley stands. He sees me coming with a guitar strapped to me, and his lips quirk, but not in the Harley Valentine way. It's sadder.

When I get to him, he holds out his arms, and I hug him how I would back in the good old days onstage—like we were brothers. With the guitar, it's more a one-armed, nice to see you type hug, but the sentiment is there.

"You made it," he says quietly so no one can hear.

"I know what Cameron would've wanted."

I step back, glance over my shoulder at the other three, and then my gaze lands on Denver.

I lift my chin and nod for them to join me. They glance at each other but then get up. As they approach, I realize it's the first time we've all been in the one place since we split.

I look up at the sky. *You did this on purpose, didn't you, you asshole?* That man was so stubborn, I wouldn't put it past him to *die* so he could get his way.

Ryder and Blake meet me with back slaps, but Denver throws his arms around me and holds me tight.

"You made the right decision."

"We'll see about that. I'm not excited about this going viral, but we know it will."

"What is this?"

"A tribute. Cameron's last wish was for us to get back together, so I thought I needed to give it to him. Even if it's only a song."

Suddenly, it's like it was years ago, and we step into place. We know where to stand. We know how to play up our angles, and when I start strumming "Memories" by Maroon 5, we don't need to look to each other for cues even though we've never performed this song together before.

It's reflexive. It's instinctual. It's what happens when you perform with the same four people for seven years and have a formula.

I kick us off with the opening chorus while playing the melody, Harley sings the first verse, and then we back him up with harmonies on the second chorus. Ryder sings the bridge, Denver takes the second verse, and Blake takes lead on the final harmonies.

The song is about loss, about celebrating those no longer with us, and toasting to the memory of loved ones, wishing they were here. I'm relieved I led this and took the opening because as the song goes on, tears sting my eyes, and I don't trust my voice anymore.

It feels like the perfect goodbye to Cameron, but it also feels like a goodbye to something else.

On the outside, it would've looked like this was rehearsed. No one would imagine this was an impromptu performance. It's why we worked so well as a boy band.

Sure, there were fights. There were hard times. And it wasn't an instant thing. It took work to get where we were, but if this has shown anything, it's that our connection hasn't wavered. We're still us.

Yet, even so, something is also missing. I want to say it's Cameron, but my gut tells me it's more than that.

Over a year ago, I walked away from this life wishing I had another chance.

I missed performing with these guys, and I missed the fans. Hell, I even missed the long hours in a studio.

But ever since I've been back, I haven't been comfortable with signing any deals other than the temporary ones with *Fandom*. I'm not jumping at the chance to get back in the spotlight.

Something has been holding me back, and I know I asked for a sign, but this one doesn't make me want to scribble my signature on the dotted line. Cameron's death makes the idea of going back to a life where I was constantly exhausted pointless. Why do I want to go back to being judged on my image, my voice, and my choices?

I haven't been sure of why until this moment. This moment where I let it all go.

The resentment toward the industry. The desire to be who everyone wants me to be.

Hollywood isn't me anymore, and there's no way I can do it without Cameron.

I think I'm done here.

CHAPTER 27
DENVER

CAMERON'S WIFE is hosting a gathering at Cameron's and her house after the funeral, but the five of us decide to do our own thing and honor him together back at my place.

Both Harley and Ryder offered theirs, but Harley has Brix's dad living there, and Ryder has Maggie and Kaylee. Blake's currently living out of a hotel because … reasons. I guess with him working nonstop on location for the last two and a half years, he's used to it. My house is the logical decision.

We're all mentally exhausted after the service. I don't think we've muttered more than a couple of words to each other since the end of it. Blake's lying on the floor in my informal living room, Harley and Ryder are on one couch, and Mason and I are on the other.

It's just the five of us. Ryder's and Harley's partners went home because they wanted to give us all the space we need to mourn together.

"I thought our reunion would be a bit happier than this," Blake says.

Harley scoffs. "No shit."

For whatever fucked-up reason, I find that hilarious.

The others do not.

"Okay, Denny clearly had a flask on him this whole time and hasn't shared," Ryder says.

Ah, they know me too well. I reach into my suit pocket and pull out the flask, throwing it to Ryder.

Mason's eyes burn into me, and I don't want to turn to see whatever expression he has on his face. It'll either be disappointment or anger, and I can't deal with either right now.

In my defense—

"Wait." Ryder lifts it and tries to look in the hole. "This feels full."

"It *is* full," I say. "I had it just in case." And I only went to reach for it about six times.

It's the one day I can be thankful for paparazzi and news crews. I'd like to say I refrained from drinking because I was strong enough to hold back, but I can't be sure that's the case. Eyes were on us the whole time, that's all.

Ryder lifts the flask. "Well, cheers." He takes a large swig, and I glance away.

"Give me that." It's Harley's turn now, and then he caps it and throws it to Mason.

"I'm good." Mason passes it to Blake on the floor.

"I already told you that you can drink around me," I murmur.

"What's happening?" Harley asks.

"Denver gave up drinking," Mason says. "Well, he *had*."

"It was *full*," I point out. Now the other four are staring at me. "Go on, guys, make a bigger deal out of this. That won't have me reaching for the bottle or anything."

They continue to blink at me.

"Jesus Christ, so I decided to be sober for a while. Is that really a big deal?"

"It is," Harley says. "But … in a good way. Are you going to meetings and stuff?"

"Fuck no. I don't want that shit getting out." It's not like I'm an alcoholic or something. I just really like it, want to turn to it, and love that it makes me feel *nothing*. Okay, that totally sounds like I'm an alcoholic. Well, fuck. "Statistically, one of us was going to become an addict. *You're welcome.*"

Though, I still don't see it completely that way. Then again, my outlook on addiction is probably skewed. My vision of an addict is those who can't look after themselves or their kids, having them taken away by the government and placed with other relatives or put into the foster system.

It's entirely possible I'm a high-functioning addict. It would be healthier for me to stop before I do become destructive and helpless.

"I have a brilliant idea," Blake says. "The more we drink, the less there is for Denny to drink."

Harley jumps up. "Good idea. I know where he keeps a stash of the good stuff. He hides it when he throws parties."

The three of them leave the room.

"Annnd now they're raiding my bar," I say. I turn to Mason, who's watching me intently.

"You were going to drink?"

"I didn't, did I?"

"How do you feel now?"

"Fine. You can go join them if you want." I wave in the others' direction. "I'm stronger now I'm home. I'm not going to lie, I had moments there today, but I'm good. It's passed. I'm cool."

Mason purses his lips like he doesn't completely believe me, but then he reaches for my hand. "I ..." He blows out a loud breath. Then he looks away.

Oh, fuck. Fuck no. No, no, no. He's been talking about leaving, and I can see it in his set jaw and soft, defeated eyes. He can't do this now. Not here. Not with everyone else in the other room.

"Whatever you have to say, you can wait until the others are gone." I pull my hand away from his.

Mason opens his mouth to say something, but it closes when

the guys come back into the room, glasses full of my top-shelf stuff in hand. That's okay. They're allowed to drink the good stuff.

I'm not cheap by any means, but my sixteen-hundred-dollar bottles of Macallan are way too good to waste on the Hollywood wannabes who turn up to my parties.

This whole situation hits me with some hard truths. Since Mason's been back, I haven't thrown a single party. I haven't invited anyone over.

And no one has contacted me. No one has asked where I've gone. No one is blowing up my phone.

Looking back on it, the organizer I'd used to contact to get people here was using me just as much as I was using him. If I ever needed to feel validated in my place in Hollywood, I'd contact Charlie, and then up-and-comers, models, and Hollywood chasers would turn up on my doorstep a few hours later. It's all about networking.

Only, I'm suddenly realizing *no one cared*.

Charlie hasn't contacted me in almost two months, and come to think of it, the only time we ever talked was when I would contact him.

I suddenly have a new understanding of what Mason went through when he went running home. The only difference is I don't have a home to run to. This is the only life, the only place, the only thing I have.

"Did you guys know Cameron offered to adopt me?" I say out of nowhere.

"What?" Harley asks.

"After my grandmother died, and we were going through all that court stuff where I had to prove I could look after myself, Cameron said if it didn't work, he'd adopt me so nothing in my life would change. It was only going to be on paper, but still … he was there for us. Always. Now …"

"That's depressing." Blake downs his glass.

"Now we should be there for each other," Harley says.

We all look at him in various states of *what the fuck* because he can't be bringing up the reunion at a time like this … could he?

Harley looks pissed at our implied expressions. "I'm not talking about getting back together or mentioning that the performance today was magic. I mean that when we broke up, we were so focused on ourselves and our careers and what we were going to do as individuals, we lost that brotherhood. It was no one's fault, and we all did it. I can't help thinking we went about it all wrong. It's been two and a half years since we've been in the same room together. Let's not do that again."

We look around at each other, each of us nodding or murmuring some state of agreement except for Mason, who's stoic.

"That might be a bit hard," Mason says. "Unless you guys are ever in Montana. Then by all means, stop by for dinner." His tone and his words are so final. It's definite.

"You're going back?" Harley asks. "For a visit?"

Mason shakes his head. "Performing with you guys again was great, I'll admit it, but beyond that… I don't see my future in Hollywood. I should be home. With my family."

"We're your family too," I point out. Or, I thought at least *I* was.

"After years and years of playing the same game, what are we going to do? Push ourselves, work our asses off? And then what? Work to death? Die of a freaking heart attack at fifty-two years old? The way Cameron would always talk about the industry, that you need to strike while the iron's hot, you need to market to the majority, to be successful you have to compromise on the things you want … He pushed himself for all of his acts, and look where it got him. I don't want to live that life anymore."

"We're not going to be about that this time," Harley says.

"I know from experience if you're not, this album you want to get done will fail. What then? If Cameron taught me anything, it's that you have to play this industry's game or fuck right off. I'm choosing self-preservation on this one."

That's it, then. No reunion. No more Eleven. And no more us.

I thought we were the type of couple who would consult each other on these types of big decisions, but maybe that was a delusion. We never defined what we were.

Cameron's death has affected all five of us differently, and maybe some perspective is what Mason needed to realize what I've thought all along.

Holding on to something because you don't want to lose it, not because you love it, is no way to build a relationship.

This thing between us is over.

I knew it all along, and yet I still hooked up with him anyway. Losing him a second time isn't just painful; it shatters the already broken pieces of my heart he left two and a half years ago.

I hold it together because I don't have any other choice. And later, once the other three are drunk, Brix comes to pick Harley up to take him home, Lyric comes for Ryder, but Blake asks to crash in one of my guest rooms. That means Mason and I also go to bed separately so Blake doesn't find out about us.

It's probably for the best anyway because I can't get into everything with Mason tonight. I'm too mentally exhausted to think clearly, and I'm too emotional over Cameron to deal with more grief on top of that.

And there is no doubt that I will grieve over Mason. The part of my heart that has always belonged to him let me have hope.

Fucking hope. That optimistic bastard.

I knew better than to believe in it.

Trying to sleep is pointless because all I can think about is the end. The end of my career if Fandom fails. The end of Eleven because we're pulling a Taylor Swift and never, ever, ever getting back together.

Worst of all, it's the end of this deluded fantasy I've been living with Mason.

My body yearns for his, and I contemplate sneaking out to the guesthouse to climb into bed with him so I can pretend he's not leaving, but my head knows that's a bad idea. My heart breaks at the thought of it. I can't pretend when I'm utterly heartbroken.

Yet, when my bedroom door opens and Mason slips inside, pretending seems a lot easier than facing it. I'm not ready. Not yet.

"Denny?"

I revel in the way he says my name.

"You awake?"

I'm tempted to stay quiet. Maybe he'll leave. Then I realize he might walk out that door and keep going. "I'm awake."

"I know we have stuff to talk about—"

"I don't want to. Not now."

"That's fair." Mason steps closer to the bed, but in the dark room, I can only see his shadow. I can't see his face as he says, "Can I sleep next to you?"

"Always." No, not always. Stupid mouth. There is no *always* when it comes to Mason and me.

He moves agonizingly slow as he strips down and gets into bed, to the point that by the time he finally settles, I can no longer take not touching him.

I inch my way closer until I'm pressed against his side, and he wraps his arm around me.

Tears spring to my eyes, but it's unclear what they're for. Cameron? Mason? *Everything*?

"I want you to know—" Mason starts, but I can't. I *can't* deal with this.

"Not now. Don't do this now," I beg.

"I think we need to. You're trembling."

"Because I know what's coming. You're going to leave again, only this time, you're not going to come back."

"I'm not leaving you."

I pull back with glassy eyes, trying to figure out what he means.

"I'm leaving Hollywood. I'm leaving fame. I'm not leaving you. I ..." He bites his lip. "I want to ask you to come with me, but I can't ask you to give up your life for me."

My brain is too tired to comprehend what he means. "So, you're not leaving me, but you are going back to Montana. You want me to go with you even though you know I can't because I'm under contract. You're under contract too, or have you forgotten about that?"

"I'll get out of it. Pay the money back they gave me."

"You're not even going to stick around for the finale?"

"I ... shit. I don't think I can. I'm not ... I'm not strong enough to deal with this. When I came back, I was literally just looking for somewhere to escape the paparazzi."

I lean up on my elbow. "If that were true, you wouldn't have come back to LA. You would've escaped to some other secluded place."

"Okay, maybe I wasn't only looking to escape. I also wanted to see you. After you turned up on my doorstep, I wanted to make things right. I came here to fix us. But now ..."

"Now you want to break us again. Got it."

"No, I don't. What are your plans for when *Fandom* wraps? You could maybe come to Montana and—"

"And what? Grow Christmas trees? Live off royalties that will eventually die off over time? Go back to being so poor we have to eat ramen every meal—that's if we even get to eat every day."

"I'm not that broke, you know. Besides, eating ramen in a mansion isn't exactly the end of the world."

"I am this life." I am because I have to be. Because I know what it's like to have an empty stomach for what feels like days. I remember exactly what it was like to be poor. To worry about being a growing boy and eating so much food that Nanna couldn't afford rent because she'd spend it all on groceries.

Logically and rationally, I know it's a long fall from where I am now, but the fear of it is what keeps me motivated to try everything to hold on to some sort of a career.

"Do you know why I've kept that ugly-ass duck all these years?"

"Because your taste is seriously questionable, and you love that thing?"

"No. Well, yes, but the main reason is because it reminds me that I came from nothing and built my way up in this industry to the point I could afford a useless, ugly, basically only good for a paperweight *duck*. It reminds me why I do what I do."

The deeper meaning of Bill finally registers in Mason's eyes.

"You don't think you belong here," I continue. "Or, you don't right now because of Cameron, but settling down in Montana isn't me. I don't think it's you either, but it's not my place to tell you why you're leaving. You have your reasons, and I'm sure you believe them, but maybe one day you'll wake up and realize you're lying to yourself."

Mason's silent for a beat. "I don't want to live my life for someone else. Not a label. Not Harley. Not any of the other guys from Eleven."

Way to punch me in the heart.

"But you ..." His breath comes out shaky. "I ... I don't want to leave you."

"So you said. It's not going to stop you, though, is it?" I'm important. Just not important enough.

"I need to do this. Singing with you guys today, it made me realize I really am done."

Yeah. So am I.

I'm done trying to make him fall in love with me.

I'm done thinking this has any type of real future.

I'm done talking.

"Kiss me?" I ask.

If this is goodbye, I'm going to do it properly. With only the small amount of courage and strength I have left, I pour it into kissing him instead of what I really want to use it for which is to beg for him to stay.

All of those arguments run through my head, each one easily dismissed. He could stay here and live with me but stay out of the spotlight—not likely. A life in LA means being pursued by paparazzi wherever we go. Plus, he has a support system with his family back home.

He could stay until the *Fandom* finale, but that will only drag out our heartache. Seeing him every day, knowing our time is running out, wouldn't sit well with me.

He should stay so I don't reach for a bottle. *Yeah, really healthy, Denny.*

Mason's only been here a short time, but I don't remember how I ever did this being famous thing without him. For over two years I've been floundering while trying to keep my head above water. Mason lifts me up in so many ways. I'm more confident around him. I'm optimistic. And watching him come back from practically nothing to being in the tabloids again, while a pain in the ass for us, it gave me hope that if *Fandom* was a huge mistake and my career takes a hit, finding the next big thing could put me back on top.

A little seed of resentment plants itself in my gut because I think the answer to my career problem is Eleven getting back together. But I can't ask Mason to suck it up and take one for the team when I can't bring myself to even contemplate moving to Montana with Mason. My heart's not there, and his isn't here.

It's a no-win situation, but I'm going to try to turn it into one.

At least a temporary one where we both win.

I roll on top of him and push my tongue into his mouth. He

groans in response and grips my ass, forcing me to grind on top of him.

This is the end, so I go slow, wanting to make it last. A small part of me actually believes if I can keep doing this forever, he won't leave me.

If my hands grip hard enough, they could brand his body. If I kiss him gently, his heart could know I'm his. And if I love him long enough, his head could tell him to stay.

But deep down, I know he won't.

I sit up, straddling his waist, and I run my hands over his torso, committing every curve to memory.

Then I reach into my boxer briefs and pull out my cock, stroking it slowly as my imagination gets away from me. "I want to mark your skin. I want to come on you so I can remember what you looked like covered in me."

Mason doesn't react, so I take that as an affirmative. I lean over him, my free hand on the pillow next to his head, but as I dip down to kiss him, his big hands land on my chest to stop me. "Or you could come inside me."

His words take me off guard, and my hand on my dick falters. "Are you sure?"

He nods.

I ignore the voice inside my head saying if we take this step, it really will be goodbye, and I half want to hold out so I can give him a reason to come back to me, but the other half of me doesn't want to give up this chance. It might be the only one I get.

I kiss him hard but make it brief because I have work to do.

I reach for the lube in the bedside drawer and shuffle my way down his body and settle between his legs. His hands tremble as he hooks his fingers into the waistband of his boxers and shoves them down. I help him out of his before taking mine off.

Then we're both naked, together, which is something I'm still getting used to. My eyes rake over his sexy body, and unlike the other times where I've been worried about making him feel self-conscious about his weight, I let myself really look.

He puts his hands on his knees and lifts them, exposing his hole. Mason lying there, bare and waiting for me to make my move, it might be the hottest thing I've ever seen in my entire life.

It makes me want things that aren't possible.

I contemplate what a relationship with Mason would look like, but it consists of long months in between brief visits. He might come back to LA to see me occasionally, fuck me for a couple of days, tell me how much he misses me, but he'll always get back on that plane and fly home.

It will tear me apart, and I can't do it. Even if it's only a three-hour flight.

It could be doable, no doubt, but how long will it take to become too hard? Too much?

What will I do when I get that itchy sense of failure and throw Hollywood parties to forget I'm fading into the background? How long will it take for me to bed someone to feel validated?

"I have a confession to make," Mason rasps, and I'm brought back to the present. To what's important. Making Mason feel good is the only thing I should be focusing on. My gaze flicks to his.

"I, umm …" He averts his eyes from mine. "While you've been working, I've been … experimenting."

Heat pools in my gut. "Tell me more."

"You don't have to worry about going slow. Wait, no, go slow, please, but you don't have to wait for me to get used to the sensation of your fingers."

A shudder runs through me. "I kind of want to be mad because I totally could've helped you experiment, but at the same time, I'm thankful, because it means this should go a lot easier."

And it does. When I press a lubed finger to his hole, teasing his rim to try to work my way in, he relaxes and accepts it easily.

"Damn, that's tight," I mutter.

"I'm good. Work me open." Mason's chest rises and falls in

long, controlled breaths, but as I slip my finger inside deeper and then move it in and out slowly for him to adjust, his breathing becomes faster.

His face flushes, sweat drops off his brow, and the muscles in his neck tighten as he grits his teeth. "I need …" He grunts.

"I know what you need." I lean over him and suck the head of his cock into my mouth.

His hips jackknife off the bed, and then I'm knuckle-deep inside him.

"Holy shit," he whispers.

I suck him while I continue to work him over, going in stages. One finger and then two. When I get to three, it's like a synchronized dance as my free hand joins in. I stroke him while finger fucking him, and every light press of his prostate only makes him beg for more.

And Mason panting and chanting, "More," over and over again sends a thrill through me.

But when I move my mouth to his balls, sucking, licking, teasing, his body trembles in the way it always does right before he comes.

As if on cue, Mason says, "Stop. Stop or I'm going to come."

I lift my head. "Is there something wrong with that?"

"I don't want to until you're inside me."

There is literally no argument for that. "Fair enough. Are you sure you're ready?"

"Yes. I need something to bring me back from the damn edge."

The weight of goodbye tries to press down on me as I lube my cock, but I push it away.

Whether it's in twenty minutes, twenty hours, or two days, Mason will leave me, and there's nothing I can do about it.

Pushing inside him, I resist the urge to fight for him. To ask him to stay even though it would be guilting him into it. I want to beg and plead. I want to ask for more than he can give me.

But this? This I can do for him. I can fuck him until he can't think, until he can barely breathe, until the only thought running through his head is that he could never leave me.

I want someone who's compelled to tell me how their day was. Who needs to cuddle on the couch because they miss my touch. Someone who will be there for me no matter what happens, who dies, or whatever obstacles get thrown in our way.

I was beginning to think that person was Mason, but it's not. No matter how much I want it to be.

And as I make love to him, cherish his body, and try to take this for what it is—a goodbye fuck—it will be hard to look back on tonight and see it as anything more than my heart breaking.

It's only when we both come that I let myself collapse on top of him and release the tears I've been trying to hold back.

We don't talk when it's done. He doesn't acknowledge the tears.

All he does is wipe one away with his thumb, kiss another, and then he disappears into the bathroom to clean up.

I should probably do that too, but like everything else going on with us, I'm leaving it in future Denny's hands to deal with.

Hopefully, I'll wake up stronger than I am right now so I can handle it, but when I wake to an empty bed, I just know.

Mason's gone.

I thought last night might have convinced him to stay even if only a few more days. I thought I had time to persuade him that Hollywood still has things to offer him. Like … me.

It's the story of my life.

I'm talented enough to maintain a career in Hollywood, but I'm not phenomenal enough to come out on top.

I'm available enough to be used for party promoters and up-and-comers in the industry, but not enough to actually be friends with.

My mom loved me enough to have me but not enough to keep me.

I've never been *enough* for anyone.

I'm torn between fighting for Mason and letting him go, but two and a half years ago, I let us fall apart. He tried to fight for me. He called and texted. He put in the effort, but I let him go.

Even though I know deep down he's gone, I check the house anyway. He's not in the kitchen, the living rooms—either one—any of the guest rooms or out by the pool. The last place to look is the guesthouse, but I can't bring myself to go out there. Because then it will be real.

I stare across the pool at the tiny square hut and fold my arms. My feet itch to go out there, but my brain tells me it will only hurt.

"What are we looking at?"

For some stupid reason, my heart flutters with hope even though Blake sounds nothing like Mason.

Blake steps up next to me, looking a little hungover. He rubs his eyes. "Is Mason not up yet?"

"He's gone."

"What do you mean, gone?"

"My guess is back to Montana."

Blake frowns. "Already? He talked about it yesterday, but I thought he meant *eventually*."

"So did I."

"Are you sure he left? Maybe he's getting breakfast."

"I haven't been out there, but his truck is gone. His stuff ..." From my room. Can't say that. "Like, all the things he had lying around the house are gone."

"Maybe he tidied."

I cock my eyebrow like *Really?*

"Right. Good point. Okay, I'll go check." He tries to walk off, but I grab his arm.

"Don't bother. He's not out there."

"How do you know?"

I know because my heart aches the way it did every moment I lived without him before. I know because that connection I've always felt for him is severed. I know he's gone because if he was here, I'd still have hope.

I have nothing to hold on to, and it feels like I'm drowning.

That's how I know.

"I just do," I say.

"What are we going to do?"

I want to give him up. I want to say we should let him run away. But I've done that once before, and I won't let it happen again. "We fight for him."

It's as easy as that to make up my mind.

CHAPTER 28
MASON

AFTER BEING intimate with Denver in a way I never thought would or could happen, saying goodbye is fucking hard. *Too hard.* It's why I slip out of his room and out of his life before the sun rises.

I need to leave. I can't … I can't be here.

The hard truths of the industry and the chaos isn't worth the pain. I used to be able to handle them, but after coming back with fresh eyes, I see this lifestyle for what it really is: the cruelest form of manipulation. I refuse to play Hollywood's games anymore.

And sure, there were only about a thousand times last night, while Denver was moving inside me, while he was breaking down afterward, and silently begging me to stay by holding on to me so tight, that I thought I could stay.

I could live with him in his Malibu home and hide just as well as I do back in Montana, but I'd know every time I'd step outside that house, I'd be drawn back in, and the public would ridicule me the way they've always done.

There's absolutely no doubt that I love Denver Smith for who he really is—Denny Mariano, a damaged boy from South Los

Angeles who craves to be wanted. I love him for the artist he's become, for his work ethic, and for his strength.

I love all of him. But love doesn't stop people from leaving, love couldn't stop my father or Cameron from dying, and love can't make everything magically better.

Love is a useless emotion that only brings heartache, and even though the thought of losing Denver crushes my soul, I have to do it. I have to protect myself.

I only wish I'd thought to save driving these agonizingly long hours until I'd had a better night's sleep.

When I drove to LA, I was on a mission. I was focused, determined, and it's how I made it to LA in sixteen hours with only a couple of breaks for the bathroom and to fill up on gas.

This time, I'm running away from someone I don't want to leave, the evidence of our love still there in the way my body aches. Leaving feels wrong and right at the same time, and I find myself wanting to change direction over and over again.

I want to go back. I want to keep driving north.

I want to find a way I can have both—my quiet life and Denver.

I'm about an hour from hitting Utah when I have to stop. I've only been on the road for six hours, but I can't take it anymore because it feels like there's a solution, but I can't quite grasp it yet, and the farther I get from LA—from Denver—the more it seems out of reach.

There are a few hotels and casinos in Mesquite, Nevada, so I choose the least sketchy-looking one and check in. Considering it's barely lunchtime, I have about eighteen hours to fill. Other than telling myself to stop doubting my decision, maybe I'll try to get some sleep. And if I get to sleep now, I might be able to check out later and drive the rest of the way tomorrow. It should only be another ten hours or so before I'm back where I feel safest.

I'll be safe to be myself and safe from all the bullshit.

Safe from being hurt.

I groan. *That's* the real reason I'm running away, isn't it? Denver was right. This has nothing to do with the LA shit.

If I throw myself fully into this Eleven reunion, I'm terrified I'll end up where I am right now.

Alone.

Which is why I'm doing it first. I'm protecting myself from reliving the hurt by doing it on my own terms and not theirs.

Maybe I should go back. If I leave now, I'll be back in LA before dinner. I can swallow my pride and pretend I didn't have this grief-induced panic attack.

But the crappy thing about panic is it doesn't magically disappear because you acknowledge the cause.

I can't face Hollywood alone, and even if I'd have Denver by my side once again, I can't help reminding myself how he left me once before. All the guys from Eleven abandoned me.

After eating crappy food in the hotel restaurant, where I'm thankfully not recognized, I make my way to my room to try to nap, but it's pointless.

I check my phone a dozen times, and I'm thrown back to the last time I went running home with my tail between my legs. I waited a long time for someone in Hollywood to notice I was gone or for someone to care. After a while, the stark reality hit me that no one did.

Except for Cameron.

Then, of course, I start thinking about what I am going to do seeing as I can't go back to my old life. Expand the Christmas tree farm? I like working with my hands and being outdoors, but it's not like it has ever been my calling to be a lumberjack. After Dad died, the lumber side of the business took a huge hit and had dried up by the time I left for college. If it hadn't been for Eleven, we would've lost the land that's been in our family for generations. The loans and land taxes were building up, and thanks to my career, I saved it.

But what am I going to do now?

Sleep eludes me, which leads me down the rabbit hole of checking entertainment news. Big mistake. Masochism and impulse control issues are really fun.

The internet is blowing up with rumors of an Eleven reunion after our performance, and as I watch back the video of us singing together, that spark of *this is what makes the bullshit worth it* tries to ignite inside me, but it flames out fast.

We were saying goodbye to one of the biggest music managers in the industry—someone important to us—and all the media can talk about is whether or not we're going to cut another album. It's disgusting.

When I do finally drift off to sleep, it's not the media, the life, or performing that I'm thinking of. There are only thoughts about a boy. A man. My best friend, my rock, and the only person in this world I could break the vow I made myself when I climbed out of his bed this morning.

I said I'd never let myself go back, but I've been away from him for mere hours, and I already miss him.

Aside from my brief appearances on *Fandom*, I wasn't working while I was staying in his house, but unlike in Montana where not working dragged me into depression, with Denver by my side, I didn't long for something to fill my time.

He balances my life just by being there.

Fuck, what am I doing?

When someone dies, you abandon everything they wanted for you. It's totally emotionally sound and completely logical.

Despite my brief what-the-fuck moment I had last night, when I finally crash out and wake in the middle of the night, I push on and keep driving north even if the voice inside my head has changed its tune and wants me to turn around.

I should be relieved when I pull into my street, or, I don't know, I should feel like I have accomplished something. It's a big choice, leaving behind the glitz and glam of fame. I did it once before with regrets. This time there's nothing but finality. Or … there *should* be.

When I open the gate to my home, I'm numb. As I drive along the winding road leading to the monstrosity I built, still numb. And when I stop the car in the circular driveway, I stare out at the five-bedroom wood-and-stone structure and remember a time where I wanted to fill it with kids and a wife and have that ever-lasting kind of love you only see in movies.

When I learned the reality, that love is messy and happily ever afters are hard work, I gave up that dream. But looking at my empty house, I realize that sometime while living with Denver, those thoughts of forever might have crept back in.

It was so easy to be with him. It was confusing but easy. We know each other inside and out, and being intimate with him only brought us closer together. Our bond deepened to a level I never knew existed. I've thought I've felt what forever feels like before, but it's incomparable to what I began to feel for Denver.

Why am I here, a thousand miles away, running from that?

I'm a fucking idiot.

I'm so distracted by the millions of thoughts running through my head, I barely notice when I bypass another car parked in my drive and think nothing of it.

Not until I slide my key in the front door and open it to the sound of people goofing off in my kitchen do I think, *Oh wait, no one should be at my house.*

But they're not just people. They're *my* people. The guys from Eleven are here. I can hear at least Harley and Blake. Does that mean …

My heart pitter-patters loudly as it jumps to conclusions, but as the door shuts behind me and the noises stop, Harley pops his head around the corner from the kitchen. Then Ryder appears.

One by one, they each come around the corner. They're in my house. They're *here*.

The last one is Denver, his head held low, his hands in his pockets. I hate seeing him like that.

"Denny." The name gets stuck in my throat.

"Don't be mad at him," Blake says.

Mad? Why would I be mad? He's … he came for me.

"As soon as he told me you had left yesterday, we called Harley, and we were all planning to come and get you back. Your mom let us in."

"You … you all came for me?"

This is what I wanted eighteen months ago. This is the missing piece that had me running away from Hollywood.

We stand there, staring across the room at each other, the four of them and then me, hovering by my door.

"You're one hundred percent right about Hollywood," Harley says. "It's toxic, it's intrusive, it's exhausting, and it's shallow."

"Can't argue with that," Blake says. "Before they offered me the Coby Godspeed movies, they told me to gain thirty pounds of muscles because 'Nobody will believe your lanky boy band body could hang from buildings and kick asses.' Then they don't let me kick any asses anyway! Damn stunt doubles."

"My point is," Harley continues, "there's a lot of shit we have to deal with to live our dream, so we understand why you want to run when things go wrong. But unlike last time, the four of us don't have our heads too far up our own asses to see you need support."

"We fucked up," Ryder says. "We all fell out of touch because the second the band split, we reveled in being independent for once. We were selfish, and when one of us failed, we forgot that even though we were apart, we will always be a team. All five of us."

"We weren't going to make the same mistake this time," Harley says.

My throat feels thick as I try to swallow, and I glance at Denver, wondering if he feels the same way. "Denny?"

He's been quiet, not having said a word since I stepped inside this house. He's barely even looked at me. His eyes finally lift, and as he pierces me with his aqua gaze, I'm hit with clarity and guilt and regret all at once.

Everything—the industry, Cameron, Eleven, even what Denver and I have—all of it is bigger than me and my stupid fear of failure and isolation.

"I'm sorry," I blurt at the same time he says, "I should have asked you to stay."

"What?" I ask.

"I didn't want to talk about it last night because I didn't think I could change your mind, but knowing you were going to walk out of my life, I didn't want to run away again without talking about it first. Because ..." He bites his lip and looks at the others and then back to me.

I spare a quick glance at Harley, Blake, and Ryder, just long enough to see their confused expressions, and then my gaze is back on Denver.

"Last time, I thought I was in love with you. This time, I know I am." Someone gasps, but Denver ignores them and keeps talking. "I'm not going to give you up without a fight. That's what I did two and a half years ago, and like Harley says, we're all here because we've learned from past mistakes."

Fuck. I drop my bag and cross the room, rushing into Denny's arms. "I'm sorry."

Everyone leaves him in one way or another, and here I am doing the same because of stupid fears and insecurities about him and the rest of LA doing it to me first.

"I'm sorry, I'm sorry, I'm sorry," I murmur into his neck. "And ..." I breathe him in and hold him tight because the millions of apologies aren't enough. So I build the courage to say the words I've only ever said to one other person before she ripped my heart out. But I remind myself this is Denny. My feelings for him might be new, but our bond isn't. "I love you too."

He freezes in my arms and goes statue still.

I pull back and cup his cheeks. "Did you hear me?"

"Say it again."

"I love you."

Then his mouth is on mine, and kissing him is like second nature now. I've memorized the feel of his lips, his commanding tongue, and the way he pushes against me just that little bit harder than anyone else would. Everything seems right with the world.

Until Blake's voice cuts through the din. "I, uh, get the impression Denver left a lot of the story out when he told me Mason was leaving."

We should probably deal with that.

Denver tries to keep kissing me, but I gently break away from him to face the others. I don't go far, though. I pull him into my side and hold tight because I never want to let him go again.

Harley and Ryder blink at us and then at each other as if asking in silent question, *"What are we looking at right now?"*

But Blake is on the end with his arms folded. "I don't know whether to be happy for you guys or mad."

"Mad?" Ryder asks. "What, are you pissed you're the only straight one?"

I love that Ryder doesn't feel the need to question us. It's so him. He has always been of the mind that anyone can fall for anyone, though. He's definitely always been fluid-focused, putting sexuality on an ever-moving spectrum.

With Denver and me, it seemed like a natural progression, but when labels get thrown around, I'm uncomfortable and uneasy because of reasons I don't understand. Societal standards maybe?

The notion we have to have everything figured out being shoved down our throats?

"I've been hanging out with Jordan, and he's adamant there was something going on with you two at the club," Blake says. "I said he was crazy. Even made a bet with him. Please tell me you're at least staying closeted so I don't have to do his movie."

Denver laughs. "You bet the movie role?"

"I didn't think I'd have to take it!"

"Well, maybe you still won't." I turn to Denver. "He's right, isn't he? It's not like we have plans to come out at all. If ever. These two haven't." I point at Ryder and Harley. "And if we did, what would we even say? We're just two best friends who fell in love?"

"Aww," Harley says. "You should totally do that."

My forehead scrunches. "What?"

"Oh, only if you're ready. Don't use Ryder and me as an excuse or an example. We're from a different time. It's only been ten years, but a lot has changed since we started in the industry."

"But you're still not coming out," I point out.

"I will be, but you know me, I'm meticulous and risk averse. I have plans in the works, and Gideon, Brix, and I are trying to work out the best way to do it. For me. That's my experience only. You two should do what feels right."

Ryder nods. "Being with Lyric, I'm getting closer to wanting to come out because I think he deserves the world, but then Kaylee … she's still so young and vulnerable."

"Dude, I've spent time with your spawn," Harley says. "She could take over the world. I don't mean in the future. I mean right now."

Ryder snorts. "I actually believe that could be true."

Harley turns back to us. "Our point is don't use our excuses to hold you back. That's if coming out is something you even want. Going forward, if we do this reunion, we're all going to be choosing our own narrative. And yours is actually really sweet.

You were always close, but I thought it was, like, a brotherly thing."

"Funny, so did I," I say.

Denver wraps his arm around me. "He's just really slow to pick up on these things. I was in love with him for years."

I look him in the eyes. "I've handled a lot of things wrong when it comes to us, but I want you to know that I left for selfish reasons. With Cameron gone, I'd convinced myself if something went wrong, I'd be alone again, so ..."

"So you hurt me before I could hurt you by ghosting you again." Denver's arm around me holds tighter.

"I may hate Hollywood, but I love you, and with you turning up like this, showing me we can both make the effort ... I want to find a way to make it work. I don't know how, but—"

"If you still need space, you can take it, but just know I'm here for you this time," Denver says. "All of us are."

"Why don't we all take a step back," Harley says. "Give each of us enough time to grieve, and we'll talk about the reunion happening once Denver's schedule opens up."

"Promise me one thing," I say. "We don't get sucked back into the heavy schedule where it's album, tour, album, tour. I can't go back to that."

"We won't," Harley says. "This is about doing what we love for fun. Sure, I want us to make money, but I believe we can do that and still enjoy what we're doing without burning out or killing ourselves trying."

I trust Harley, I do, but I know how easy it is to spout one thing and have labels do another. If Harley's new label tanks, he might resort to desperate measures.

"I'll have it in your contracts," he says, as if reading my mind.

That's enough for me. "One more thing. If we're doing this whole own narrative thing, I don't want a personal trainer being shoved at me. I'm not interested in calorie counting or worrying about my appearance. This is me. I'm happy this way."

"And I love you in any shape." Denver's arm around me tightens as he squeezes me.

"I think you're going to be an amazing role model," Harley says.

"Then I think we have a deal. At least on my part." I glance at Denver, and he nods.

"I'm in."

"I've already signed," Ryder says. Of course he has.

Blake sighs. "I guess I did promise if the rest of you were in, I'll be in too."

Harley's mouth drops open. "Wait … did … no way … Did that really happen? Should I draw up contracts now before you all change your minds?"

"You can send it to an entertainment lawyer first," I say. "Hmm, I should get me one of those."

Ryder steps in. "I can hook you up. Lyric's brother is pretty big in the industry, and he's trustworthy."

"Nice." I move toward the kitchen but bring Denver with me. "You all staying for a bit? I'm exhausted and need caffeine."

"We can stay for coffee," Harley says. "Lyric has a few appearances I need to be back in LA for. I'm his manager until I can find someone good. I almost lent him mine, but Gideon's helping me with this label business."

"I have to get back to Kaylee," Ryder says.

Blake points at them. "They're my ride."

Denver presses against me. "I'd like to stay … if that's okay with you? I know you said you need air and time alone, and—"

I lean in and press my lips to his. "I want you to stay."

"It can only be for a few days. Then I have back-to-back appearances on talk shows for *Fandom*."

Me, Denver, and my little cocoon of safety? I can't think of a better way to let go of all the sorrow, the hurt … the *fear*. I just hope a couple of days is enough.

"We can go back to LA together." Because Denver needs

someone too. He may not act like it, and hell, he probably doesn't think he does, but I know him better than he might even know himself.

Denver wraps his arms around my middle and buries his head in my neck. "Whatever you need, I'll give it to you. If you need longer, we'll work it out. I'll come back after my obligations are done. I'll get out of them if I can. Whatever it takes for you to come back to me."

Failure still hangs over my head, and with it, the hesitance to even try, but the guys turning up on my doorstep means everything to me. It's what I needed a long time ago. And maybe under different circumstances, it would have been easy to say *too little, too late*. Only difference now is, Denver's here vowing to make us work, promising we do it together, and that's what's giving me the strength to fight. For us, for the band, and for a life I thought I said goodbye to already.

CHAPTER 29
DENVER

THE WEIGHT of Mason's body against me shifts, and like I have every morning for the last three days, I reach for him to try to keep him wrapped around me. It's barely dawn, but he's wide-awake.

Mason peppers kisses from my cheek, down my neck, and then to my lips while his hand wanders over my body and into my boxer briefs.

I'm half-asleep but still awake enough to enjoy him bringing me pleasure. By the time I come, I'm ready to pass back out, and I think that was his plan all along because I feel him slip out of bed not long later. I don't have the energy to stop him this time.

He has spent the last few mornings outside with his trees, but by the time I've made my way out onto the back deck, he's come to the house with rosy cheeks and a bright smile on his face.

The difference between Mason in LA and Mason in Montana is astounding. He's more relaxed, less pessimistic, and while it's obvious he's still grieving, he's not so shut down and reclusive.

We're leaving tonight, though, and I'm worried he'll go back to that bad headspace. I think it's too soon for him to come with me, but I know he'll do it if I ask him to.

I don't really want to be alone, but I have two choices here: go home and make these appearances on my own so I can have a happy Mason return for the *Fandom* finale, or drag him with me and risk having him revert to the guy who left LA a few days ago determined never to return.

I know what I need to do. I just don't want to do it.

When I wake properly and after I get clean in Mason's monstrosity of a shower, I make my way downstairs to the kitchen where a pot of coffee awaits me along with Mason's mother sitting in her usual spot at the dining table.

Mrs. Nash smiles warmly at me like she always has. She comes by the house every day to check on us to make sure we're doing okay with all the Cameron stuff, and if she's noticed that only one bed in this house is being used, she hasn't said anything.

I'm not sure if Mason has plans to come out to her or not, but it's not my place, so I've said nothing.

"Mason's still out there." She glances out the glass-paneled doors toward the neatly planted rows of trees.

There's something in her brown eyes that resembles how I feel —a quiet wariness about Mason's mental well-being.

"We're supposed to fly back tonight," I say.

"Ah. That explains it. He's probably saying goodbye to all his babies."

For some reason, I picture him out there raising a whole bunch of Groot trees that give him attitude.

I lean against the kitchen counter with my coffee and eye Mrs. Nash. "I'm thinking of telling him to stay for a bit longer."

"It would be good for him, but I'm not sure how much without you here with him." Okay, now she's staring at *me* with the same wariness in her gaze.

"I'm sure he'll be fine." I sip from my cup and avoid eye contact.

She stands and approaches me. "Mason took his father's death hard, and with Cameron, he's going through it all over again. He needs some time. What about you? How are you dealing?"

I shrug, but it's stiff. "Is it possible to become desensitized to loss? I've never really had anyone in my life permanently. I'm sad and I miss him, definitely, but … life goes on. I have no family—"

She reaches for me, wrapping her thin fingers around my arm. "That's where you're wrong. Mason is your family, and so am I. You're always welcome here, and who knows, maybe one day you'll be comfortable enough to call me Mom."

I suck in a sharp breath because I don't understand. Is she saying she knows about Mason and me, or is she being the doting mother hen she has always been—to all of us in Eleven. She might not have been around much, but when she was, she fussed over us like we were her own.

"I see the way Mason looks at you. I saw how miserable he was when you two had your falling-out. I'm not blind."

"Oh."

"Not to mention I clean this house. You're either less messy than you used to be or you're sleeping in my son's bed."

Is it suddenly hot in here? I tug at the collar of my shirt.

"I'm sorry. I didn't mean to put you on the spot." There she goes with that mothering tone again, and tears sting my eyes, but I try to hold them back. I don't know what I want more, for her to accept me and Mason as a couple or to be considered part of her family no matter what.

"I've been in love with Mason for years," I admit.

"And he's been in love with you too. He just hasn't known it. But he knows it now, doesn't he?"

I nod, but it's subtle.

She wraps her small arms around me just as the back door opens and Mason steps through. Shit. I wipe at my eyes when she pulls away.

Mason frowns. "What's wrong?" He doesn't hesitate to come to my side.

"Your mom knows. I didn't tell her. She *knew*."

He blinks.

His mom puts her hands on her narrow hips and cocks an eyebrow. "And when were you going to tell me that you found a person you can be truly serious about?"

"Now?" Mason squeaks.

"Were you worried I wouldn't approve?"

"No, no, not that. I was scared you'd *worry*. We're already ridiculed in the media, and you hate it. This—"

"Is nobody else's business, just like all the other bullshit in your industry. Here should be your escape from all that, and I don't want you to be uncomfortable in your own home or feel you need to keep secrets."

"It's not that."

"Good. Now give me a hug, and then I'm going to leave you boys to it."

Mason holds her. "We'll come by tonight before leaving for the airport. Ria said she'd drop us off."

His mom glances at me, and I don't have to read her mind to know what she's thinking. He needs more time here.

When she's gone, Mason pulls me to him. "Well, that was an easy coming out."

"If all of them would be like that, I'm sure Harley and Ryder would've done it years ago."

"Probably," he murmurs into my neck and then kisses me there.

I'm going to miss this affection—the softer side of him that's really starting to come through now he's more relaxed and at peace. He's well on his way to being his old self, the guy I looked up to. I don't want to ruin that. It's why I have to tell him to stay.

"So, I've been thinking …" I hedge.

"Don't do that."

"Think?"

"Thinking only leads to trouble."

"Mase …"

He pulls back. "That's your serious tone."

"You know I love you, right?"

"And now you're freaking me out."

"I … I think you should stay here longer."

"What?"

"If I didn't have to go back, I'd stay with you, but I'm under contract."

"So am I. I never ended up calling and getting out of the *Fandom* finale." He squeezes me a little tighter. "We'll go back together."

"The finale is still a while away. I don't want you to come back too soon. I've seen how well you're doing here, and I think you owe it to yourself to take this time and come back completely fresh."

His lips purse.

I cup his face. "This is totally different than you leaving LA. I know you'll eventually come back to me. I have trust in that. In *us*."

"You're okay with me staying?"

The fact he's so quick to give in shows how much he needs it. "I'd love to have you with me, but not at the cost of you not being ready. I didn't understand why you came here until these last few days where I've seen you in your element. Lumber might not be your calling, but it runs in your blood. It calms you."

"It really does. I don't know why."

"You know, I've actually been picturing us living here."

Mason's eyes widen. "You what?"

"Not permanently. But if we set our own Eleven schedule like Harley wants, escaping to the mountains during our downtime seems like a perfect solution to our problems. When LA is pissing us off, we come home to Montana. When it gets too quiet here, I can go back or both of us. This thing is only going to work between us if we compromise and give each other what we need. And you need more time here. You're allowed it."

He holds on to me so tight as if he fears he'll lose me if he lets me go. "I want to be better for you. I want to be there."

"And you will be. When it counts most. I have no doubts about that."

"I'll be there for the finale. I promise."

"It's only two weeks."

I lived without him for a lot longer than that.

Two weeks. That's all.

I know Mason being in Montana has been good for him, but if he doesn't get his ass to the studio soon, I'm going to both kill him and kiss him when he finally gets here. Maybe not in that order, though. Kiss, then kill.

He promised he would be here, but the closer it creeps to our stage time in the show, the more nervous I get. When I left him, I had no doubts, but if I get another "My flight was delayed again, but I still have time" text, I'm going to lose my shit.

This isn't just another performance. It's not a publicity grab. It's ... bigger than that. Eleven reunion rumors have been circling since Cameron's funeral, and they haven't slowed down. This is going to amplify them more, even if it is only the two of us out on that stage.

If Mason gets here in time.

The contestants have all performed. Alondra has sung her greatest hit. We're due to go on next. Mason only has two commercial breaks and five minutes of the host rambling that we're only moments away from finding out who won. It's never "moments away." It's an eternity.

I'm waiting in the wings, staring out at the audience, who are all a shade of blue thanks to the low lighting.

During the commercial break, the stage lights are down, so I can see nearly all the crowd's silhouettes. I take a deep breath. This is ridiculous that I'm nervous. If Mason doesn't get here in time, I'll go out there and sing by myself. It's no big deal.

It's not performing alone that's getting to me, though. This song *is* Mason and me. And after everything we've been through, from past mistakes to the future ones I anticipate we'll make, singing it with him in front of millions of people will mean something. Even if we're not saying the words aloud, we're hoping the song will speak for itself.

The guitar Mason's supposed to be playing sits on a stand by my side. I want to pick it up and throw the strap over my shoulder to prepare to go this alone, but that would be admitting defeat.

The insecure part of me tries to tell me he never got on the plane and he needs even more time. Maybe that he never made it to the airport, but he's been texting me updates all day. If he wasn't coming, he would've told me.

Time away from each other will always be hard, but it's been harder than I anticipated. It's like the more time apart we have, the more those doubts try to come back. But we've spoken every day, we've FaceTimed, we've texted … Logically, I know it's my nerves trying to ruin this. Well, that, and the fact he *still isn't here*. But he will be. I *have to* believe that.

We need to have that trust, or this will never work.

One of the PAs nearby talks into their headset, telling them to "send him through, ASAP," and my heart gallops with hope they're talking about him.

Then when I see him round the corner, fiddling with the earpiece they've already fitted him with while trying to shake off the makeup artist, the relief that floods through me almost knocks me off my feet.

Two weeks has felt longer than the two years we were apart.

He smirks at me as he approaches. "You're looking a little worried. Thought I wasn't going to make it, huh?"

"Cutting it close, don't you think?"

His smile widens, and damn, he looks good. His beard is neatly trimmed, probably the shortest I've seen it yet, his hair has been cut by a professional this time, and it's styled to stick up with product. He looks remarkably happy.

"Are you ready to go out there?" He nods toward the stage.

Am I ready? Two minutes ago, I wasn't sure. But now that he's here? I could take on the world.

"I'm ready," I croak. Okay, like ninety percent ready. I clear my throat.

Mason picks up the guitar and throws the strap over his shoulder and then leans in. "I missed you, by the way. If it weren't for all these cameras and people, I'd kiss you hello."

My gaze darts quickly around the backstage area, but no one can hear us. Our microphones are onstage, sitting in their stands, so there's no need to be paranoid, but it's there anyway. Always there, I guess.

How have Harley and Ryder kept their sexualities secret for so long?

"Soon," Mason says.

Chances of making it to my bedroom later tonight are slim to none. I envision quick BJs in the foyer. Even Mason's hand on my cock might be enough to come in one second flat.

I've missed him.

I've missed the way he holds me.

"Double-checking here," Mason says, "we're still finishing this how we planned?"

We came up with a stupid … or brilliant idea.

Maybe this will change things too much. Maybe we shouldn't. We should perform it how the show wants us to. But then Mason smiles, and nope, no way.

"We're so doing this."

His happiness is breathtaking. Damn, I want to kiss him right here and now.

"We're ready for you." A production assistant appears in front of us out of nowhere, and we both flinch back. "Places. Now," she orders.

Mason turns to me. "Time to work."

Good. The sooner this shitshow is over, the sooner we can go home. And it is a shitshow. And no doubt rigged. Supposedly the fans of the show voted for Isla over Reggie, which means he didn't make it to the top three tonight.

He'd be in the greenroom, no doubt asking where he went wrong, when the reality is the show probably chose the person *they* wanted. I'm not worried for him, though. I've already spoken to Harley about it, saying if Reggie did lose, that Harley should reach out. After watching some episodes, Harley agrees. Maybe Reggie will sign with him, maybe he'll go with a bigger label. Either way, he'll get a contract, so I'm happy for him even if he's probably feeling sorry for himself right now.

Mason and I take our places on the stage, the low blue hues covering us in darkness until we wait for the show to go back on the air and the lights to come up.

Our stools are close together, our knees touching. It's the soft reminder I need that he's here. He's next to me. This is happening.

The host does his introduction, blabbering on about how we're the hottest new duo and two from five of the most popular boy band in the world which makes the crowd scream.

It never fails to make me smile and internally cringe at the same time. I love the screams of excitement. My ears don't love it, but I do. They're intoxicating, and it's like being hit with a shot of adrenaline before a performance. It boosts me to the level I need to be at to perform without any hesitance.

Mason starts with the opening chords. Unlike the impromptu performance in my music room, this time we've worked out how to perfectly harmonize our voices, which means I kick off the first verse.

I sing to the crowd and the cameras, but the words are all for him. And when he joins in, the magic sparks between us.

After all these years, his voice still has the ability to send shivers down my spine.

Lights swirl around us, and unfortunately a backup band joins in, ruining the emotions of the song, but I was told it was nonnegotiable. The audience has seen our basic acoustic version already, and this one needs to be different.

Still, I block that out and turn my focus on Mason. We're sitting toward each other, staring into each other's eyes. And as the song comes closer to the end, our harmonies get more intense.

My heartbeat kicks up a notch because I know what's coming. We're going to cause a shitstorm. Sorry to my manager, Keith, who I did not warn about this. I couldn't. He'd try to talk me out of it.

We hit the last word, and even though I must look wide-eyed and possibly scared, Mason's confident as he leans in. He strums the last guitar note, right before he takes charge and presses his lips to mine.

We knew we had to be fast because this is on a network that will be pissed over a gay kiss on live television. They will no doubt need to pay fines for this, but we weren't entirely convinced they wouldn't cut to a commercial before we got the chance to do it.

Maybe they have cut already, maybe they haven't, we don't know. So we stay lip-locked, and even though I want to dive in and push my tongue into his mouth and ravish him after weeks of being apart, I hold back because the soft, chaste kiss sends a big enough message.

The studio dies down to impossible levels of quiet when we pull apart.

The stage goes dark.

And then? The crowd fucking erupts with screams and applause.

"We did it," Mason breathes.

"We did. Blake is going to kill us."

Mason smiles, his bright teeth shining in the dark. "I guess the Eleven reunion might have to wait until after the movie wraps filming."

"I'm okay with that."

Stagehands come out to take our seats and microphones away, shooing us offstage where we're met with an alternate universe or a zombie movie. Where people are normally running around, production assistants, producers, and showrunners stand stunned.

Low murmurs from the corner of backstage filter through saying things like "Did anyone know they were going to do that?" and "Is this real? Are we all going to be fired?" "There goes the chance for season two." My favorite is probably "Is this a publicity stunt?"

Because yes. We would risk everything for a little bit of publicity. Sure.

I wish I could say they were all being melodramatic, but they're probably not. This is exactly why we wanted to do this. Things like two men kissing on TV should be normalized because news flash: it's not fucking scandalous.

I intertwine my fingers with Mason's and drag him to where Alondra and Brian are waiting in the wings. The winner will be announced next, and then it will all be over.

Hopefully we can sneak out of here, but I'm guessing by most of the shocked faces around us, we might have some trouble.

Alondra stares at me.

"What?" I ask.

"Nothing at all." She wraps her arm around my shoulder. "Don't let anyone get to you. That was brave what you just did, and don't you forget that."

"Thank you."

"Brave or stupid, I haven't made up my mind," Brian says. "Though they seemed to love it." He stares out at the crowd. He's a label exec, not on my label, so he's probably thinking how this might affect any of his acts.

Prepare for the domino effect, my friends. At least, that's the *hope*.

Hollywood and the music industry have their LGBTQ acts. They're acts who are put in boxes and marketed in a way that being gay or queer is their main identifier.

Maybe doing this will pigeonhole both Mason and me too, but I honestly believe the more it's normalized, the better the future will be. Maybe one day soon, a new act could come along, kiss whoever they want on live TV, and no one will even blink.

We're called back onto the stage, and Mason kisses my cheek before I leave him in the wings.

Our contestants are brought out with us for the announcement, and as Isla takes her spot next to me, she mutters out the side of her mouth, "You two are so cute."

Umm, thank you?

I guess I'm going to need to find a way to respond to those kinds of comments.

When we come back from the commercial break, the host acts like Mason's and my performance never happened or wasn't a big deal. I'm guessing because it was either cut or they don't want to draw even more attention to it.

My heart's in my throat the whole time the host talks because I think I'm waiting for it to all blow up in our faces. I'm waiting for the other shoe to drop. The chaos to start.

I don't snap out of that until it's announced that Isla did in fact win the whole damn show.

I want to be mad about how unfair it is. I want to hate the whole production and everyone involved.

I smile as if I'd just won and hug her. But my glance moves to the side of the stage where Mason is, and I can't help being thankful for *Fandom*.

It helped bring Mason back to me.

It helped us fall in love.

It has made the whole stressful process worth it.

Because Mason is my everything. And you can't be mad at the thing that gave you the world.

CHAPTER 30
MASON

I CAN'T BELIEVE HALF the shit in the media about Denver and me and that teeny, tiny little kiss a couple of nights ago.

After we snuck off the set of *Fandom*, we turned off our phones, and Denver welcomed me home in the best way possible. My body is still wrung out from the rounds of handjobs, blowjobs, and every other which way we made each other come in the last few days. I lost count after the first time we passed out in a pile of cum and sweat.

Now, freshly showered and lying on Denver's couch, I'm finally catching up on everything we've been avoiding. Denver's in the kitchen making coffee and yelling at his manager on the phone, while I scroll through the ridiculousness.

Look at us, breaking the internet. Who knew the only thing I needed to get back in the spotlight was to kiss a dude on national TV?

It's not all likes and popularity, of course, but after my solo album tanked, nothing they say can hurt me. It's disgusting that so many hateful comments against the queer community can still exist, but considering I've only been a part of that community for all of five seconds, there's that disconnect there that is helping me cope. It's a good thing because it works as a shield against the haters, but we'll see how long it lasts before the hate starts getting to me.

Then there are the comments that really make me laugh. It's not the name-calling or telling us our sex lives are disgusting, but the people projecting this is all a big publicity stunt so that when the Eleven reunion happens, everyone will be focused on Denver and me instead of the "real" queer boys of Eleven: Ryder and Harley. Gay conspiracy theories are a thing, apparently. I worry what the fans will do when they find out Ryder and Harley are queer but happily in relationships with *other* people. I think they might be more heartbroken than when the band broke up.

Denver appears with a defeated sigh on his lips. He puts our coffees on the coffee table and then leans over me, touching his lips to mine. His mouth is warm, and I want more, but he pulls back before I'm ready.

He slumps down beside me on the couch.

"How'd the phone call go?" I ask.

"He wants us to play it up because 'It's a great way to get publicity. Why didn't we think to fake date a man before?'"

"Your own manager is on team *this is just a PR stunt*?" I lean forward and reach for my coffee.

"Yep. So, I told him he's fired."

I almost choke on my drink. "You *what*?"

"If we're going to do this Eleven reunion our own way, and we're going to take a direction that's risky—coming out was already a risk—I need someone who's not only about the publicity grab. That's all Keith was. His vision of keeping me famous was to throw parties and date starlets to stay in the tabloids. If we want this to be about the music, we're going to need a team of people who'll respect that."

"Fair enough. I don't think we'll find anyone as good as Cameron was, and I'm a little scared to try after my last one. He was the worst. I thought he was good, but I need someone who'll challenge me and push me."

"Harley says his manager, Gideon, is good. Maybe he can work with us all or even find someone for us."

"Speaking of Harley, how many missed calls did you have from him when you turned your phone on?"

"A gajillion."

"Same. And a couple from my mom. I didn't tell her we were planning to come out like that."

"She's all right with it, though?"

"She loves you. Probably more than me."

"Not true."

I smile. "No, but she does see you as one of her own. She's happy for us but wary. Like she always has been when it comes to this industry."

"You know who's not happy for us? Blake. Wanna see the pic he sent?"

I move in closer so I can look at his screen as he pulls his phone out of his pants pocket. It's a photo of Blake signing a ... "Is that a cocktail napkin?"

"Yep. He was apparently out at a bar with Jordan last night. He made him sign a napkin saying he'll do his movie. It's official. He hates us."

"We'll see how he feels after the movie comes out. I'm no expert by any means, but I think it could be good for his acting career so he doesn't get pigeonholed into action flicks."

"Maybe he'll thank us in his Oscar speech."

I snort. "I wouldn't go that far, but maybe. Did you call Harley back?"

"Not yet."

And as if Harley himself was waiting outside, or he can sense whenever his name has been said three times in a span of twenty seconds, the buzzer for the front gate sounds.

"Took too long," I say. "That has to be him."

"Or Blake."

"Hmm, or paparazzi."

"Nah, they know not to actually buzz. It'll be Harley for sure."

We both get up to answer the front door, and there's Harley's bodyguard, holding back paparazzi while they take photos of Harley, Blake, and Ryder. They're probably taking photos of Lyric too, seeing as his first single is selling well, but they have two other guys with them as well. Someone who looks like Lyric and also Harley's manager, Gideon.

I hit the button to open the gate for them to come in, but this is just going to add to the mania.

As Harley reaches us, he smiles sweetly. "Band meeting."

When they all file into the house and we close the door behind us, Denver grabs my arm. "It's three years ago again. Help. PTSD. Harley's meetings telling us what we could be doing better or different."

Harley pauses in his tracks and turns to slap the back of Denver's head.

"Oh, the head slaps are back too," he cries dramatically.

I pull him to my side. "Don't worry. I'll protect you." I kiss the side of his head.

We all file into the informal living room and sprawl out, much like we did after Cameron's funeral. It's surreal being in the same room as these guys now, but I'm sure the feeling will pass once I get used to being in their presence again.

I realize now it wasn't them I was angry with; it was myself. The need for sales, the need for likes, the need to be successful, I let it all get to me last time, and I won't let that happen again. All I want is to be happy.

Harley stays standing with the guy who must be Lyric's brother. "Everyone, this is Chord Jones. He's an entertainment lawyer, and he'll go over the contracts for you to give to your agents, managers, whoever you've got."

Denver and I share a look.

"About that," I say.

Denver bites his lip and says in a low voice, "We don't have one."

"Neither of you?" Harley asks. "Even after kissing on TV? I would've thought your phones would be flooded."

"Oh, we switched them off so we didn't have to deal with it," I say.

His eyes widen, and he turns to Gideon with a pleading expression.

Gideon smiles. "Want me to take care of this?"

"Yes, please."

"Do you see the kind of shit you've put me through? You managing Eleven is going to make me so happy. You're going to come crawling to me begging for my forgiveness because of everything I deal with being your manager."

"Whatever, I'm delightful." Harley's words are mumbled as if he's already feeling exactly the same way Gideon says.

Gideon's attention turns to us. "I'll set you two up with a publicist, and I'll be at all meetings. The kiss might need to be clarified through some sort of other media outlet. Article, TV interview, *something*. You can say as little or as much as you want, or if you really like, you can let the media continue with their crazy conspiracy theory crap. Though, with there being truth behind those conspiracies, it might be better for Harley and Ryder if you come forward and clarify."

I stare at Denver, who seems unsure. "I wouldn't have kissed him in public if I wasn't ready to face all that."

Denver's shoulders sag in relief. "Me too."

"Good. That's settled." Gideon takes out his phone. "I'm going to make some calls. Be back soon. You got an office I can use?"

Denver leads him down the corridor but returns moments later and sits closer to me so our thighs are pressed against each other. I reach for his hand, and our fingers intertwine.

It's interesting to me that Denver and I are easily showing

affection when Harley and Ryder don't with their partners. I think being closeted is so ingrained into them that they're used to refraining in public. We are all trained to be that way to an extent because the public wants to know everything about our lives, but there's a difference between holding a woman's hand and looking lovingly into another man's eyes. Harley's and Ryder's guards have been up for over a decade, and I think that's why Denver and I were able to come out when they couldn't.

The industry is evolving, but Harley and Ryder have had years of "You should do this" or "You shouldn't show this side of you" to get over.

"So, schedules permitting," Harley says, "we're hoping to spend the rest of summer and part of the fall writing while Blake's doing his movie."

Blake uses his Coby Godspeed *I'm about to kill you* face. "Thanks for that, by the way."

I grin. "You're welcome. Who knows, you might *like* kissing Jordan."

He waves me off. "It's not the gay stuff that I'm worried about. It's mainly how the public will react to it. Homophobes might stop watching Coby Godspeed, the queer community will hate that I'm a straight dude representing a gay guy … There's a lot more to be worried about than kissing Jordan Brooks. I'm comfortable enough in my heterosexuality to get the job done."

"Famous last words," I mutter.

"What?"

"Nothing."

"Anyway," Harley cuts back in. "We write and record for the album, drop a single or two over winter, and then tour next summer. Next year will actually be the ten-year anniversary of our first album, so it's perfectly cheesy and symbolic."

Straight back to business as always. We may mock him and mess with him about all this stuff, but I trust him to get the job done right. He's meticulous, like he says, but it's because he cares so much. I want that in my corner.

"Mason already has some songs," Denver says, and I swear I've never glared at him harder.

"No, I don't."

Denver nudges me. "Yes, you do."

"Let's hear them," Harley says.

They're all going to pay for this. "I lost them. Oops."

Every set of eyes land on me.

"There was a fire." I gesture an explosion with my hands. "Poof." They don't believe me. I throw my hands up. "Fine. But remember that you said we're allowed to do our own sound. I recorded this in Denver's music room, so the quality is crap, but you get the gist." I take out my phone, but instead of going to where I have actually recorded rough tracks, I pull up YouTube and type in the search bar "Songs with animal sounds" and click one of the top results.

Then, as a version of "What is Love" comes through the small phone speaker, I watch as every single face in the room drops. I have to bite my lip to stop laughing out loud.

"I'm really proud of it," I say, my voice only cracking a little. I'm surprised I even manage.

Harley presses his lips together, probably trying to choose between telling me to fuck off and remembering that I haven't actually signed a contract yet. "It's … uh … interesting."

Right as he says that, a rooster crows in the song, and I lose any composure I had left. I completely let my laugh fly, and then suddenly, Denver's decorative pillows he has on his couches are being thrown my way. From everyone in the band.

"Asshole!" Harley says. "I thought you were serious. I'm sitting here trying to remind myself that I'd give you creative freedom!"

I'm still laughing, so much so, I'm too distracted to notice

Denver going for my phone. "No!" I try to get it back, but he holds it above his head.

When I climb into his lap, he throws the phone to Harley.

I stand to go after him, but he calls for Brix, who immediately steps in my way. I have to stare *up* at him. Has he always been that tall and wide?

"Mase," Harley says. "We're going to be a team, and I promise we won't tear your songs apart."

I slump because that's not actually what I want at all. "No, you should. I can take the criticism. I want to put out the best songs. I just don't think my songs are that."

Harley steps around his boyfriend and stops in front of me. "Show us." He holds out my phone for me.

I sigh and pull up one of the songs I was working on while Denver was on the *Fandom* set and I was playing around. I have to close my eyes as I hit the Play button, and as my words about finding a soul mate in a best friend filter through the room, I refuse to look at Denver.

It's a pure love song. It's a queer anthem. It's not what I set out for it to be when I started writing it, but … that's where my muse led me, I guess.

Denver stands and slowly approaches me. "Is this about me?" His voice is low, but I have no doubt everyone can hear him.

I'm uncomfortable doing this in front of all of them, but I don't want to belittle us by cracking a joke.

Instead, I speak from the heart. "You know it is. I've never felt this way about anyone before. I love you with everything I have."

Denver takes me off guard by closing the gap between us and slamming his mouth on mine. I stumble back a couple of steps, but he comes with me, not letting up. His tongue enters my mouth, and then his hands grip the back of my head to hold me to him.

It's enough to make me forget we're in a room full of people.

But then Denver pulls back, his lips puffy, his eyes glassy. "I love you too."

The song ends, and the room is silent.

I keep looking at Denver. "What do their faces look like? Are they trying to figure out how to tell me it sucks and it's obvious why my solo career tanked?"

"It's amazing," Harley says.

I slowly turn.

Harley nods. "We need it on our album."

"Really?"

"I want to play with the melody a bit, but the lyrics are … I'm blown away."

I didn't know how much I needed validation from Harley until this very moment.

"So this is really happening?" Denver asks. "We're signing contracts, we're *doing* this?"

"Let's celebrate with some drinks." Harley heads for the bar.

"Uh—" Denver starts, but Harley's gone before Denver can stop him.

"Where's all your alcohol?" And Harley's already back.

Denver rubs the back of his neck. "I, umm, had to get rid of it."

I frown. "Why?"

"When I decided I should give drinking a break, it was a lot harder than I thought it was going to be. And then when Cameron died … it was almost unbearable. But while Mason was gone …" Denver's aqua eyes meet mine. "I poured myself a drink."

Oh, damn. "I didn't know," I whisper.

"I didn't drink it," he says quickly. "But you all were right. I would drink way too much and way too often. The biggest problem was I'd drink to forget. When I was numb, I wasn't stressed about my career or having friends or …" He turns to me. "Missing you."

I squeeze his hand.

He keeps talking. "I thought I had it handled, but I really

didn't. And while Mason was gone, I realized if I couldn't handle being alone without drinking, that maybe sober living needs to become a permanent thing for me."

I'm speechless. Denver and alcohol have always gone hand in hand, but I know he has issues with it, and I'm proud of him for taking it seriously and doing something about it.

"You all are welcome to drink around me, but, yeah, you won't find any in the house. I had to pour it all down the sink so I wouldn't drink it."

Harley gasps. "All your Macallan?"

"Okay, no, that I sold to a party promoter friend of mine for half price. Throwing that out would've been blasphemous."

"We all support you," Harley says.

Ryder moves from his spot next to Lyric and stands next to Harley. "Agreed."

Blake joins next. "We're a team."

I shake my head. "We're a family."

Denver holds out his arms. "Group hug?"

As we step into more of a huddle instead of a hug, I'm taken back to all those times we've been onstage together.

We really are a team. We really are family.

And while my feelings for Denver have changed and evolved over the years, there's absolutely no doubt in my mind that he's the one for me.

I'll support him and love him, cherish what we have and never give up fighting for him.

We're going to create a life together that we want, and I can't wait.

Harley steps out of the group hug first. "Okay, let's get to work."

Here. We. Go.

THANK YOU

Thank you for reading *Fandom*!

What a ride, huh? Mason and Denver were the types of characters who just ... were. They led their own story, and I loved writing them even if they took the story to places I didn't think they'd go. (Sorry Cameron)

I'll try to make Blake and Jordan less ... murdery. But no promises. There is that pesky boyfriend of Jordan's ...

Want to stay up to date on what's coming next?

Join my reader group here: https://www.facebook.com/groups/absolutelyeden/

Join my mailing list here: https://landing.mailerlite.com/webforms/landing/d4e2a5

ALSO BY EDEN FINLEY

https://amzn.to/2zUlM16

https://www.edenfinley.com

OTHER BOOKS BY EDEN FINLEY

FAMOUS SERIES

Pop Star

Spotlight

Fandom

Novellas:

Locked Heart

Thorned Heart

CO-WRITTEN WITH SAXON JAMES

Power Plays & Straight A's

Face Offs & Cheap Shots

Goal Lines & First Times

Line Mates & Study Dates

FAKE BOYFRIEND SERIES

Fake Out

Trick Play

Deke

Blindsided

Hat Trick

Novellas:

Fake Boyfriend Breakaways: A short story collection

Final Play

VINO & VERITAS

Sarina Bowen's True North Series

Headstrong

STEELE BROTHERS

Unwritten Law

Unspoken Vow

ROYAL OBLIGATION

Unprincely (M/M/F)

ACKNOWLEDGMENTS

I want to thank my long list of betas, especially Leslie Copeland from Les Court Services, Blue Beta Reading, and Sandra from One Love editing for copy-edits.

Thanks to Lori Parks for one last read through for those ninja typos that have the ability to sneak through four rounds of editing.

My PA, CC Belle.

And lastly, a big thanks to Linda from Foreword PR & Marketing for helping get this book out.

www.ingramcontent.com/pod-product-compliance
Lightning Source LLC
Chambersburg PA
CBHW050440200726
48295CB00024B/741